TWISTED VOWS

By Bonita Y. McCoy

Dedicated to:
My Aunt Ruby
Who taught me about the importance of family heritage.
"I remember your genuine faith, for you share the faith that
first filled your grandmother Lois and your mother, Eunice. And
I know that same faith continues strong in you."
2 Timothy 1:5

CHAPTER ONE

A scream.

I froze with the ivory-handled cake knife plunged into the middle of the second tier of the three-tiered wedding cake I was cutting. Had I heard a scream, or was it part of the pulsating music coming from the speakers by the dance floor?

The quick swish of silk taffeta coming from the hall to my left grew closer.

I glanced over my shoulder to find the bride, Betsy Jacobs, or I guess Betsy Williams now that the ceremony was over, emerging from the hallway with a look of horror on her face. "What's wrong?" I pulled the knife from the center of the cake without making the circle needed to ensure all the slices would be the same length. A trick Julia Jacobs, my best friend and owner of Pure Sweetness Bakery, taught me for this occasion.

"Amy Kate, I … I …" She grabbed my arm before I could lay the knife down on the table. "Come with me." Pulling me down the dark hallway behind her, she dashed to the office door which bore the name, Reverend George Boggs, in large gold letters. Betsy let go of my arm and swung the door open, bursting into to tears. "What are we going to do?"

The groom stood behind the desk, holding a bloody cake knife identical to the one in my hand. He hovered pale and wide-eyed over the body of George Boggs, the man who had pronounced them man and wife less than an hour earlier.

"I swear I didn't do this. It's not how it looks." Jimmy Williams held the knife away from his body as if it were toxic and he was unsure where to put it. Releasing the weapon, he dropped it on the desk. "I came in here to sign the marriage certificate. And found him this way."

"Why did you touch the body?" I asked. "That's TV murder 101. You never touch the body." Hadn't he ever seen a crime show?

"I thought I could save him. So, I pulled the knife out of his chest." Jimmy's complexion turned from ashen white to a pale green as if he might barf. "I had my phone ready to call 9-1-1, but then I didn't."

I moved into the room and grabbed the trash can shoving it toward him. "Here, use this."

His hands trembled as he hugged the black can and leaned his hip against the desk for support.

"We need to think. Did you touch anything else besides the knife?" I kept the groan stirring in me pushed down.

"No. But when Betsy screamed, I dropped my phone. I don't know where it went."

"We'd better find it before we call the police. Once this becomes a crime scene, it'll be days before you'll see your phone again, if ever."

Dropping down on her hands and knees with her wedding train bunched at her feet, Betsy looked by the bookcase to the right of the door.

Jimmy sighed, put the trash can down, and fell to his knees to search under the desk.

I still held the knife covered in icing that I had been using to cut the cake. Not sure where to lay it, I held it in one hand and squatted so I could see under the front of the desk, trying hard not to get any on my dress.

No phone.

I duckwalked to the filing cabinet and searched on either side. Not an easy task in a hip-hugging satin dress. Then I peeked behind the cabinet to make sure the phone hadn't bounced there somehow.

"What on earth is going on here?" A deep male voice asked from behind me.

I shut my eyes wishing with all my might that I could be invisible.

"Amy Kate Anderson, this had better be good," Lieutenant Gabe Cooper, my date, stated.

Standing, I pivoted on my light blue high heels, a pair of Bottega Veneta knockoffs I had dyed especially for this wedding and faced him.

Gabe filled the doorway with his broad shoulders and height. He looked so debonair in his black suit and silk tie, but the red rising in his cheeks and the throbbing nerve right below his tight jaw did nothing for his overall appearance.

Jimmy and Betsy rose from their positions on the floor.

Betsy's eyes filled with tears, causing her mascara to trickle down her cheeks. "I can explain." She sniffled.

Jimmy jumped to rescue her. "She has nothing to do with this. You can leave her out of it." His chin thrust out. "I came in here to sign the marriage certificate and found the reverend dead in his chair."

"What were all of you doing on the floor?" Gabe cocked an eyebrow.

"Good question," I said but pressed my lips together the moment Gabe shot me an icy glare.

Jimmy crossed his arms. "I took my phone out to call 9-1-1, but before I could, Betsy came in and found me by the body. She screamed, and I dropped the blasted thing. We were looking for it."

"You were looking for your phone? The one you were going to use to call 9-1-1 but didn't?"

"That's right." Jimmy shrugged.

"Why did you enter the room once you saw the body?" Gabe asked.

Jimmy studied the floor. "I didn't actually find the reverend exactly like this."

"Well, tell me, how did you find the body, exactly?" Gabe growled.

"The chair was facing the window." He pointed to the pane behind the desk overlooking the children's park. "I called his name. When he didn't respond, I thought he might have had a heart attack or a stroke or something. The guy wasn't a spring chicken."

"Just stick to the story and leave off the commentary." The nerve by Gabe's jaw twitched.

I knew better than to interrupt. But knowing better and not doing it are two entirely different things. "We were going to call the Pine Lake P.D. the minute we found the phone."

"Oh, I see." Gabe shoved his hands into his trouser pockets. "So, you moved the body or at least the chair the body is in, since it now faces the door. What else have the three of you done?"

Jimmy winced. "I took the knife out of his chest."

"You what?" The nerves on both sides of Gabe's jaw now throbbed in unison. "Out, get out! Everybody but you." Gabe pointed to Jimmy. "You, I'm taking in. Jimmy Williams, you're under arrest for the murder of George Boggs, obstruction of justice, tampering with evidence, and anything else I can find to hold you on until I sort out this mess."

Gabe stepped toward Jimmy, but Betsy flung herself at him. Holding tight to Gabe's arm, she pleaded, "don't do this. It's our wedding day. Can't this wait? He didn't do it."

"He should've considered that before he tampered with a crime scene."

"Gabe, you can't believe Jimmy is guilty." I pointed the end of the cake knife at him.

"Right now, I don't know what to believe. And put that knife down. Knowing you, it's probably evidence." He unwrapped Betsy's arms from his own, then grabbing Jimmy's arm, he pulled a pair of handcuffs out of his suitcoat pocket and snapped them around Jimmy's wrists.

"Do you always come so prepared?" I huffed, settling my fists on my hips while still holding the knife.

"Yes." He glanced over his shoulder. "And I meant what I said. Leave the knife. I want to make sure all the evidence stays in the room until Floyd and I can go over it."

"Fine," I barked. "And how am I supposed to cut the wedding cake without a knife?"

"I'm sure you'll think of something." Gabe pushed Jimmy into the leather chair in front of the large maple desk.

Great, just great. I'd splurged on the dress and dug into my savings for the shoes, and all for nothing. My trouble magnet seemed to be working at top capacity today. And to think I'd planned to have a talk with Gabe about being exclusive. Fat chance of that happening now.

We'd been dating for a few months, but the subject hadn't come up. We sort of danced around it. Neither one of us wanted to push the relationship further than the other one wanted to go.

I placed the knife encrusted with hardened icing on the desk next to the one Jimmy had pulled from the minister's chest and turned to find Betsy with her arms wrapped around her middle. She looked more like the zombie bride I'd seen in a recent film than the beauty who had floated down the aisle earlier this afternoon.

The black streaks of mascara stood out against her ruddy complexion, and her nose, red from all the crying, nearly glowed. Spotting a box of tissues on the end table next to the loveseat, I snatched several sheets out of it and handed them to the poor girl. She wiped the fresh droplets drizzling down her cheeks, smearing the black even more.

"Come on, Betsy, let's go. Gabe will tell us when he's ready to talk to you." I slipped my arm around Betsy's shoulders and directed her out the door. Outside in the hall, I could hear Gabe's voice on the phone. "Floyd, can you get over to The Methodist Church? We've had some trouble."

Betsy glanced up at me, and I placed my finger to my lips. Her eyes widened, but she didn't make a sound.

"Yeah, Reverend Boggs is dead. Someone thrust a cake knife into his chest. I've made an arrest." Gabe went silent for a moment then he said, "the groom. And bring your laptop. We'll need to take statements from the guests and do background checks on those who stand out."

I peeked back into the room. Gabe leaned his hip against the desk. "Yeah, there are some out-of-town guests, so we'll have to do a little digging." He disconnected and tucked his phone back into his pocket.

Horror mixed with disbelief played on Betsy's face. She

opened her mouth to speak, but before she could, I dragged her down the corridor toward the fellowship hall.

"Oh, Amy Kate, what am I going to do? Jimmy didn't do this. He'd never hurt another human being, ever. The man can't even kill a spider. There's no way he could've … done … that." Her voice went up several octaves, and she waved wildly in the direction of the office. "This can't be happening. Not now. Not on my wedding day!" Hysterical, she screeched. "I've planned for months and months, dreamed of the perfect day, but … but …" She swayed to the left then to the right. Her skin suddenly matched the color of her dress, and before I knew what happened, Betsy fell into my arms in a dead faint.

~

I struggled to drag her to one of the cushioned folding chairs surrounding the tables sprinkled throughout the hall. The train on her dress didn't make it easy. It tangled around my heels causing me to shuffle my feet to move forward. Shuffle, shuffle, drag. Shuffle, shuffle, drag. She'd be ninety before I ever reached the chair.

With my attention on Betsy, I bumped into one of the groomsmen, Mark, jostling the drink in his hand. He managed to keep it from spilling on Kristin, the matron of honor. Turning, he noticed I was wearing the bride. "Is she all right?"

"No, can you help me get her to a chair? She's fainted." My tone sounded a little sharp even to my own ears, but I thought our predicament was self-explanatory.

Mark set his drink on the refreshment table next to him. Gently, he placed one arm around her shoulders and slid his other arm under her knees. I gathered the train the best I could to keep it from getting in the way. He took the few steps needed to reach the table and waited for my help.

I skirted around him to pull out the chair, so he could slide Betsy into the seat without having to do any form of contortions. As he placed her in the chair, I guided her upper torso, so it draped to the side over the white tablecloth, carefully laying her head on her arm like a schoolkid taking a rest at her desk.

All the jostling around hadn't awakened her.

Not sure what to do, I patted her exposed cheek. "Betsy, Betsy." But she didn't stir. I tapped a little harder, but she remained still. The thought of giving her a good, firm pop came to mind, but there was no way I was slapping the bride after the day she'd had. "Can you bring me a glass of water? I have an idea."

"Sure, anything." Mark rushed to the drink table and snatched one of the small bottles of water from the elegant tub of ice where it sat chilling. Grabbing one of the clear plastic cups next to the punch bowl, he poured the contents of the bottle into the glass and dashed back to the table. "Here."

Taking the glass from him, I dipped my fingertips into the icy water and flicked drops onto Betsy's face.

"Are you sure that's what you're supposed to do?" Mark's brows pulled together, and his lips twisted into a frown. "I don't think that's right."

"Look, it's not like I have a lot of experience with people fainting." I cut my eyes in his direction. "Saw this in a movie once." I repeated the process but still no movement. Finally, not sure what else to do, I threw the entire contents of the cup into her face. It worked, but now, the top half of her beautiful silk taffeta dress looked as if she'd been caught in a monsoon.

"What happened?" She sputtered touching her wet face as she straightened in the chair. Looking down, she saw the watermarks on the silk. "What have you done?" Her eyes darted from me to Mark and back to me.

"You fainted." I shrugged.

"And you couldn't find some smelling salts or something that wouldn't wreck my dress?" Her lips quivered, and a new cascade of tears rolled down her cheeks.

Mark tugged at his collar and said, "I'm not good with this sort of thing," then darted off in the direction of the cute blonde bridesmaid.

Typical, first sign of tears and the man bailed. I shook my head.

"What does it matter? Jimmy's going to prison." She sobbed. "And we'll never be together. Our beautiful life is over before it ever started." Her eyes widened, and she gasped. "I'll be a prison wife, scheduling visits." She wailed and her body shook.

Fearing she might faint again, I slipped into the chair next to her and tried to calm her. "Aw, now don't give up hope. I'm sure his lawyer will spring him in no time."

"I don't know. I mean—" she made a weird, guttural noise. "He stood there holding the bloody knife. Why couldn't he have left everything alone? Why did he touch the blasted thing?" She turned toward me and without warning, an eerie calm settled over her. "You've helped our family before when we came for the reunion. Julia told me about several instances where you've helped to solve a case."

More like almost got myself killed, but I thought it best not to quibble over semantics with her in her present state. "Yes, I've helped here and there." I didn't like the gleam in her eyes.

She grabbed both of my hands in hers. "You must help Jimmy. He's innocent. I know it. And without you, he'll go to jail. My one true love …" She placed the back of her hand over her mouth in a dramatic movie-star style, then dropped it to her lap. "My soulmate."

Okay, she wasn't playing fair. Every one of my heart strings quivered with sympathy. Plus, a man's future dangled on the line. If he was innocent, he deserved someone on his side. Groaning, I leaned back in my chair and crossed my arms. Gabe wouldn't like me interfering with his case. That was a no-brainer.

Betsy's eyes softened, and she clasped her hands together as if praying. "Please, please?" She begged.

My heart tugged in my chest, but my head screamed, *don't do it. It won't end well.* Since when did I listen to my head?

"Please," she mouthed.

"Fine, I'll see what I can find out. But I'm only helping because you're Julia's cousin, and she'd never forgive me if I could've helped and didn't."

"Oh, thank you. Jimmy and I will never forget this. I just can't imagine—"

Before she could get another word out, three uniformed police officers burst through the large wooden doors of the First United Methodist Church Fellowship Hall with Floyd Simms, Gabe's partner, close on their heels carrying a laptop.

Floyd looked to be in his mid-forties, and the slight paunch hanging over his belt spoke of the many sedentary hours spent behind a desk or on a stakeout.

The older ladies seated at one of the tables turned to see who had shown up so late to the celebration. When they discovered the uniformed officers standing inside the door, the whispering commenced. No doubt the Pine Lake grapevine would be ablaze tonight considering what was about to take place. The murder of Reverend George Boggs would be big news in our small town.

Assessing the situation, Detective Simms huddled up with his men to give them some instructions before he headed toward the DJ in the far corner. The thirty or so individuals dancing the Boot Scootin' Boogie slid to a halt when the music stopped. Floyd pulled the mic from the stand, sending a squawk reverberating through the hall.

"Sorry for the interruption, but we've had some trouble here today." He frowned.

Droplets of sweat formed on his forehead. Boy, I did not envy his position. How do you tell seventy-five wedding guests that the minister whom they'd seen alive not less than an hour ago lay dead in his study? And the prime suspect was the groom.

I shifted in my seat trying to get a better view of the stage.

Floyd yanked at his button-down collar and loosened his tie. "It seems Reverend Boggs—" His brow puckered, and he took a deep breath.

The people on the dance floor gave him their full attention, and those who had been seated stared at the detective, me included. No one said a word.

"—Is dead. Murdered," Floyd said.

Gasps spread around the room faster than head lice at a sleepover.

"So, you can understand why we'll need to get a statement from each of you before we can let you leave. We'll also need to see any pictures you might've taken with your phone cameras, and any candid shots the photographer took." He scanned the crowd and nodded when he spotted the woman with a camera hanging around her neck. "All right, we're going to try to do this in an orderly manner. I need everyone whose last name begins with A through H to see Officer Pete Howard."

Officer Pete waved, letting the out-of-towners know who he was.

"And everyone with last names I through Q see officer Jane O'Neal."

She held her hand above her head and gave a quick nod to the crowd.

"Officer Clyde Paris will take the rest." Floyd moved to put the mic back on the stand, then hesitated, and added, "Thank you for your cooperation."

I peered at Betsy. Her lips quivered, her shoulders shook, and she made that weird guttural sound again. Thinking quickly, I offered, "I'll go check on Jimmy. See what Gabe has to say," hoping to calm her down.

Betsy nodded, pressing her lips together, unable to speak.

I spotted one of the bridesmaids, Monica, making her way toward us and waved her over.

"Oh, Betsy, you poor dear," she cooed. "At least it wasn't anyone related to you."

Betsy threw back her head and howled.

I stepped away before I lost the opportunity, pushing down the guilt rising in me. Now that I'd agreed to help, I needed to see the crime scene again. But how? Gabe had barred me from the reverend's office. Perhaps a little good ole southern compassion would do the trick.

CHAPTER TWO

When I entered the study, Gabe sat in one of the two leather chairs meant for visitors which were positioned in front of the reverend's dark maple desk. Jimmy sat in the other one, handcuffed with his face looking pale against his black tux lapel.

Reverend Boggs still occupied the cushy office chair behind the desk. If it wasn't for the gaping wound in the reverend's chest, the scene could've been mistaken for a business meeting.

"You can't be in here. You'll have to wait out in the fellowship hall with all the others." Gabe leaned his forearms on his knees.

I stopped in my tracks unsure of what to do. Although I'd barely stepped into the room, I needed to get a closer look at the body. Gabe could be such a stickler for the rules, so I played the compassion card. "I told Betsy I'd come check on Jimmy."

Glancing toward Jimmy, I nodded. "There's a very frightened and confused bride out there, doing everything she can to keep calm." Okay, so she fainted and then howled like a banshee when she regained consciousness, but what was I supposed to tell her groom? He had enough on his plate without having to worry about Betsy.

Gabe nodded and motioned for me to enter. "You have one minute."

"I can only imagine how she feels." Jimmy stared out the window. "Tell her I didn't do it."

"She knows." I stepped further into the room careful not to disturb anything, hoping to get a look around without being too obvious.

I'd been so busy with Betsy earlier I hadn't had the presence of mind to look for any clues. Of course, I didn't know I needed to be looking for them either. Dropping onto the arm of the loveseat adjacent to the desk, I had a great view of the body drooping in the chair. "What's going to happen to Jimmy?"

Gabe leaned back, his eyes shifting from me to the accused. "Until we sort this out, I'm taking him into custody."

My eyes drifted over the reverend's gray hair and paused on the injury to his chest. Blood stained his robe. The fact there was only one puncture wound didn't escape my notice. Whoever stabbed him had to know their anatomy. To hit the heart, the knife had to be pushed between the fourth and fifth rib and through the cartilage. The killer had to be precise. "You mean he'll be spending his honeymoon night in a jail cell?" Gabe believed in the law and justice, but this seemed a little cold-hearted.

With the stopping of the heart, there was no blood spatter.

"There's nothing I can do. He was caught standing over the body holding the murder weapon. This isn't a game of Clue where I can let him have a do-over. It's out of my hands." He shook his head. "Besides, I think it's for his own good. If what he says is true and he didn't do it, it'll give us a chance to find out who did without him getting himself into more trouble." Gabe lifted his eyebrows. "And it'll give him an airtight alibi if anything else should happen."

A uniformed officer stepped into the study. "I'm here for the suspect."

Jimmy's head snapped around, and a look of panic rose in his eyes. He caught my gaze. "Let Betsy know I love her." The officer moved forward and took Jimmy by the elbow. Jerking free, he stepped toward me, grabbing my arm. "Tell her not to give up on me. I'm innocent."

"I'll tell her. Don't worry. You won't be in there long. I'll see to that." Realizing what I'd said, I clamped my lips shut and watched as the police officer reclaimed Jimmy's elbow and escorted him through the doorway into the dark hall. When I looked back toward Gabe, he was studying me with a bemused expression on his face.

"Amy Kate, you're not thinking about getting involved in this case, are you?"

Caught between a rock and a brick wall resembling Gabe Cooper, I decided to change the subject.

"He's innocent. You know it." I shrugged and chanced another glance at the body. The reverend hadn't removed his stole from around his neck that he'd worn during the ceremony. Everything on his desk appeared to be in place. Even the marriage certificate for Betsy and Jimmy still sat with a pen on top of it, undisturbed. So, he hadn't put up a fight. Which meant he knew his killer.

"I'm not so sure about that." Floyd leaned against the door jamb. "I got a hit on one of the guests. You're not going to believe this."

"Who is it?" Gabe asked.

Floyd shook his head. "None other than Frank Morelli, head of the Atlanta Morelli crime family."

"Not possible. Frank Morelli's dead."

"Not according to my laptop. He's alive and sitting in the fellowship hall."

"No, your information has to be wrong." Gabe shook his head.

Floyd shrugged. "You can't argue with fingerprints."

"Really? Frank Morelli's out there while Minister Boggs is in the study, dead. Interesting." Gabe motioned with his thumb toward the corpse. "When's the forensic team going to arrive?"

"They're on their way. Doc was out fishing when he received the call." Floyd said.

"So, Frank Morelli is here." Gabe rubbed a hand across his jaw.

"That's not the half of it. He's Jimmy Williams' grandfather."

"Jimmy's gramps is a crime lord?" I gasped. "You've got to be kidding. That nice old man with a walker runs a syndicate?"

Floyd hesitated and glanced my way then turned toward Gabe. "Maybe we should speak privately."

Gabe nodded. "Go ahead. She's already in it this far."

"Jimmy's mom, Aurora Williams, is his daughter. She has no

record, never been in trouble with the law. Seems to be a respectable citizen." Floyd shrugged. "Go figure."

"Wow, sweet Gramps, a mobster." I shook my head in amazement.

"Not everything is as it appears. Maybe the apple doesn't fall as far from the crime family tree as you'd like to think." Gabe stood and sighed. "I'd better go talk to Betsy and see how much she knows about his family. Wouldn't want her to hear this from anyone else." Facing me, he said, "Sorry our date turned into work."

I shrugged and gave him a smile. "It's not your fault."

He walked over and pulled me to my feet before placing a light kiss on my forehead.

Floyd chuckled. "I'll go finish running those ID checks. I have three uniforms taking statements and downloading pictures from phone cameras." He pushed off the doorjamb and headed toward the fellowship hall.

"We should clear out. Doc hates it when there are people in the crime scene while he's working."

I walked to the door. Glancing back, I caught sight of the marriage certificate. "Did you happen to notice if Betsy and Jimmy had both signed the marriage certificate?"

Gabe stopped and caught my shoulder. Meeting his gaze, I read the internal struggle on his face. "I shouldn't be telling you this. Jimmy signed it, but—" He bobbed his head. "Betsy and the reverend didn't."

"Oh, no." My thoughts raced to poor Betsy. Were they even married? "Are you going to tell her?"

"Not yet. She's already pretty traumatized, and I don't want to upset her to the point I can't get any information from her."

"Gabe, you have to tell her." The woman deserved to know her nuptials weren't as solid as she thought.

"I will but not now." Dropping his hand from my shoulder, he met my gaze. "And you're not going to tell her either."

Not able to make that promise, I turned and hurried through the doorway.

Gabe trailed behind me. I could feel his breath on the back of my neck. "Don't tell her, Amy Kate. I need her to be focused on Jimmy's family and the events of today."

I didn't turn around or acknowledge him or even nod my head. I concentrated on the light at the end of the dark hall, hoping for a quick escape.

Before Gabe could stop me, Officer Paris caught him and asked for a minute. Relief flooded over me. Selfish, but I hated making promises I couldn't keep.

Standing in the center of the fellowship hall, I scanned the area. To my amazement, the guests had divided themselves into two factions. On the right side, we had the bride's family, and on the left, the groom's. I spotted Betsy surrounded by her mom, dad, and aunts and uncles. Our talk could wait. Not about the marriage certificate, but about the crime family thing.

Surely, she wouldn't know about Jimmy's history, or maybe she did and didn't care. I searched the groom's family on the left for Gramps. If Floyd was right about him, the older gentleman would be wound up tight right now with all these cops buzzing around the place. It might be the ideal time to have a chat.

"Hey, where've you been?" Julia's dress rustled to a stop with one last swish.

"I've been checking on Jimmy for Betsy. Saw him for a minute before they took him to the police station."

She lowered her voice. "How is he?"

"Shaken. But all right considering what's happened."

Julia's eyes widened. "I know. Can you believe this mess? My heart aches for Betsy. I felt so sorry for her that I …" She hesitated. "I invited her to stay with us for the next few days. You don't' mind, do you?"

"Of course not." How could anyone expect this brokenhearted bride to stay alone on her honeymoon? She needed to be with friends. Plus, it would give me the opportunity to ask her the questions flying around in my mind.

"She'd already checked out of the hotel because they're supposed to be on their way to Cancun. Their flight leaves at six." Julia frowned. "What a terrible way to start a marriage."

It took all my will power not to tell her about the certificate. My tongue bled from biting it so hard.

"I didn't even take a single picture of the couple." She glanced over at Betsy who sat holding her mother's hand while she talked to Gabe. Her wedding bouquet sat on the table behind her, crumpled and forgotten. "This was supposed to be her day."

"Well, let me at least take a picture of you in your dress. Man, the Kelly green makes your eyes shine."

"I feel like a leprechaun." Julia pulled at the bodice of the floor-length dress.

"That's all right. No bridesmaid ever loves their dress. It's tradition." I laughed and scurried to the cake table to retrieve my phone from my handbag.

Catching sight of the delicious masterpiece Julia had created, I remembered I needed to find something to cut it with later so I could serve it. Returning to the spot where I had left her, I got Julia to pose near one of the flower arrangements decorating the buffet table. As I snapped the shot, one of the groomsmen passed behind the table, photobombing the picture.

"Wait, I need to take another one." I pressed the button and snapped a fantastic picture of my friend. As I deleted the photobomb of the groomsman, an idea emerged.

Starting at the hallway, I worked my way around the room taking photos of all the guests. If I was going to help Betsy find the truth, I needed a record of all the guests. And I couldn't depend on Gabe the Babe to share his information.

"What are you doing?"

"Gathering evidence." I smiled, glancing at her.

"Betsy told me she asked you to help. But I didn't know if you would or not, considering how serious things are between you and Gabe." A twinkle played in her eyes. "And then I remembered who we were talking about."

Giggling, I clicked the final shot I needed to have a complete record of the guests. "Come with me." We headed to the table where the guest book lay open. Julia turned the pages and kept an eye out for any police while I snapped a shot of each page with the names and addresses of the attendees. "We'll work on matching names with photos tomorrow after I return from my dad's house." Pivoting, I faced the guests who were huddled around several tables giving interviews to the police.

Julia leaned close. "Do you think one of the guests is the killer?" She scanned the room, her brow puckered.

My gaze landed on Jimmy's grandfather, and our eyes connected. A slight smile inched across Gramps' lips, creating deep lines at the corners of his eyes, and without any provocation, he winked at me.

I bit my bottom lip to keep from spilling the beans about him to Julia. If he was a don, how many of the wedding guests were part of his organization? Gee, the whole blessed event could be *The Godfather* on steroids. Shrugging, I kept my cool. "It's possible the killer's sitting in this room." To redirect her attention, I pointed to the cake table. "Do you think I should finish cutting the cake?"

"No, after what's happened, no one's in the mood. Besides, I'm not sure we'd have enough with the extra people."

"No, I guess not." I scanned the room taking note of who had that mobster look. Somewhere in the room lurked a killer, and for Betsy's and Jimmy's sake, I needed to find him no matter what, even if it led me to a charming old man with a Hello Kitty pouch on the front of his walker. From the crime scene it was clear the killer knew his anatomy, which pointed to a professional. And if Gramps was involved then one question topped the list, why would a crime boss from Atlanta want a reverend in Pine Lake dead?

CHAPTER THREE

Dragging the covers off me and swinging my feet over the side of the bed, I fished around with one foot for my slippers. Gizmo, my black Scottish terrier, wiggled his short body deeper into the comforter ignoring the bouncing of the mattress.

The night had been rough. Julia and I had fed Betsy a gallon of Triple Chocolate Delight and started on a gallon of Death by Fudge before turning to the cookies.

Boy, can the woman eat cookies. We'd bought out the Kroger bakery when we'd stopped at nine last night to stock up, thinking we'd have enough for the next few days. Not a crumb remained, not even a crumble on Betsy's lips. She'd consumed them all before she passed out in a sugar stupor around three, still wearing her wedding gown.

I shoved my feet into my fuzzy pink slippers and grabbed my robe.

Gizmo groaned and opened his eyes without lifting his head.

"Fine. Stay in bed, but you'll miss out on Julia's eggs."

The door creaked as I slipped out of my bedroom and tiptoed down the hall to the bathroom. A ball of white fluff draped in a brown and red blanket lay motionless on the couch. My heart ached for Betsy. I couldn't bring myself to tell her about the marriage certificate or the crime family last night. But today, I'd have to tell her so we could focus on finding the real killer before the trail grew cold.

My dad, Joe Anderson, a retired detective, had taught me that the window of opportunity stayed open for about two weeks. After that, people's memories tended to fade, and physical evidence became contaminated making it harder and harder to solve the crime. Plus, we were dealing with people from out of town. The police could only keep them here for so long.

The thought of Jimmy spending his life in prison made my stomach churn. Or it could be all the junk food I consumed consoling Betsy.

I inched my way through the living room into the kitchen for coffee. Checking the clock on the microwave, I sighed. Late to church again. The fact my dad insisted we sit up front so he could hear better didn't help the situation.

Grabbing a filter, I poked it into the basket and scooped out three spoons of coffee, added water, and hit the go button. The gurgling of the water sounded like music to me. Rubbing my tired eyes, I decided to skip church. I'd catch up with the family at dad's house for our Sunday dinner.

"Hey, I thought I smelled coffee brewing." Julia gave me a limp smile.

"How did you sleep?" I kept my voice low, so I wouldn't disturb our guest on the couch.

Julia rolled her shoulders and stretched. "Like I was wrestling an alligator."

"Oh, that well." I grinned.

"I surfed on a tidal wave of sugar for at least an hour before I could relax. Then I heard Gizmo in your room. One of those bark snores he does." Julia leaned her forearms on the counter.

Giggling, I pulled two mugs from the cabinet above the coffee machine. "Yeah, the little guy is sleeping in. Gizmo didn't know what to do to comfort Betsy last night. He wore himself out licking her hands and face, trying to console her."

"I think he wanted the splotches of ice cream on her chin." Julia melted into one of the chairs at the kitchen table. "How did we ever do those all-night slumber parties when we were teenagers? We could stay up, eat pizza and a gallon of ice cream, and still function the next day—no problem."

"I believe the key word is teenager." I poured a cup of brew for her and placed it on the table along with the creamer and sugar before I filled the second mug.

The rustling of silk taffeta caught my attention, and I turned to find Betsy standing in the doorway with the brown and red throw wrapped around her shoulders. Streaks of dried-on mascara still smudged her cheeks.

Opening the cabinet, I pulled out another mug and filled it as Betsy shuffled her way to the small kitchen table and plopped into a seat. The train of her gown piled next to the leg of the table.

I carried the two mugs over and sat across from Julia. Umpteen things to say ran through my mind, but none of them fit the situation. Betsy's dull eyes studied the mug sitting in front of her.

"Are you hungry?" As a chef, Julia thought food could help every problem.

Betsy shook her head and took a sip of coffee. "I don't think I could eat. Ever." She looked down at her gown. "How did it go so wrong?" The question that had been her mantra all night sprang to her lips again. "So terribly wrong?" She ran her hand down the silk. Her bottom lip quivered.

After all the waterworks yesterday, the poor girl had to be as dry as a bone. But no, a few tears trickled out.

"Aw, sweetie, that's what we're going to find out. We'll clear Jimmy of the murder, and you two will be starting your happily-ever-after before you know it." Julia squeezed her cousin's hand. "Right, Amy Kate?"

I froze. It's true I didn't think Jimmy had murdered the reverend. But the pesky facts about his family being a criminal element in Atlanta kept buzzing around in my head. What if I were wrong? What if Jimmy wasn't the nice guy I thought him to be? After all, I'd thought Gramps was a teddy bear, and look how that turned out.

"Amy Kate?" Julia nailed me with a withering glare.

"Sure. Certainly. We're going to clear Jimmy. Of course. But I do have a few questions I need to ask you before we go any further. A few minor points I want to straighten out."

The corners of Betsy's lips plummeted into a deep, deep frown. "What do you need to know?" She tensed. "Jimmy is my husband, and he needs your help. Yesterday you told me you'd help. You're not backing out on me, are you?" Panic dripped from her words.

"No, I'm not backing out. I have every intention of helping. But …" I glanced from Julia to Betsy then back. Julia nodded, encouraging me to continue. "There's something you need to know about Jimmy and his family."

"I know they're a little eccentric, but whose family isn't?" Betsy rested her elbow on the table and placed her chin in the palm of her hand.

Figuring there was no easy way to spill the beans, I went for it. "Gramps Morelli is Frank Morelli—head of one of Atlanta's most dangerous crime families. They're mobsters. Plain and simple."

Betsy slammed back in her chair like someone had pushed her. "No, not sweet old Gramps. He's as harmless as a ladybug."

"You do know ladybugs bite, right?" I asked.

Julia rolled her eyes. "That's not helpful." Turning to her cousin, she patted her hand. "Gabe told us yesterday when they were interviewing everyone in the fellowship hall. I know it's a lot to take in, but it is true."

Betsy's eyes grew as round as bagels. "Jimmy told me he wanted out of the family business and that's why he went away to college. I assumed he meant the chain of dry cleaners they own." She shook her head. "Mobsters?"

Gizmo sauntered into the room and trotted to his food bowl. Finding it empty, he came to investigate the pile of silk next to the table. He nudged the soft material with his nose and snuggled into it. Laying his head on his front paws, he closed his eyes.

Seeing where he'd decided to nap, I picked up his bowl from the mat and filled it. The clinking sound of the kibbles hitting the ceramic perked Gizmo right up, and he left the soft bed of the wedding dress train for meatier pastures.

I rolled the top of the dog food closed and clipped it shut. "So, you don't think Jimmy has anything to do with the family business?"

Betsy squared her shoulder. "I'm certain of it. My Jimmy would never be a part of such an awful endeavor. He's too kindhearted. The man can't even watch those specials on the Animal Channel where the mother bird has to push her babies out of the nest. He tears up every time and hides his eyes while he waits for them to fly to safety." Her eyes hardened. "No way that man is a killer. You can't fake that kind of compassion."

"All right." I sat back down at the table. Smiling, I motioned toward Betsy. "The first thing I need you to do is to get cleaned up. I have an assignment for you and Julia while I'm at my dad's house this afternoon. You need to go through the pictures of the guests I took yesterday and match them with the names from the guest book. Especially those related to Jimmy. I'll email the pictures of the guests and the guestbook pages to Julia's computer before I leave for my dad's."

"Do you think his family had anything to do with the reverend's murder? I mean, what's the connection?" Hanging onto the throw, Betsy leaned over and picked up her train then wound it around her arm. "Why would a mob family from Atlanta want to harm Reverend Boggs?"

"I don't know. But it's a good place to start."

"Will you go see Jimmy?" Betsy pushed her chair back and stood, waiting for me to answer.

"Yeah, tomorrow. First thing." And while I was there, I planned on chatting with Gabe to see what he could tell me about the good reverend. Perhaps something in his background would give me a lead—how long he'd been in Pine Lake and where he'd lived before coming here for starters.

Betsy moved to the kitchen doorway. "I think I'll grab a shower."

"Sounds good." Julia leaned back in her chair, and we watched Betsy disappear into the living room.

I picked up my mug letting the steam swirl under my nose as the questions about the reverend swirled in my head. Then it dawned on me. I had a better source than Gabe for gathering the information I needed—my assistant at Twisted Plots bookstore, Flora Smith-Jones. A confirmed member of both the First Community Church and the Pine Lake grapevine, nothing got by her. If Gabe couldn't or wouldn't give me the scoop, Flora could.

Taking a sip of my coffee, I made a mental note to pick up a loaf of cinnamon raisin bread on my way into work. It was Flora's favorite, and she always chatted more with a piece of cinnamon raisin bread at the end of her fork.

~

The aroma of chicken and dumplings wafted through the house drawing me straight to Dad's kitchen. I tossed my purse onto the couch as I passed by the living room.

Sundays for the Anderson family meant church and dinner at Dad's house. Ever since Mom's death six years ago, Dad insisted we stay connected, and our weekly dinners at his house kept us up-to-date with one another's lives. Sure, most people text or email these days, but Dad says there's no replacement for a good bear hug. As he wrapped his arms around me, I agreed with him. The scent of his cologne tickled my nose and made the stress of the last few days dissolve. Home and family—it felt good.

He released me and picked up his wooden spoon to stir the bubbling white gravy in the pot. "How are you, honey?"

I leaned against the island in the middle of the kitchen. "I'm all right. It's Betsy I'm worried about."

Alexia, my younger sister, stood by the stove dropping dough into the bubbling mixture.

I picked up her son, Grant, from his spot on the floor and swung him onto my hip. It seemed he'd grown another two inches since I saw him last week. I blew a raspberry on his pink, chubby cheeks, and he laughed showing his two bottom teeth.

"How is the bride?" Alexia asked.

"How do you think? Awful. She cried half the night. Julia and I fed her ice cream and cookies until she passed out in a sugar coma. But no amount of chocolate is going to fix this mess."

"Bite your tongue." Alexia grinned. "Chocolate can solve all the problems of the world if people would give it a chance." Taking her son from my arms, she snuggled close to him and baby talked. "Isn't that right, Grant?" The baby giggled and squealed.

Dad swirled the delicious-smelling concoction, pushing the chunks of chicken out of the way while I stepped in to take Alexia's place dropping the last of the dough into the pot.

Cole, Alexia's husband, walked in from the backyard, carrying a giant bowl of sliced watermelon. "Amy Kate, I hear your trouble magnet has been working at top capacity again." He slid the bowl onto the kitchen island and stood behind Alexia, placing his hands on her shoulders. Leaning down, he planted a kiss on her cheek. "A murder of a reverend at a wedding." He shook his head and tsked. "I bet Gabe is thrilled to have you involved in another case."

I raised my hand. "It's not my fault I attract trouble."

Cole grinned. "Wouldn't it be nice if you attracted money instead."

"Yessss. It would be." I sighed. "But instead, I have a weepy bride-to-be and a wannabe groom sitting in a jail cell."

Alexia's brow puckered. "What do you mean a wannabe groom? He *is* the groom. From what Carol said this morning, the ceremony happened. Right?"

"Yeah, but …" I bit my bottom lip, trying to decide if I should tell my family about the marriage-license debacle. Or wait until I had told the bride and groom. But before I could decide, the front door slammed, and my older sister, Elizabeth, called down the hall.

"Where is my favorite nephew?" Elizabeth sing-songed.

Grant wiggled in Alexia's arms, and she placed him on the floor on his hands and knees. He rocked back and forth, revving up his engine to take off.

Dad's laugh rumbled deep in his chest as he tapped the long-handled spoon on the edge of the pot. Yes, family did feel good.

Alexia and Cole followed behind Grant as he crawled towards the living room in search of his aunt.

Alone with Dad, I decided to take advantage of these few minutes and pick his brain about the Morelli family and the mob crimes in Atlanta. Being a retired detective, he had to know something.

"So, Dad, how much do you know about the Atlanta crime families?" I walked to the sink and washed my hands before joining him by the stove.

After resting his wooden spoon in the bright red ceramic holder shaped like a chili pepper, Dad picked up the metal lid and placed it on the pot before turning the heat to simmer. "I know enough to know they're dangerous. Why? What's this about?"

I glanced up and met his gaze. "It's part of the investigation. Apparently, Jimmy's Gramps is the head of the Morelli crime family in Atlanta. Can you believe it? Sweet Jimmy related to a bunch of thugs."

Dad scoffed. "Thugs. Those people have no respect for the sanctity of life. I've seen what they can do. They're not thugs.

They're criminals of the worst kind." The sparkle in his eyes dimmed, replaced by concern. "You don't want to mess around with those folks. Sit this one out."

"But Jimmy and Betsy are counting on me. Jimmy figures the police will think he did it since the circumstantial evidence is so overwhelming. Add that to his family ties, and he has no hope even though he never went into the family business."

"The evidence is that bad?" Dad crossed his arms and leaned his hip against the counter of the island.

I straightened and shifted my weight. "It's bad. The bride found him hovering over the body with the knife in his hand."

"You're kidding? He touched the murder weapon?" Dad's eyebrows winged up.

"Yep, and he moved the chair with the body in it, too," I said.

Dad peered down at his shoes and shook his head. "Poor guy. He's in way over his head. Are you sure the family wasn't trying to make a point?"

"What do you mean?" The lid on the pot rattled under the steam.

"Do you think they wanted to make an example of him for not wanting to be part of the family business? It's a rare thing for them to let anyone walk away from that life. Most people who want out wind up testifying in court against their own flesh and blood and go into witness protection—WITSEC, giving up everything and everyone they know. I'd be surprised if they ever let Jimmy Williams out." Taking a potholder from a hook on the wall by the stove, Dad moved the lid to the side leaving an opening so the steam could escape.

"Oh, I'm sure he's out. Jimmy couldn't do anything like that."

"Maybe not, but I'd make sure before I went any further in the investigation if I were you." Dad turned off the heat under the pot and tossed the potholder onto the counter. "I suppose it won't do any good for me to tell you to stay out of it."

I shook my head. "I told them I'd help, and I have to honor my word. You wouldn't have it any other way." A smile pulled at my lips.

Dad nodded. "If that's the way of it, remember to watch your back. Jimmy keeping his distance and choosing a different road for his life could be reason enough for the Morelli family to make an example of him. And what better way to make their point than killing the reverend who performed his wedding and framing him for it." Dad gathered the silverware and went into the dining room to set the table leaving me to ponder his words. Was this revenge for Jimmy's decision to leave the family business? And if so, could Gramps be behind it?

CHAPTER FOUR

"Our Father, for what we are about to receive, make us truly thankful." Dad's rich voice rumbled the well-known prayer. And we all sang out, "Amen."

The spoons clattered against the bowls as we dug into the thick white gravy. Baby Grant sat in his highchair between Alexia and Cole on the left side of the table. Elizabeth sat beside me on the opposite side, and Dad sat at the head. We left the chair at the other end of the formal dining set open. It'd been Mom's spot, and unless we had company, we filled in the other chairs.

"So, where's Gabe today?" Elizabeth's bright blue eyes shone with mischief. "He's been such a regular. I've gotten used to seeing him here." Her lips parted into a wide grin.

"He's busy working today. You know, on the wedding murder."

"Those two words do not belong together." Alexia grabbed the basket of garlic bread and took a piece before passing it to Dad.

"No, they do not." I blew on my spoonful of chicken and dumplings. "But that's what we're dealing with."

"We?" Cole spooned a small bite into Grant's mouth while the tyke pulled at his piece of bread.

"Yeah, Amy Kate has agreed to help Betsy and Jimmy figure out who could've done this to Reverend Boggs." Dad glanced at me as he passed the basket to Elizabeth.

Cole chuckled. "I knew you couldn't stay out of it."

Alexia swatted Cole's forearm. "Leave her alone."

The worry in Dad's eyes brought on a wave of guilt. I hated to upset him. Ever since Mom's death in a hit-and-run accident, he'd been the quintessential protective father. Add to that his knowledge of the underbelly of our little town, and I was surprised he ever let us out of the house.

"Do you think that's wise?" Alexia asked.

"Doesn't matter what I think." Dad cleared his throat and took a sip of his iced tea. "Amy Kate can take care of herself. I'm confident with Gabe keeping an eye on her, she'll be fine."

"Right," I agreed. "It's not like I'm doing this all on my own." I cut a sideways glance at Elizabeth, one of the best defense lawyers in the state. "In fact, I'm hoping Elizabeth might have some time to talk with Jimmy. See if she can help with his case."

Elizabeth leaned back in her chair with her spoon in midair, staring at me. "Sorry, I have a full docket. I had to move things around to come here to eat. In fact, when I'm done, I need to go meet with my team to discuss our strategy for the Upton case that starts tomorrow." She shook her head. "I don't see it happening."

"Okay. Can you suggest someone who could do the job as well as you?" I tilted my head, waiting.

Elizabeth prided herself on her work ethic. She gave each case a hundred percent, fought to win, and treated her clients with respect. Using these facts to my advantage wasn't very nice. But desperate people do desperate things, and I needed her as my safety net in case I failed to prove Jimmy's innocence.

Besides—and this was a tad selfish—I couldn't endure another night of consoling Betsy if he didn't get off.

Elizabeth slipped her spoon back into her bowl and clasped her hands under her chin. "Of course, there is Rodney or Keith or Gus, but none of them would be as thorough as my team." She scowled and turned her shoulders toward me. "I hate when you do that."

"Do what?" A grin stretched across my lips as a chuckle escaped. "I'm sorry, Elizabeth. But Jimmy needs the best, and you're it."

Groaning, Elizabeth rolled her eyes and picked up her spoon. "Flattery won't help your cause."

"It's not flattery when it's true." I nudged her elbow with

mine. "Come on, sis. I need you."

"Fine, but I'm going to need to know everything you know. And no running off alone. If it hadn't been for Gabe, your goose would've been cooked the last time you helped a relative of Julia's."

"Understood. I'll keep you in the loop, and Gabe will know what I'm up to."

"I doubt that. But I'll do it." Elizabeth pulled her spoon through the dumplings, but before she took a bite, she asked, "So what do you know so far?"

Hesitating, I made a split-second decision to tell her the whole truth. "Gramps, Jimmy's grandfather on his mother's side, is the head of an Atlanta crime family, and Jimmy was found standing over the body holding the murder weapon, a cake knife."

Caught in the middle of taking another bite, Elizabeth spewed and coughed. White gravy flew from her lips and landed in the middle of the table.

I pushed out my chair and patted her on the back. Everyone else sat frozen except for Grant who squealed at his aunt's antics.

Between coughs, she sputtered. "What? A crime family?" Two more coughs followed, and she took a long drink of her water.

Dad stood and went to the kitchen to retrieve some paper towels.

"That's right. But Jimmy's not a part of the business. In fact, he's done everything he can to stay out of it." Now that Elizabeth seemed to be breathing better, I pulled my chair back under the table and picked up my own spoon.

"You must be kidding. A crime family here in Pine Lake?" Alexia dropped her hands onto the table. "Why would they want to murder poor old Reverend Boggs?"

I glanced at Dad who had returned with the paper towels and dabbed at the spots of chicken broth on the tablecloth. "There could be a number of reasons." The one Dad had pointed out earlier flashed like a neon sign in my mind. "But that's why Jimmy needs my help to figure it out."

"I don't want you to do it," Alexia pleaded. "It's too dangerous. Mobsters, a crime lord. Uh-uh, this one is too hot. Don't do it. Dad, you talk some sense into her."

Dad raised his eyebrows. "Not me." He took his seat and placed the paper towels in a small heap beside his bowl. "Look, I agree with you, Alexia. It is dangerous, but Amy Kate gave her word." Turning to me, he said, "And she has to keep it." A twinkle of pride glistened in his eyes. "Like all Andersons, she has to be true to her word."

I reached over and squeezed his hand. "Thanks."

"So, with that in mind, this is what I know about the Morelli family. They specialize in smuggling goods. Everything from guns to artifacts to people. Frank Morelli has been untouchable. Over the years, there were a few times the Feds thought they had a case against him, but the witness always seemed to disappear, or some minor miracle would happen, and evidence would go missing. So, he'd walk."

My heart moved to my throat forming a lump. What had I gotten myself into? The little old man who had a walker with fuzzy yellow tennis balls on the feet and a Hello Kitty pouch could make witnesses and evidence disappear. I couldn't connect my dad's words with the image in my mind.

"The only time I ever remember one of the Morelli crew being indicted was Frank's younger brother, Tony. He received ten years for fraud and tax evasion. While serving his sentence, he got into a fight with his cellmate or something and died in prison."

I blinked twice trying to digest what I'd just been told. The lump in my throat grew to the size of a grapefruit. Apparently, if the Morellis were part of this, I would need to tread lightly. The thought of disappearing without a trace didn't appeal to me, not one teeny-tiny iota.

~

When I arrived home, Julia and Betsy were seated on the floor around the coffee table with Julia's tablet propped up, assigning names to the people in the images on the screen. A faint smell of cookies hung in the air.

Betsy looked up from the papers in front of her. "Oh, hi. You're back already?"

"Yeah, it's almost seven." I hung my monster of a purse on the coatrack behind the door and leaned down to pet Gizmo who had jumped from the couch to greet me. "How's my boy doing?"

"He's in love with Betsy." Julia leaned back against the

couch behind her. "She's spent the afternoon rubbing his belly and feeding him cookie crumbs."

"A friend for life." I gave Gizmo one last scratch between the ears and straightened. The fact Betsy wasn't drowning in tears didn't escape me. Perhaps having them work through the photos of the wedding guests and the names in the guestbook had taken her mind off the ruined wedding and redirected her thoughts toward helping Jimmy.

I moved into the living room and took a seat in one of the overstuffed chairs. "So, how's it going? Any luck identifying all the people in the photos?"

"Well—" Julia crossed her legs Indian-style and leaned her elbow on the coffee table. "So far, we've been able to match most of the people and the names. But there are a few guests Betsy doesn't recognize."

"Yeah, one of Jimmy's cousins and his family didn't make it in until a few hours before the ceremony. So, I didn't have the chance to meet them. I figured the ones I didn't recognize in this photo were them." Betsy swiped the tablet. "See?"

Moving from the chair, I knelt on the carpet beside her and looked at the picture before me. A man and woman with two elementary-aged children sat around one of the tables near Gramps.

Betsy swiped to another shot. "I didn't know this woman." The lady stood with her head turned at an angle. "Or this guy." She swiped to the next picture and pointed to the shadowy area near the stage where the DJ had set up his equipment.

A second figure stood close to the stage, but the lights on the dance floor made him hard to make out. The man was a little more than an outline.

"And I don't know this guy either, but he could be with the DJ," Julia said.

Betsy glanced toward me. "I mean you can't see much of him except for the side of his face. But he isn't anyone I've met in Jimmy's family, and he's not part of mine. Too tall."

Leaning forward, I squinted. "Hm, I think I recognize him. I mean I don't know who he is, but I've seen him around town. Maybe, he's been in the bookstore before, or perhaps I've seen him eating at the bed-and-breakfast. So, you're right. He might be with the DJ. Maybe helping with the setup and the teardown. But we'll still need to check it out."

Julia nodded. "That's been part of the process—trying to figure out who were guests and who were staff members. So, we made a list. There was the wedding coordinator, Pauline DeVaney, the DJ, Jeffrey Bright, and the caterer who handled the appetizers along with the waitstaff."

"The waiters were easy to spot because of their uniforms, but anyone who tagged along with the DJ or the wedding coordinator, we've had a harder time identifying," Betsy added. "But by the time of the reception, I think Pauline had sent most of her extras home."

"That makes sense." I moved my legs out in front of me, crossing them at the ankles and leaned my back against the couch to get comfortable. "And of course, all the people connected with the florist had left before the ceremony started. I saw The Cracked Flowerpot van pulling out as I arrived. So how many people are left to identify?"

"Maybe three. Not counting the cousin and his family," Julia said. "But one of them we believe is a member of the catering staff without their bow tie."

"Not bad for an afternoon's work." I smiled.

"Afternoon and evening," Betsy corrected.

"Well, I do have to confess we took a break to bake some cookies." Julia grinned. "We ran out, and you know how demanding Gizmo can be about his cookies."

Gizmo's head popped up from the chair cushion when he heard his name.

"Yes, he's so demanding." I giggled.

"It wasn't all wasted time. While I baked, Betsy typed the names from the guestbook photos onto a list on the computer, so we could match the names easier. Some of the handwriting was atrocious."

Betsy handed the printed list to me. "We put checkmarks next ·to each name as we matched it to a photo. All the names have been matched to a photo, but we have three people in the photos who don't have names in the guestbook."

I pursed my lips and nodded. "Meaning those three people weren't supposed to be there or they were part of staff."

"Right," Julia said. "And once we finished matching the photos and names, we decided to do a little sleuthing of our own."

Betsy wiggled her eyebrows, a smile splayed across her lips. "You'll never guess what we found."

Julia tapped the keys on the keyboard. "We looked up Reverend Boggs in the online edition of the paper, and look what we found? One of our mystery guests is none other than Reverend Boggs' secretary, Tammy McNair." Julia's grin spread from cheek to cheek. "Not bad, huh? For a couple of amateurs."

"Not bad at all." I rubbed my chin as I studied the photo of Tammy McNair standing next to the reverend outside the church in front of the nativity scene.

Several questions rolled around in my mind. First, why was she in the fellowship hall during the Williams' wedding, and second—and the most important—did she have a reason to want her boss dead?

CHAPTER FIVE

The Beans and Leaves Coffee Shop sat right next door to my bookstore, Twisted Plots, on the west side of the town square. Each side of the square housed three shops of varying types. Elizabeth's law office sat on the east side right across the town green, diagonal from my business.

I can't count the number of times I've said a silent prayer of thanks for the Beans and Leaves location. Many mornings, it saved me when I ran late and didn't have time to make my much-needed cup of joe at home. Stepping inside, I spotted Matt Murphy, the owner, and waved.

"Amy Kate, your usual?" Matt wiped his hands on the green apron he wore with the store logo on it. The coffee bean and tea leaf dancing the tango always brought a smile to my lips.

"Actually, I'll need to add two slices of cinnamon raisin bread to the two coffees today. If you have some."

"Not a problem. Julia dropped off several loaves this morning along with an apple crumb cake that smelled yummy. Can I interest you in a slice?"

Julia, my roommate, worked as the head chef at Whispering Pines Bed-and-Breakfast. In her off time, she ran her own bakery, Pure Sweetness, out of the Whispering Pines kitchen. The arrangement was perfect. She had the use of a commercial-grade kitchen, and they got first dibs on all her delicious baked goods for their customers.

The offer of the apple crumb cake tempted me for a moment, but I knew cinnamon raisin bread was Flora's absolute favorite, so I stuck with the plan. "No, just the cinnamon raisin bread, please."

After paying, I picked up the beverage tray in one hand and the brown paper bag in the other and walked toward the door. My purse hung from my shoulder and my keys to the bookstore were clutched in the same hand as the paper bag. A juggler, I'm not.

At the door, I spotted a copy of the *Pine Lake Daily* lying open on one of the tables. The picture on the front page caught my eye. There I stood in the background watching the chaos as the uniformed officers questioned the wedding guests. "Hey, Matt, is it all right if I take this copy of the newspaper with me?"

Smiling, he nodded. "I saw the picture. Betsy's wedding reception sure turned sour. I can't imagine how she must feel. And the groom. Such a shame."

Balancing the beverage tray in one hand and letting my purse slide to my elbow, I grabbed the paper from the table with my forefinger and thumb. I had to work hard to keep the brown bag with the bread slices and my keys from falling to the floor.

Wrestling the paper to where I could see the headline, I read, "Murdered Reverend Found at Wedding Reception." The first line named Reverend George Boggs as the deceased.

"It's strange to think the reverend won't be coming in every afternoon for his cup of Lavazza."

"Lavazza? What's that?" The newspaper slipped in my hands, but I gripped it a little tighter, rumpling the pages.

"It's a type of Italian coffee that will put hair on your—" Matt stopped and grinned, glancing up from wiping the counter. "Well, you know what I mean. He loved the stuff. I special ordered it for him from a company in Atlanta. I told him I could get it from my regular vendors, but he insisted it come from the one in Atlanta. He said it had a special flavor, since they ordered it straight from Italy."

"I didn't realize he was a regular." The reference to Atlanta blazed bright.

"Oh yeah, he came in almost every day." Matt slung the damp white rag across the top of the display case.

I shifted the items in my hands, and a thought presented itself. "Did you notice if he was acting strange last week? You know, anxious or nervous? Anything out of the ordinary?"

"Not that I could tell. But we didn't do much chitchatting. If others were in the shop, they tended to monopolize his time." Matt stopped and leaned his elbows on the counter. "But since you mentioned it, he did behave out of character a few weeks back. Reverend Boggs came in and snapped at one of the ladies having tea when she asked him about the annual craft show in September. He apologized on the spot but seemed a bit preoccupied. When I asked him if anything was wrong, he said the bishop was coming for a visit to check on some church business. When I asked if he'd been surprised by the bishop's upcoming visit, he said no, he'd been the one to ask him to come."

"Well, that doesn't sound too distressing." My arm ached under the weight of my purse, and my hand threatened to cramp if I didn't get moving.

"No, but I did have to wonder why he wanted the bishop to visit." Matt shrugged and straightened. "When I saw him the next afternoon, he seemed fine."

"Hmm. I'll have to make a note about the bishop's visit and see if Gabe knows anything about it. Thanks for the information and the coffee." I swung my hip to push open the door, but before I made contact, an older woman in a bright purple jogging suit opened it for me.

Stumbling through the door, I tripped over my own feet sending me lurching toward the sidewalk face-first. But before my knees gave way, a strong arm caught me and kept me from wearing two cups of coffee.

"Easy there." A low rumble near my ear sent goose bumps skittering down my arms. In one sweeping motion, the man righted me onto my feet.

Looking up, I recognized my rescuer as one of Jimmy's groomsmen, Mark. He had an olive complexion, a lush thick head of dark hair, and brown eyes like Gabe's. He'd been the one to help with Betsy when she'd fainted.

"Oh—" I beamed. "Thank you so much. That could've been a real disaster." Heat crept up the back of my neck and warmed my cheeks. "I seem to have a knack for bumping into you."

"Hey, you were the one helping Betsy at the wedding, right? When she fainted."

"That's right. That's me. Little Miss Helper Bee." What was I saying? Someone stop me before I make an even bigger idiot of myself. "I'd better go. My assistant hates when I'm late."

"Well, it was nice 'bumping' into you." His lips spread, revealing a brilliant white smile. "Again."

"My pleasure." Groaning, I pivoted and marched the few steps down the sidewalk to the front door of Twisted Plots.

The lights were on, letting me know Flora had arrived on time as usual. The bell jingled when I pushed the door. The sign next to the bell still read *Closed* to the outside world, but Flora believed in promptness as much as she believed in loyalty to her friends and family.

Over the last ten months of working with her, I'd learned to be more punctual, even though I was the boss. Well, I tried to do better, but when I looked at my watch, I found my stop at the coffee shop and my encounter with the handsome groomsman had pushed me well past my usual arrival time of eight-thirty.

"Flora, you in here?" I carried the beverage holder and the brown paper bag to the back of the store to the workroom. Of all the many things I loved about my bookstore, the workroom rated at the very top of the list, next to the smell of new books and right below the feel of old paper.

I slid the gray cardboard tray and the bag onto the long workstation where we kept the computers we used for inventory. The steel table gave us plenty of room to process in the books, both used and new. Two swivel stools with padded seats and backs covered in a floral China blue pattern sat on either side of the worktable. Comfortable for those days when we spent too much time hunched over the keyboards.

In the corner, my overstuffed chair covered in a plain blue pattern sat surrounded by four end tables of various shapes and sizes. I'd salvaged the tables from the fire earlier this year. They held a cascade of books I'd pulled to read. A floor lamp sat beside my chair giving a warm glow to the area. But the item I most treasured was the second chair, covered in a bright blue floral material because it was where my friends and family would sit and talk about their lives.

"I'm in your office checking my email," Flora called out. "Hope you don't mind. Herman told me he'd send me the receipt for the new dishwasher, so I could print it. It's like all the electronics in our house have gone haywire. First the dishwasher, now the printer. This morning the oil light on my car dashboard flashed on." Flora's face glowed a gentle shade of pink under her short silver locks, and she drummed her fingers on the desk where she sat.

"Well, I guess it's a good thing I brought cinnamon raisin bread for you then," I said.

She leaned back in the office chair and punched the print button. The printer roared to life, and the hum of the paper being sucked into the machine caused Flora to smile. "At last, something works."

"I would hope so. The thing's only a few months old." My eyes grew wide.

Flora gave a weak laugh. "That's true. The fire did force us to replace several items which in truth needed to be."

My assistant was no stranger to technology. Even though she was in her sixties, she did a fair amount of the ordering and financials for Twisted Plots online. She'd come part and parcel with the bookstore when I bought it last year, which had proven to be both a blessing and a curse.

It surprised me she appeared so flustered. "Come on. Let's have our coffee and treat before we open the store."

Settling into the second overstuffed chair, Flora placed her plate in her lap and hugged her tall latte between her hands. "So, I heard what happened at the wedding." She drew in a breath and shook her head. "What a terrible thing for a young bride on her wedding day."

I slipped into the chair across from her and pulled the chain of the floor lamp. The smell of the cinnamon raisin bread beckoned to me, and I took a bite before answering. "I know, right? Betsy's been a mess ever since she discovered Jimmy standing over the reverend holding the cake knife."

"Who could blame her? Anyone in her position would be devastated." Flora took a bite and closed her eyes. Pure delight painted her face.

"Good?" I grinned.

"Um, very good." Flora sipped her coffee. "So, do you think Jimmy did it? Or was it someone else?"

"Betsy swears he's innocent, so it must be someone else unless she's a bad judge of character." I glanced down at the foam cup in my hand. "But I'm not sure who. That's why I wanted to talk to you this morning. I don't know much about Reverend Boggs, but I hoped you could fill in some of the gaps for me." I pressed my lips together, waiting.

"Well, what do you want to know?"

"Stuff like how long he's been here? Maybe, a little bit about his character. Things like that." I didn't want to insult her by asking for the latest news firing up and down the local grapevine, but I wanted to know that too. "And what can you tell me about his secretary?"

Flora leaned back in the chair and tilted her head to the right. "Let me think. I know he's been in town for about twelve years."

"Oh, so he's still a newcomer." I chuckled.

"Exactly." Flora grinned. "I've heard several ladies from his congregation speak very highly of him. But of course, they were widows and the reverend, as I understand it, was single." She winked. Placing her coffee on top of one of the books on the end table, she pursed her lips and squinted. "As far as his secretary goes, she's lived here all her life. Grew up with one of my sons. They went to school together. Sweet girl. Now, she could give you a much better idea of what sort of man the reverend was. You know—what his habits were, who he spent time with—that sort of thing."

I hesitated. "Do you think she'd have a reason for, you know, wanting the reverend gone?" I tried to phrase the question as delicately as I could since Flora had known the woman all her life.

"No, not Tammy McNair. She's the kindhearted type. The idea of something sinister wouldn't even cross her mind."

"Oh, I see." I took another bite and changed the direction of the conversation. "Do you happen to know how old the reverend was? To me, he looked to be in his late sixties." Glancing up, I caught Flora peering at the wall clock. She'd want to open the bookstore soon, so I needed to move to the big question.

"I think he was sixty-seven, but I'm not sure."

"Flora, have you heard any ..." I hesitated out of politeness and avoided the word gossip— "news about the reverend in the last few weeks? Matt mentioned the reverend came into the coffee shop not too long ago and acted out of sorts, even snapped at some ladies. When Matt asked about it, the reverend said something about the bishop paying a visit."

"Oh, yes, I'd forgotten. There was talk about a Methodist bishop coming to town—something to do with the building committee. Carter mentioned it to me. They've been putting money into the fund for years. I can't imagine what happened to draw the bishop's attention to it now."

"Really? They've been working on it for years?"

Flora nodded. "Since the time Reverend Boggs came on. He was the driving force behind the building plan. The reverend thought they needed a larger fellowship hall and wanted to turn the present one into a daycare facility to help the working moms in the community."

"Wow, twelve years is a long time to be gathering funds. Guess if I were the bishop, I'd be curious, too." I grabbed my coffee from one of the four end tables and took a sip, deciding not to share the fact that it was the reverend who had invited the bishop to town. "You don't happen to know who's on the building committee, do you?"

"No, but I'm certain Carter would know since he's a member of the First Methodist Church."

"True. I've heard Carter talking about the reverend and some of his out-of-the-box sermons. He loved his unique take on things." Standing, I took my plate and empty coffee cup to the trash can at the end of the workstation. "Too bad Reverend Boggs won't be around to deliver any more messages."

Flora sighed. "Yes, it is too bad. From everything I've heard over the years, his congregation loved him. A breath of fresh air."

"Carter comes in at two, right? Can you stay a few extra minutes, so I can talk to him alone? It might be better to do my nosing around on the down low."

Flora laughed, a twinkle dancing in her eyes. "Yes, dear, we should keep it on the down low. Since it's been in the paper, and half the town saw you at the wedding, plus people know you're dating the detective on the case, so you're right we should definitely keep it on the down low."

Quashing the urge to roll my eyes, I crossed my arms. "Fine, point taken. Can you stay or not?"

CHAPTER SIX

Standing in the waiting area of the Pine Lake Police Department, I spotted Officer Wallace sitting behind the front desk, skimming today's paper. He glanced up, and I waved as I headed toward the elevators.

"Hey, the star of the hour," he called across the empty lobby and motioned for me to come over, holding up a copy of the newspaper. I veered in his direction.

Usually, the lobby teemed with activity, but today it seemed as if the small-town criminal element had received the news a bigger fish was in town and had collectively decided to stay home. I glanced around the area before meeting Officer Wallace's gaze. "Weird. Has it been this quiet all day?"

Wallace nodded. "Yeah, ever since the news leaked about Frank Morelli being here, the crime rate has dropped to an all-time low. We've issued a few traffic tickets, but anything more than jaywalking has halted."

Peering over the tall counter, I scoffed. "It won't last. In a few days, everything will be back to normal. You'll be picking up Stan so he can sleep it off before he goes home to Rose, and Seth will be back to spray-painting the alleys—" Making air quotes with my fingers, I added, "—leaving his mark on the world. And Mrs. Culpepper will be in to complain about her neighbor, Mr. Fortenberry."

"Probably." Wallace chuckled. "but I'm going to enjoy it

while it lasts." His gaze drifted back to the paper. "Not a bad picture of you." He pointed to me standing in the background as the officers interviewed the wedding guests in the fellowship hall. "Nice dress."

Flattered, I smiled. "Thank you, Wallace. That's nice of you to say." I leaned toward him across the counter and lowered my voice, "I had the shoes dyed special for the occasion. But no one noticed." I waggled my eyebrows. "If you know what I mean."

Wallace leaned back in his desk chair and made a gun with his thumb and forefinger, shooting it in my direction. "Gotcha. So, are you here to see Detective Cooper, or are you here to speak to the prisoner?"

The conversation had been so friendly I almost said to see Jimmy. But I stopped short and didn't say anything. If I told the complete truth, Wallace wouldn't let me go up to the second floor to the detectives' bullpen. He wouldn't appreciate my need to talk with the prisoner. So instead of lying, which I detest, I answered a different question. "You're right. I shouldn't be here to see Gabe after everything that happened on Saturday. He didn't even mention how nice I looked—not once. Then he arrested the groom, leaving me and Julia with a basket case of a bride. I can't tell you how upset Betsy is over this. A royal mess. So, yes, that's why I'm here. But thanks for noticing." I patted his hand resting on the counter and zapped him with my 100-watt smile.

"No problem." Wallace chuckled.

Turning, I made a beeline for the elevator and pushed the button for the second floor. I snuck a peek around the corner in Wallace's direction. Confusion played on his face. He looked my way, but I snapped my head back before we made eye contact. The wheels of the desk chair rolled across the hard tile and footsteps echoed in the lobby behind me. "Come on," I muttered.

The doors to the ancient elevator parted, and I stepped inside not waiting for them to open fully. Pushing the close door button repeatedly, I glanced toward the lobby. A frowning officer rounded the corner as the doors drew together.

I stepped off the elevator onto the second floor wondering what type of reception I would receive. After all, Gabe and I hadn't parted on the best of terms Saturday night. He'd called to check on me and the bawling bride after we'd arrived home, but before the conversation had gone too far, he said something about me not getting involved, and I'd made a crack about him being the worst wedding guest ever. Things spiraled from there. Okay, not my finest moment, but in my defense, I was dealing with a howling, brokenhearted heap of white taffeta. I didn't need an overprotective, close-to-being exclusive boyfriend added to the mix.

I paused outside of the detectives' bullpen. Peering through the glass doors, I glanced toward Gabe's desk near the back and found the chair empty. Scanning the rest of the room, I didn't see him.

As I pulled the door open, the smell of aftershave, old socks, and sweat wafted around me, bringing back memories of my mom and me delivering dinners to Dad on nights he had to work late.

Movement behind the glass in one of the interview rooms caught my attention. Gabe stood on one side of a rectangular wooden table, and Jimmy Williams sat in a metal chair on the other. The frown on Gabe's lips and the tightness of his jaw gave me the information I needed.

My appearance here wouldn't be welcomed. I peered back at the door and thought about retracing my steps. But an image of Betsy with her big green eyes pooled in tears as she stuffed her face with cookies drifted into my brain. I'd made the woman a promise, and I needed to make good on it. Leaning my hip against the desk closest to the interrogation room, I watched.

Gabe's tight jaw and straight stance told me Jimmy wasn't talking. As I watched the exchange, Jimmy's face turned red, and he jumped up and pushed the chair back with his legs. Leaning over the table toward Gabe, he stabbed his finger into Gabe's chest.

Gabe didn't back down. He leaned towards Jimmy and said something that made the young man turn pale. Jimmy dropped back into his seat and buried his face in his hands. Picking up the file in front of him, Gabe exited the room, leaving a very shaken Jimmy in his wake. As Gabe rounded the corner into the bullpen, he caught sight of me. "What are you doing here? Never mind. I'm sure I can guess." He strode past me toward his desk.

"Nice to see you, too." I followed hot on his heels. "Look, I know this goes against all the regulations, but I promised Betsy

I'd talk with Jimmy."

Gabe tossed the file in his hand on top of the pile sitting on the corner of his desk. "No."

"What do you mean, no? The least you could do after our disaster of a date where you ruined everything by arresting the groom is to hear me out."

"You need to let that go, all right? I said I was sorry, but my job is my job."

Heat crept up the back of my neck to my cheeks. He was right. I needed to let it go. After living with my mom and dad, I knew what a cop's life was like. And I'd known Gabe the Babe lived and breathed being a cop before I ever agreed to our first date. I dropped my purse on his desk with a clunk and held my hands up in surrender. "You're right."

"Um, I'm glad you agree, but for some reason, I have the feeling there's a but coming my way." His brows knit together into a tight V.

"But—" I leaned my hip against his desk.

Plopping into his chair, he leaned back and crossed his arms. "Okay, I'm listening."

"Betsy is beside herself with worry. She thinks the circumstantial evidence is too overwhelming, and Jimmy will be sent to prison for a crime he did not commit. I promised her I'd talk to him, and you know how I feel about keeping my word."

"I hope you straightened her out."

"About what?" I asked.

"About the fact we don't make a habit of sending innocent men to prison. About the fact we investigate the details and the people involved to determine who our suspects should be. And yes, we use circumstantial evidence, but we also look for motive." Gabe heaved a sigh and straightened. "Look, Amy Kate, I'm sorry work ruined our date. But I hope you'll let me make it up to you as soon as this case is closed."

A sweet smile spread across his lips and a warm light entered his eyes as he leaned forward taking my hand in his. My knees went weak, the traitors that they are.

He stood and drew me to him. "What do you say? Will you give me a chance to take you out somewhere nice, so you can wear that blue dress again?"

"Oh, did you like the dress?" I raised my chin and averted my eyes even though he stood inches from me.

"Yes, I did. It made your eyes sparkle." Gabe tucked a strand of my hair behind my ear. Leaning close, he whispered, "I liked it very much."

I leaned my full weight against the desk so I wouldn't drop straight to the floor. Weak knees and a racing heart can make for a scene, and I didn't want to have a case of the Southern vapors in the middle of the detective bullpen. A picture of Scarlet O'Hara flashed through my mind. Inspired, I batted my eyelashes and placed the palm of my hand on his cheek. "I tell you what, you let me see Jimmy and you've got yourself a date. And I might throw in a batch of my oatmeal raisin cookies you love so much, just for fun."

He removed my hand from his cheek but held it. "Are you saying if I don't let you see Jimmy, you won't go out with me?" A large crease spread across his brow.

"Of course not, but I'm desperate here. I promised Betsy I'd speak with him."

Gabe let go of my hand and stepped back. "Then you shouldn't make promises you can't keep." Sitting down, he rolled his chair closer to his desk.

The set of his jaw clued me in that I'd cooked my own goose. "So that's it? You won't let me speak to him?"

"Nope." Gabe leaned forward and pressed a few tabs on his keyboard.

Not wanting to leave things as they were, I asked, "Are we still going out soon, so I can wear my dress?" I tried to sound upbeat.

He cut his eyes in my direction. "I have a ton of work to do, so can we talk about this later?"

Was he kidding? He expected me to wait to find out if he'd take me out or not, leaving our relationship status in complete flux? What was I supposed to put on my social media profile? Single? In a relationship? Waiting to wear the pricey blue dress? I slung my Goliath of a purse over my arm, stamped my right high heel on the tile floor, and gave him one firm, "Hmph." Pivoting, I marched past the desks littered in my way and straight into the interview room where Jimmy sat wringing his hands.

My temper raged to the point the roots of my blond hair boiled. The nerve of the guy thinking I'd be sitting around waiting on him. "Who does he think he is?" I muttered, slamming my purse on the wooden table. "I can't believe I almost had the 'let's be exclusive' talk with him." I jerked the chair out, swiped my hand across the seat in case there were any cooties left behind, and sat.

Concern filled Jimmy's eyes. "Are you all right?"

"Of course, I'm all right." I scooched my chair under the table and sat straight. "The question is how are you?"

Gabe tapped on the glass window of the interview room. I ignored him.

Jimmy glanced from me to the two-way mirror and back. "Does someone need you for something?"

I lifted my chin. "Apparently not." Rolling my shoulders, I turned my full attention to Jimmy. "First, let me tell you to expect to hear from my sister, Elizabeth Anderson. She's the best lawyer in the state, and she's agreed to help."

Jimmy's whole body sagged with relief. "Gramps is sending one of his guys as well, but thank you. Any help is appreciated."

"You're welcome." Out of the corner of my eye, I kept a lookout for Gabe. "Now, tell me again what happened. Don't leave anything out. The smallest detail could be something important."

Running his hand down his face, Jimmy exhaled. "Betsy and I finished the dances. She danced with her dad, and I danced with my mom. Then we danced our first dance as man and wife." He clasped his hands together on the table. "As we left the dance floor, Reverend Boggs came over to tell me we needed to sign the marriage certificate.

"When I told Betsy, she said she needed to go to the powder room and would meet me in his office. So, she headed back to the bride's dressing suite, and I went to the reverend's office to sign the document. When I got there, the door was open, and he was seated in the chair at his desk. It was turned toward the window. I said hello as I stepped into the room, figuring he was watching the kids in the park across the street. When he didn't respond, I signed the marriage certificate on his desk but kept chattering. When he didn't answer, I walked around the desk and found him stabbed with the cake knife."

"Why did you turn the chair?"

"So, I could pull the knife out. I'm right-handed and was standing on the left-hand side. Thought I could save him." Jimmy leaned back in his seat, shaking his head. "I don't know how an act of mercy has become so boggled." He met my gaze. His eyes pleaded with me to believe him. "I swear I didn't kill the man. Why would I? He'd just given me everything I wanted in life. Betsy."

"There are a few things I need to know. For starters, how long did it take you to get to the reverend's office? Did you see him ahead of you in the hallway or did you stop to talk to someone?"

"Well, I saw him go down the corridor, but he disappeared. I remember watching Betsy as she and one of her bridesmaids headed in the other direction toward the sanctuary and the bride's suite, thinking she would be a while, but I'd wait for her. So, I grabbed a glass of punch because I was thirsty from the dancing."

"A time would be good. Three minutes, five minutes?"

Jimmy huffed and leaned his forearms on the tabletop. "Why does it matter?" Frustration colored his words.

"Because you were the last one to see the reverend alive besides the killer, and you were the one who found his body. I need to know how long between these two events, so I'll know who had the opportunity to murder him."

Wincing, Jimmy swallowed. "Maybe five minutes. No longer than that. I drank my punch and Mark came over. We talked about the car Betsy and I were taking to the airport. I'd rented it and had begged the guys not to use any shaving cream on it when they decorated it for our departure. I didn't want to take a chance of ruining the paint job."

"Okay, so five minutes give or take. Which means it had to be someone at the wedding for them to know the reverend was alone in his office. Someone in the fellowship hall who had seen the reverend go down the hall." Facts swirled in my head. "You said you were going to wait for Betsy. Why didn't you?"

"She took too long. The wedding coordinator interrupted my conversation with Mark to tell me we were supposed to toss the bouquet and garter next, so I thought I'd sign the marriage certificate before the next event, and she could go afterward."

Jimmy's eyes widened. "Oh, something else, I thought I heard a door close somewhere down the hall when I entered Reverend Boggs' office."

"So, let me see if I have this straight. The reverend catches you after the couples dance and asks you to come sign the certificate."

Jimmy moans. "Are we even married? I don't think she ever signed."

Not wanting to jump down that rabbit hole, I continued. "Then he goes down the hall. Betsy goes with someone else to the bride's suite to powder her nose, and while you wait, you grab a cup of punch. Mark stops and talks with you, and the wedding coordinator interrupts. Aware of the time, you decide to go sign the certificate first and tell Betsy to go sign after the throwing of the bouquet. And to the best of your knowledge, five minutes elapsed between the time you saw the reverend in the fellowship hall and finding his body in his office."

"Yes, and don't forget about the door shutting," Jimmy said.

"No, I won't." I reached out and patted Jimmy's hand. "It's going to be okay. Now, can you tell me why someone like your grandfather might want the reverend dead?" I had every intention of pinning this on the Atlanta mobster. After all, it had to be him or someone who worked for him. With the precision of the stab wound, it had to be professional.

"Look, I keep telling everybody I'm not part of the family business. I've kept clear of it. Mom wanted more for me. She'd seen too many people she loved end up in the morgue." Jimmy stared at the table as he ran his palms down the top of his pant legs. His words screamed innocent, but his actions told a different story.

"What aren't you telling me, Jimmy? You need to tell me everything—any detail no matter how small—if you expect me to get to the truth."

He rubbed the back of his neck. All the color drained from his face. "This is going to make it look worse."

"Doesn't matter. I'm not a lawyer. I'm a friend."

His eyes met mine. "I recognized the reverend. Not at first, but after spending some time with him at the rehearsal dinner. He was older and a little wider around, but the eyes were the same.

And he had a chipped front tooth.”

"How did you know him?"

"I met him at Gramps' place a few times one summer when I was eleven and was visiting during the break. Do you think someone at the wedding did this?" Jimmy's eyes widened.

"Yes, but not necessarily someone *with* the wedding party." Tammy McNair's photo popped into my mind. If she was there, who else had come without an invitation?

Sounds outside the two-way mirror caught my attention. I needed to hurry.

"Jimmy, is there anything you want me to tell Betsy?"

He lifted his chin. "Tell her I love her, and I'm going to make this up to her if it takes me the rest of my life to do it."

The door of the interrogation room swung open, and Gabe and Officer Wallace entered.

"Amy Kate, I've been asked to escort you out of the station." Wallace looked apologetic. His eyes crinkled at the corners as he smothered a smile.

Super, my boyfriend was having me thrown out. "Isn't that odd? Usually, police officers escort people into the station." I stood to my full five foot two and pushed my chair under the table.

Wallace cut his eyes toward Gabe who stood inside the doorway. "Simply doing as I'm told."

"I understand." Picking up my purse, I draped it over my shoulder and tightened my lips. As I passed Gabe, I stopped. "I can take a hint when I'm not wanted."

"Don't. I told you not to speak to the suspect, but you wouldn't listen. Don't make me the bad guy." Gabe's warm brown eyes drilled into mine, and I didn't find even a hint of anger in them, only concern. "I can't take any chances with this case. There are other factors in play here. You need to trust me on this one. I can't keep you out of trouble if you're caught interfering, not this time."

Unhappy with his explanation, I lifted my chin. "Well, at least I've learned one thing from this interrogation."

Gabe frowned. "What's that?"

"My relationship status on social media will have to be changed. Do you know if limbo is a choice?"

Wallace let out a half-strangled cough and covered his mouth to hide the smile threatening to appear.

"Oh, and I also learned there was someone else in the hallway when Jimmy found the body. You might want to do a thorough search of the other offices. Seems Jimmy heard a door shut." Score one for the limbo-status girl.

CHAPTER SEVEN

Aggravation and embarrassment swarmed around me like buzzing bees. The nerve of the man. I'd never been so humiliated in all my life. Throwing me out of the police station.

The bell on the front door of Twisted Plots bounced against the glass as I barreled through it. Well, okay there was the dumpster-diving incident and maybe the time I'd been bound and gagged by Julia's cousin. But honestly, this pushed all my buttons.

Carter Cooper, Gabe's dad and one of my mature employees, stood behind the counter hunched over the computer entering the new inventory, his short silver sideburns framing his face. He glanced up. "Hey."

"Hey, yourself." I snapped, dodging the display table featuring this month's summer reads and swerving around the rack holding the hand-painted greeting cards I sold for the senior citizen center. I marched past him straight to my small office across from the workroom and shut the door. Tossing my purse on the desk, I counted to ten, taking slow even breaths before heading back into the main area. Gabe could be so infuriating.

Carter greeted me with a warm, understanding smile. "Better?"

My frustration melted. "Yeah, but your son is skating on thin ice."

He held up his hands in surrender. "I'm not responsible for my son's actions. But I do know he has a lot happening with this case." Carter went back to tapping on the computer keys.

"I picked up on that when I saw him at the police station," I said.

"I take it things didn't go so well?" Carter's eyebrows pinched together as the little crinkles around his eyes appeared. "Did you get to speak with Jimmy?"

"Yes, but not with Gabe's consent."

"Oh, I see." Carter pursed his lips, not glancing up from the screen.

"The funny thing is, though, he didn't seem angry. He seemed more concerned like I was in danger." I shook my head. "Which is absurd. Jimmy isn't dangerous."

"No, but I know for a fact his family is. Maybe Gabe doesn't want you mixed-up in something that could turn deadly." Carter leaned his elbow on the counter and met my gaze.

"Maybe." I trusted Carter's judgement, and who knew Gabe better? But a little spark of doubt about his motives still simmered in my mind. "Where's Flora?"

"Oh, she went ahead and made the two o'clock mail run."

Grabbing my phone from my back pocket, I noted the time.

"She waited for as long as she could but didn't want to get caught in the after-school traffic." Carter slid the stool from behind the counter and took a seat. "Flora also told me you had a few questions for me about the First Methodist Church."

The door jangled, and we both turned. Three teenage boys strolled over to the small comic-book section I kept stocked for them, since they were regulars. One of them waved.

I peered at Carter. "Flora said there was talk of a bishop coming for a visit and it pertained to the building committee. Is that true?"

"Yes, the bishop arrived yesterday." Carter nodded. "It's sad, but the reverend believed there might have been some mishandling of funds and wanted the bishop to look over the books."

"Is there any substance to the accusations?" I leaned my forearms on the counter, drawing closer to Carter so the teens couldn't hear.

He bobbed his head from side to side. "Possibly. After all, the church has been collecting funds for the building project for twelve years, long before Maureen and I were on the scene. You'd think they'd have started the actual building by now. There could've been some miscalculations over a period that long."

"True. I wonder who pointed out the discrepancy to the reverend?"

"I'm not sure, but I believe it was one of the members of the building committee. There are five sitting on the committee and I know of one who would complain, if she thought something was fishy."

"Really, who?" I asked.

"Ada Culpepper." A lopsided grin rose to his lips.

"Yeah, you're right. If she thought something was fishy, she'd be the first to speak up, loud and clear." The idea of pumping Mrs. Culpepper for information about the building committee appealed to me about as much as the idea of eating worms. At least the worms would be easier to swallow.

"So, you've decided to help Jimmy?" Carter grinned.

The man knew me too well. "Yes, but I'm not sure where to begin."

"At the beginning." Flora entered from the back workroom.

"Where'd you come from?" I turned, wondering why she'd entered through the back alley.

"Oh, Doris had her floral van parked across three spaces. So, I parked in the lot across the street. Thought the walk would do me good."

"Well, I'm glad you came back instead of going home."

"I didn't know when you'd return from the police station, and I didn't want to stick Carter with all this week's inventory. Figured he'd need help shelving everything. Besides, Mrs. Darcy is on the hunt for another classic."

"Which one is it this time?" Carter punched some numbers on the keyboard and placed the book in his hand on top of the third pile.

"*The Three Musketeers*." Flora's eyes sparkled. "Men with swords saving the world." She moved past me and reached for a stack of books on the counter.

"Oh, that's a good one," he said.

Flora stood with her hand on the stack of books. "So, where are you going to start with Jimmy's case?"

"I don't know. Gabe is acting strange. And I don't want to do anything that could jeopardize our dating relationship."

"Gabe always acts strange when you get involved with one of his cases. That's nothing new." Flora shrugged. "He worries."

"This is different. He's acting weirder, more protective." I glanced down as the heat of embarrassment rose to my cheeks. "He threw me out of the police station."

Carter straightened on the stool. "He what?" The twinkle in his eye vanished as his lips hardened into a straight line. "That does sound out of character for him. Does he know something about the case he can't share, and he's trying to protect you?"

"Could be." What Carter said made sense, but my pride still smarted from the humiliation of the whole event. And what made it worse was that Officer Wallace, who I've known my whole life, was the one to escort me to the door. "Maybe I shouldn't help Jimmy. I don't want to cause Gabe any problems."

Flora stood blinking at me with her mouth hanging open. "First, when has the probability of causing Gabe problems ever stopped you?"

Carter chuckled but kept his eyes on the screen.

"And second, if you told Jimmy and Betsy you'd help them, you have to be true to your word." Flora crossed her arms, nailing me with her stare. "As I recall, your Aunt Maude said Anderson women were made of Southern iron, real tough stuff. You're not going to let Gabe's behavior keep you from holding up your end of the bargain, are you?"

Now, guilt washed over me for even considering sitting this one out. "No." I groaned.

"Besides if you don't, the DA has a slam-dunk case. The paper said Jimmy was found standing over the body holding the bloody knife." Flora pivoted and headed toward the True Crime section.

"She has a point." Carter nodded. "The DA does have a beaut of a case. Gabe won't leave any stone unturned, but the DA isn't going to want him to look too hard." Standing, Carter placed his hand in the crook of his back and winced.

I picked up the other stack of books to help Flora shelve them. "Are you all right?"

"Maureen said I tossed and turned most of the night." He

rolled his shoulders.

With the books in hand, I joined Flora in the True Crime section.

"I guess it's having Frank Morelli in town. Brings back bad memories."

Flora stopped, her arm in midair, the book dangling, and she shot me a look.

We both dropped the books in our arms to the floor and scurried back to the counter.

"What do you mean? Why would Frank Morelli being in town cause you to have a restless night?" I asked.

"Yeah, spill. How do you know him?" Flora raised a single eyebrow while casting him a scrutinizing glare.

"No need for all this excitement. Maureen and I lived in Atlanta during the trial of his brother, Tony Morelli. That's all. It took over the local news for months. Frank's and Tony's pictures were plastered on every station. Then one of the witnesses turned up dead."

"Well, that's enough to keep you awake at night." Flora nodded.

"Yeah, the only reason they got a conviction was because someone else who worked for the family business turned state's evidence at the last minute for a deal."

"Who?" Flora's eyes glowed. She loved being in the know, and this tidbit would give her added juice for the grapevine.

I wondered if it was the reverend like Jimmy had told me. Was he the one who had testified in the case?

"I don't remember his name. Since the first witness came up dead, they kept this one under wraps. Limited news coverage. No media in the courtroom. Very guarded."

Flora's face fell.

Trying to find some morsel she could use, I said, "What happened to him? I mean, after the trial."

"He went into WITSEC. It was part of the deal and no jail time." Carter's eyebrows winged up. "I remember because when the news about it leaked out after the trial, so many people were outraged he'd cut a deal. The Morelli family caused a lot of grief for a lot of people in the Atlanta area. And the community wanted the family to pay for the crimes they'd committed, as well as the lowlifes who worked for them.”

Could Jimmy have been right? Had the reverend worked for the family at one time? I needed to find out.

Flora reached over and turned the computer Carter was using toward her. “Let’s do a little research, shall we?” She typed in the Morelli name and added the search terms, *Atlanta* and *trial*. Several articles dated twelve years earlier appeared on the screen. Flora clicked on the one from *The Atlanta Journal-Constitution*. “Says here Frank’s brother, Tony, was convicted on several counts of fraud and tax evasion. He received a ten-year concurrent sentence. Isn’t that how Capone was caught? Tax evasion?” Flora glanced up and met Carter’s gaze.

“Yep, you can skirt the FBI, the CIA, and TSA, but you’d better not mess with the IRS.” Carter grinned.

Flora and I groaned at his attempt at humor and turned our focus back to the article on the computer. “Dad told me about this last night. He got like ten years and was killed in prison.”

“Says here,” Flora continued. “—the witness was connected to the Morelli family through a third party. He worked for a financial company who handled the Morelli fortune.”

Carter leaned his arms on the counter and craned his neck to see the screen. “That sounds familiar. Does it give the name of the company?”

“No, but it mentions the company handled their accounts. The daily income of the businesses—both the legitimate and illegitimate ones.” Flora scrolled down the page, then clicked back to the list of articles the search had pulled up on the browser.

Carter leaned as close as he could with the counter in his way, and I skimmed the page over Flora’s shoulder as she rolled the mouse.

Scrolling down the page, Flora stopped on an article titled “Mysterious Witness Speaks Out.” Clicking on the article, a fuzzy photo of a group of people ascending the steps of a courthouse appeared on the screen.

“See if you can enlarge that photo.” Excitement bubbled in me.

Flora fiddled with the zoom on the computer and magnified the picture by a hundred and fifty percent. But the original had been too fuzzy for the enlargement to help. I couldn’t tell if it was a younger version of Reverend Boggs flanked by law enforcement or not. Especially since the photographer had captured a side view of the main subject as the group ascended the stairs.

"Wait." Carter circled the counter and pointed to the man standing in the middle of the group. "That's him. That's the witness who put Frank Morelli's brother in jail."

CHAPTER EIGHT

Flora left a little after three, and I spent the next hour shelving the books as Carter entered them into the computer. Kirk Woodard, a college student from the nearby university, worked for me some evenings and weekends. He was scheduled to relieve me at five.

A few customers flowed in and out all afternoon, and the teens who had showed up close to two stayed until Kirk arrived. They met him at the door with questions about some popular video game everyone was playing.

As they moved to the back hallway, sputtering out their questions faster than Kirk could answer, I noticed the comic book section sat in complete disarray. Deciding to straighten it before heading home, I walked over to the magazine racks and knelt to pick up the scattered books. The bell on the door rang out, and I glanced up to see who had entered. Gabe stood in the doorway of Twisted Plots holding a bouquet of flowers, big enough for him to hide behind.

Gabe spotted me, behind one of the three club chairs bunched together in front of the magazine racks. My eyes connected with his.

He hugged the beautiful spring flowers to his chest and zigzagged across the main floor, dodging display tables and racks to the spot where I knelt holding an armful of comics. "I see you're getting your comic book-fix." He smiled down at me and offered me his free hand.

Not wanting to give him the wrong impression, I grabbed the back of the chair and pulled to a standing position in front of him. He needed a lot more than a few, okay a ton, of flowers to make up for what he had done. "What can I do for you, Detective."

Gabe groaned. "Can we talk somewhere private?"

"Why? You didn't seem too concerned about privacy when I was the one getting tossed out on my ear." The embarrassment of the moment replayed in my mind, stirring up a flame that heated my cheeks.

"You didn't leave me any choice. But that's why I'm here." Gabe stepped closer.

Kirk and the three teens emerged from the back workroom and walked straight toward us. "Okay, if you want to kill the lord of the castle in the tower, you first have to get through the night shadows on the second level. You must have the key of worthiness in order to open the stairway that leads to the other levels."

The red-headed teen sat in the chair in front of me and propped his feet on the coffee table in the middle of the grouping. The other two settled in the other two chairs, and Kirk sat on the floor with the book about the video game on his lap. None of them even noticed we were standing there.

"Can we go outside? I need to talk to you." He presented the bouquet to me.

I hated the fact I couldn't resist them. Taking the flowers, I handed him the comic books. "I'll go put these in a vase. Make yourself useful and put these back where they belong."

A grin appeared on his well-formed lips. "Consider it done."

The warmth in his eyes worked to cool my anger. The giant bundle of flowers didn't hurt either. I arranged the bouquet in a vase and placed it on the counter in the main area so everyone including the customers could enjoy the fragrant scent. Then I made a second trip to the workroom and grabbed my purse so I could leave for home once I'd heard what Gabe had to say.

When I returned to the main section, Gabe was chatting with his dad at the counter. "There she is." Carter smiled and stood. He eyed my purse. "Are you leaving for the day?"

"If that's all right. Gabe wanted to speak with me, and I thought I'd go ahead and take off once he finished." I tucked my purse under my arm and moved in front of Gabe, standing between him and his father. Acting as if Gabe didn't exist, I continued. "I figured I'd hear him out."

Carter's eyebrows winged up, and he nodded. "I see. It shouldn't be a problem." Pointing toward Kirk, he added, "Seems he has everything in hand on the customer front."

I sighed. Late summer was always a slow time for the bookstore business, but since last week, it had ground to a halt. Surveying the stocked shelves and magazine racks as well as the gift items and cards, my heart faltered. The store couldn't afford to have a slow season. We were still recovering from the fire and makeover. I needed to think of a way to pump some life back into the old girl. Standing there contemplating the possibilities, I forgot all about Gabe until he touched the back of my arm.

"Are you ready?"

"Oh, sorry. Yeah. I'm ready." In that split second, I forgot to be mad.

We headed to the parking lot across Harding Street where Gabe had parked next to my van, an old blue Caravan whose 'best if used by date' had long passed. I leaned against my van, and he leaned against Baby—his beautiful red Corvette.

I'll admit dating a handsome guy with a hot car had perks. "So, what did you want to say?" Hugging my purse to my chest, I knew I had stepped over a line when I'd entered the interview room without permission, but he'd acted so out of character. So unyielding.

Gabe moved from leaning against his car to standing beside me. "Forgive me. I went too far this morning." He took my hand and held it. "I should've handled it myself and not involved Officer Wallace, who by the way, got a great laugh from it. He must've told half the squad about what happened and the look on your face." A chuckle rumbled in his throat, but after a glance at me, he swallowed it.

Horrified, my eyes widened, and I huffed, "Is the fact he got a few laughs at my expense supposed to make things better?" Irritated, I tried to pull my hand from his, but he wouldn't let go.

Instead, he stood straight and peered deep into my eyes.

The heart is a fickle thing, but my knees—they tend to be dependable. But not today. I sagged as the traitors weakened and my iron resolve melted into a pool of mush. The concern in his face broke down all remaining barriers.

"Amy Kate, the truth is this case frightens me. I don't like where the evidence is leading, and I'm afraid you're going to get in further than you should." He squeezed my hand. "And I'm not going to be able to rescue you this time. Don't you know I couldn't stand it if something happened to you? If I lost you." Any hint of humor drained from his face. "This isn't the usual case. It involves other law-enforcement organizations, who may not share all their information with me, and the Morellis are dangerous and unpredictable. I need to know you're safe. Please—I'm begging you to stay out of this one. The risk is too high."

The intensity in his eyes made a chill run down my arms even in the August evening heat. "I've given my word. Besides, who else is going to help Jimmy? The DA has an airtight case against him. He's not going to have you look for anyone else. And my gut tells me Jimmy's innocent. A guy in the wrong place at the wrong time."

Gabe released my hand and leaned his back against my van. "That's what my gut tells me too. Which means I'll keep looking into it. No matter what the DA or the chief thinks."

My heart did a somersault. "So, you think he's innocent as well?"

"Yes, but proving it is going to be a job. If he'd left the knife alone, or called for help right away, but he didn't. And none of that plays in his favor. Add in the family ties and the fact that—" Gabe stopped.

"What? Add in the family ties and what?" I turned toward him, so I could see his expression.

He shook his head and studied the ground. "Nothing. I can't say."

"Well, if you're going to tell me Reverend Boggs was the witness in the Tony Morelli case who sent him to prison, I already know."

His head snapped up. "How on God's green earth could you know that?" His voice rose.

Looking around the parking lot to make sure no one was in earshot, I moved closer. "Shh, you don't want anyone to hear about this. *The Pine Lake Daily* would eat it up and take the opportunity to get the scoop on the other statewide newspapers. It's bad enough they've printed what they have so far."

"Fine. How did you find out?" He asked.

"Jimmy told me. He said he thought he recognized him. Reverend Boggs was older and heavier, but he had the same eyes and a chipped tooth."

Gabe held up his hands to stop me from saying anything more. "Don't tell me." He shook his head and tsked. "I can't believe it. Thought the case against him was as bad as it could get, but boy, was I wrong."

"What do you mean?" Worry crept into my voice.

"Don't you see? If Jimmy admits to recognizing the reverend, it only works to strengthen the case against him. It gives him motive."

"What motive?" I stood straight facing Gabe head-on.

"Revenge."

"Revenge? For what?"

"For sending his uncle away for life, for embarrassing the family, for proving the Morellis aren't indestructible. Take your pick." Gabe let out a long sigh. "This guy has everything stacked against him. I don't see how I'm going to clear him. He's locked himself in tight."

Feeling the full force of the southern iron running in my veins, I clasped him by his shoulders and kissed him on his cheek. "We are going to do this together. That's how. We're going to find the truth and prove Jimmy Williams is as innocent as a newborn babe. The truth is out there. We simply have to find it."

Gabe smiled and pulled me into his arms, mashing my purse to my side under my elbow. "Together sounds good. But you must keep me in the loop. There are too many unknowns, and I won't risk your safety. I'd rather see Jimmy in jail than lose you." He tucked the crook of his finger under my chin and lifted my face to his. "Understood?"

"Yes, understood."

With that, he leaned over and touched his lips to mine. For a moment, the world sang the sweetest song that flowed in rhythm with the beat of my heart.

Breaking the kiss, he stood with his hands on my shoulders. "So, are we good?"

My lips still tingled from the warmth of his kiss. "Yes, we are very good."

He chuckled. "I have to go, but I'll call you tomorrow. Remember, be safe."

As I slid into the driver's seat of my worn-out van, a small lump formed in my throat. "Speaking of truth," I murmured. My gut told me it was time to tell Betsy the truth, the whole truth, no matter how ugly it was or how bad it would hurt her.

Turning onto Adams Avenue, I pointed my van in the direction of the grocery store to load up on ice cream and sugar cookies before heading to my apartment to break the bad news to her. I couldn't help but wonder which flavor went with "you're not married,"

I grabbed triple chocolate delight and a jar of caramel.

~

"Why me?" Betsy sobbed. Tears ran down her cheeks, dripping mascara onto our white couch. She swiped away the stragglers, but a fresh batch popped up. "My perfect day demolished, the honeymoon cancelled, the love of my life in jail and now, you have the audacity to tell me I'm not married?" The last word came out as a squeak emitted at a pitch only a dog could hear.

Gizmo buried his head under the stack of throw pillows on the couch sitting next to Betsy.

"I thought you should know. That's all. And I didn't want someone else to tell you." I plopped into the overstuffed chair sitting at an angle to the sofa, hating myself for even bringing it up. "Figured it would be better coming from me than one of the police detectives. They'll be around soon enough to talk to you again."

"Detective Simms called and had me come down to the station earlier this afternoon." She hugged one of the throw pillows to her chest, leaving Gizmo unprotected. "At least, I got to see Jimmy for a second." At the mention of his name, the tears pooled.

I pulled some tissues from a box on the coffee table and handed her the wad. "Sorry, I feel like a heel, but you had to know. Jimmy told us on Saturday when we were all in the office looking for his cell phone. He'd come to sign the marriage certificate when he'd found the reverend. But you and the reverend never had a chance to sign it."

"I know, but I hoped the certificate was a simple formality like the reverend had said." Frustrated, Betsy hit the couch cushion.

Gizmo jumped to the carpet and barked. Turning, he trotted down the hall in search of a more serene domain.

Julia, who sat in the other chair, spoke up, "This is terrible. So, they're not married, and all that effort and money was for nothing?"

"Ooh, no, no, no." Betsy wailed, her body rocking back and forth with pure agony.

Julia popped up and scurried to her side. Wrapping her arms around Betsy, she pulled her close. "Oh, sweetie, everything's going to work out. You and Jimmy will get married. This can be fixed."

Hiccup. "Fixed? How? With—" Hiccup. "—Jimmy in jail?" She moaned and rested her head on Julia's shoulder, dabbing at the tears running down her cheeks.

Julia's eyes pleaded for me to help.

"I'll scoop up the ice cream with a cookie chaser." Pushing up from the chair, I walked toward the kitchen.

"Better make it two cookies." Julia said. "And throw on some caramel."

I turned to find Betsy holding up her hand with all five fingers extended.

"Five, it is." I headed into the kitchen, convinced it would take more than cookies to mend the chasm in Betsy's heart.

~

Pulling down the covers on my bed, I fluffed my pillows and grabbed the latest issue of *Today's New Woman* magazine from my nightstand.

I'd chatted with Gabe before he'd gone in for the late shift. It felt good to have everything worked out. Gizmo stretched on the bed and circled three times before settling at the foot of the comforter near the footboard. All the drama had worn him out. "I know how you feel, buddy."

I scratched between his ears before crawling under the covers to enjoy my new read. Settling in, I flipped through the pages checking out the latest in food and fashion. Then I stopped on a section highlighting the new fall hairstyles. I didn't mind my blond hair, but the length meant it was always getting in my way. Every time I leaned over, a cascade of thick hair blinded me. And if I had something in my hands, I was stuck. Sighing, I imagined how a pixie cut would look with my rather round cheeks, part of the Anderson family legacy.

I earmarked the page so I could show it to Julia the next morning for her opinion. When I did, the word *Rut*, colored in red in the title on the next page, caught my eye. Flipping the page, I read, "Five Signs Your Love Life Is Stuck in a Rut," Hm, is my love life stuck in a rut? Maybe.

Scanning the article, I spotted a test at the bottom of the second page. I love a good a, b, c kind of test. So, I picked up the pen lying beside my phone on the nightstand. With a click, I started down the path to self-discovery.

The first question asked, "Are your evenings ... a. adventurous, b. flexible, c. predictable?"

Well, on Monday nights, Gabe and I talked on the phone before he headed into the station for the late shift. And on Tuesday, we always meet at the Deli on the Square for lunch. But that's because of his schedule. I squirmed under the covers and shimmied my head against the pillow. Wednesdays he spent with his family. Funny, he never invited me. My pen drummed on the page. Then Thursdays, he'd stop by the bookstore after three to chat and bring me a Vanilla Mud coffee from the Beans and Leaves next door. Fridays were movie-and-a-pizza night. And of course, on Sunday, we attended church and my family's luncheon in the afternoon.

A yawn swept over me, bored by the very thought of our routine. Discouraged, I read on. "When was the last time you were spontaneous as a couple ... a. a few days ago, b. last week, c. over a month ago?"

I bit my bottom lip, feeling a little uneasy about my answer. We'd solved a murder together—well, sort of. But that was months ago. And we hadn't done anything earth-shattering since. But it could be argued solving a murder does set the bar rather high on the excitement scale.

The third question pried a little deeper. "Would you say when you spend time with your significant other, you … a. hold hands and cuddle, b. engage in interesting conversation, c. wilt from the day's events?"

What does a stupid magazine know anyway? Slamming it shut, I tossed it to the floor and snapped off my lamp. "There's a lot to be said for routine," I muttered and flopped onto my side. I shut my eyes, but all I could see was the bright red word *Rut* tap dancing in my head. Sitting up, I snapped the light back on and retrieved the magazine from the spot where it had landed. Thumbing to the page I had earmarked, I found the article and read the list of the five signs your relationship was doomed to the fiery caverns of Relationship Hades. It couldn't be helped. I had to look.

I skipped the whole two paragraphs full of "if this, then that' advice and moved right to the heart of the matter, the list. It began, *… your relationship may be stuck in a rut if …*

You're both too tired to cuddle.

Neither wants to try anything new.

You text more than you talk in person.

You both forget important anniversaries or events.

As a couple, your idea of 'fun' is staying in and watching a movie.

I gasped. The last one got me. That *was* our idea of fun. Our big date night revolved around marathoning the Marvel movies. Holding the magazine to my chest, I fought back the tears. I knew more about the Hulk than I did about the man I was dating. Horrified, my heart raced. Now what?

Not sure, I sent up a little prayer for direction.

Closing the magazine, I tossed it to the foot of my bed missing Gizmo by an inch. I clicked off the lamp, uncertain if I'd be able to sleep knowing my budding relationship with the handsome detective quivered on the edge of failure.

Then my thoughts turned to Betsy sleeping on the couch in the living room. The poor creature had no idea what her future held. She'd tied herself to a man she thought she knew, but it turned out love had blinded her. One thing was for sure though, they were not stuck in a rut.

As I drifted off to sleep, my final thoughts were of the cake knife with its white ivory handle, cutting down through the thick layers of cake. Shifting, the knife cut into the chest of Reverend

Boggs. Two knives…two knives. Where had the killer gotten the second knife?

Chapter Nine

Rushing out the door of my apartment, I called Flora hoping she was her usual punctual self. I'd overslept, and by the time I was ready, my phone read ten o'clock as I headed toward my ancient blue van. With the phone pressed against my ear, my steps quickened with each ring.

Relief flooded over me when she picked up the store phone. Thank goodness for her beautiful, reliable soul. "Sorry I'm running late. With Betsy staying with us, I'm out of my routine. I'll make it up to you somehow." I almost bit my tongue when I heard what I'd said.

"Not a problem. Things like this happen."

I stopped dead in my tracks. Something was wrong. Was this code for 'help me. I'm being held hostage'? I'd lost count of how many lectures on punctuality Flora had given me over the last ten months we'd worked together. "Is everything all right?"

"Sure, everything's perfect. Why do you ask?" The cheerful lilt in Flora's voice drew my attention. But I decided not to push my luck by asking about it.

"Listen, I hate to do this, but can you stay a little later than two this afternoon? I want to go to the bed-and-breakfast to talk with Jimmy's grandfather before he leaves town. Don't want to miss my chance."

"Oh, sorry, dear. I can't stay. Herman has an eye appointment, and he needs me to drive him." She giggled. "Really, he needs me to drive him home. They want to dilate his pupils. He's home now scouring the place for a pair of sunglasses. Herman hates wearing them, but if he doesn't take his own, he'll have to wear those flimsy ones the optometrist gives you. I'm sure you know the ones I'm talking about. You have to fight them just to get them to unroll."

"They can be a pain." I opened the door to the van and slid in, holding the phone with one hand and closing the door with the other. Starting the engine, I drove out of my apartment complex.

"Tell you what, why don't you head over there now? That way, you'll have your time to chat with Jimmy's grandfather, and I can still make the appointment with Herman," Flora said.

"Are you sure? I hate leaving you to handle the whole store alone again, after being gone most of the day yesterday." I did a U-turn at the next light and pointed my van in the direction of the Whispering Pines Bed-and-Breakfast.

"Don't worry. I have everything under control here. Besides, you have a sweet young couple who need your help. And keeping an eye on the store makes me feel like I'm doing my part. We want them back together and on their way to their honeymoon as soon as possible." Her words oozed joy.

"You're singing to the choir." I pushed the disconnect button, not sure what had Flora in such a good humor. No lecture on punctuality and concern for the couple's happiness. I mean, Flora's a wonderful, caring person, but something didn't add up.

Pulling into the parking lot of the bed-and-breakfast, I snatched the first available spot. I pulled down the visor and peered into the little lighted mirror. The woman staring back at me looked tired and under-caffeinated. Puffy. My whole face looked puffy like a giant marshmallow with freckles. I blamed the wedding-themed nightmares I wrestled with until dawn.

The plunging cake knife had turned into an endless row of brides marching down the aisle to the tune of "Oklahoma" until a rather large green man with ripped clothing landed in the middle of them, punching and kicking. Somewhere amid all the chaos, Gabe appeared. He stood a few steps ahead of me, but when I called to him, he never looked my way.

Shaking off the remnants of the nightmare, I closed the mirror and replaced the visor. Releasing my seatbelt, I picked up my purse. Now or never, I decided and stepped out of the van to go ask a known crime lord what he thought about the death of the reverend, the man who sent his brother to prison. My stomach lurched as a tingling sensation swept through me.

I stopped at the front desk and asked if he was in. The clerk, Sue, told me I had just missed him. "He's going to the town square, I believe. Said he needed some air."

Standing on the sidewalk, I spotted him several blocks away walking with a cane. His shoulders were hunched, and his left leg dragged a bit when he took a step. He had a newspaper tucked under his arm, and he stopped at intervals to glance in the store windows.

I decided to retrieve my van and park closer to the bookstore. As I pulled out of the parking space beside the bed-and-breakfast, Elizabeth stepped off the sidewalk and waved. I rolled down my window to see what she wanted.

"Hey, thought I'd let you know I went to see Jimmy this morning," she said.

"How is he?" I kept my eye on Gramps.

"Fine for a man accused of murdering someone. I have to be honest with you. The circumstantial evidence is pretty damaging. Have you found anything yet?"

I turned my attention from Gramps to Elizabeth. "You sound worried."

"I am. He was found at the scene holding the murder weapon, he's connected to one of the most notorious crime families in the United States, and he has motive, revenge."

"I see you've talked to Gabe," I said.

"Yeah, he told me about Jimmy recognizing the reverend." Elizabeth bit her lip.

I nodded. "But anyone in the family would've had the same motive. Even Jimmy's Gramps. Wouldn't someone like him, a known criminal, make a better suspect? It was his brother, after all, who the reverend sent away, which had to have affected his business."

"True, but Jimmy was the one holding the cake knife. We need to come up with something to give the DA or they're going to charge him soon." She pushed back away from the window. "What does Gabe think about you working on this case?"

I shrugged. "He doesn't want me poking around. Says he can't keep me out of trouble this time if things go wrong."

"With the marshals working on this, he's right. Reverend Boggs being in WITSEC does muddy the jurisdiction waters. He'd have a hard time keeping you from being charged with tampering with evidence or interfering with an investigation if you were caught nosing around."

I smiled. "Then I'll have to avoid being caught."

"Good girl." Elizabeth grinned. "Oh, also, I wanted to let you know the police found Jimmy's phone."

"Where?"

"Stuck under the leg of the corpse." She shook her head.

"We can't catch a break." I leaned against the seat.

"I know." Elizabeth stepped back onto the sidewalk. "See you later. Let me know if you find out anything useful. The sooner the better."

By the time I found a spot in the lot across the street from the town green and adjacent to Twisted Plots, Gramps was sitting on one of the park benches reading his newspaper.

"Hi, Mr. Morelli. I don't know if you remember me, but we met at Betsy's and Jimmy's wedding."

He raised his eyes from the paper and smiled. "Yes, I remember you. Betsy's friend who cut the cake at the wedding. You wore that lovely blue dress. A knockoff but lovely nonetheless." His Italian accent flavored his words.

"That's me." I clutched my purse to my chest pressing the ruffles on my blouse flat. At the wedding, he'd been a sweet old guy with a nice smile. Now, knowing about his past, being in his presence made me edgy.

Folding his paper, he asked, "Is there something I can do for you?"

My nerves jumped at the determined coolness in his eyes. Swallowing, I stilled my hands from fidgeting. "Yes, I have a few questions I'd like to ask you if I might?"

He laid the paper aside and nodded toward the empty spot on the bench next to him. "Take a seat, and I'll see if I can help you."

"Oh, thank you." The tension of the moment got the better of me, so the words tumbled out. "Isn't it a beautiful day? The park here in the town green is one of my favorite places. Of course, I get to see it every day from my bookstore. Oh, I own one of the local bookstores, The Twisted Plots. Right over there. Have you heard of it?" I waved my hand in the direction of the store then stopped. Clutching my purse in my lap, I focused on Gramps. "Why would you have heard of it? Silly question."

His dark ominous eyes held mine. "I hope not all your questions will be silly." He leaned back and studied me for a moment.

I ran my hands down the tops of my jeans trying to remove the moisture from them.

"I can tell from how you handle yourself you're someone who deals openly with others." He ran his arm along the back of the bench behind me and leaned closer, lowering his voice. "So, let's not waste precious time with niceties." Straightening, he continued, "Ask your questions, young lady. And I will choose whether to answer them or not."

If intimidation were a person, it'd be named Frank Morelli. Laying my purse on the seat next to me, I whipped up a smile. "Sounds like a deal." Tilting my head to the side, I aimed straight for the bull's-eye. "Did you kill Reverend Boggs?"

Frank threw back his head and roared with laughter. "I'll give it to you, miss. You got moxie. I like that." He sobered, but a twinkle of mischief remained in his eyes. "No, I did not kill the reverend. If I'd wanted him dead, I would've waited. No sense in ruining Jimmy's big day. Besides, I didn't even recognize the rat."

"I find that hard to believe. A man as observant as you—who noticed a dress as a knockoff—didn't recognize the man who put your brother away for life?"

"Young lady, I thrive on directness, but no one calls me a liar." His eyes darkened. "You're a nice kid, pretty. So, I'm going to ignore the insult. Instead, I'm going to tell you I didn't have anything to do with this."

"I would've thought you'd be very interested in finding the man who sent your brother away. Since he died in prison, I figured you would've blamed the witness for your brother's death."

He shrugged. "Perhaps, or it's possible his unfortunate incarceration benefited me. Maybe, he wanted what I had, and I didn't want to share. It happens between brothers. Cain and Abel, Jacob and Esau. Family rivalry isn't new."

Wow, the man knew his Bible brothers. "No, it's not. So, Tony's death wasn't cause for retribution?"

"No, his imprisonment, let's say, helped my cause."

"May I ask how he died?" I waited as the sly old fox weighed his words, knowing Tony had died in prison.

A faint smile tugged at the corners of Gramps' mouth. "There are rules in every society, even mine, and he broke the rules."

I couldn't believe my ears. The man all but admitted he'd planned his brother's death. Not wanting to go any further with a line of questioning that might get me killed, I swallowed hard and switched gears. "Did you notice anything unusual at the wedding?"

"At the wedding? No. But at the reception, yes. I saw some guy hoofing it out of the hallway."

"Which hallway? The one by the stage?" I asked.

"No, the other one by the cake table."

A sadness draped over his countenance, and his gaze lingered on the newspaper beside him before he spoke. "We value family. Especially loyalty. It is the core of who we are." He raised a fisted hand and thumped his chest twice. "And it tears my heart to pieces when someone betrays that loyalty." Anger flared in his eyes.

A fresh cascade of tingles ran rampant down the back of my neck and along my arms. "Family loyalty is important." My mouth went dry while the palms of my hands became clammy.

"My brother being in prison—it helped to keep the family intact which made me happy. But my niece, she's not so happy. She blames her father's incarceration for his untimely death." Frank Morelli leaned back against the bench and sighed. He once again looked like the sweet old man I'd met at the wedding.

"No, I imagine she didn't like her father being locked away and then to lose him. It's tragic."

"Tragic. But I've made sure she's had everything she's needed. And she's been loyal, unlike her father." He rested his hand on the newspaper beside him and scooped it up before standing. "I'm tired. If you are done, I think I'm going to go for a rest or perhaps stop in the little coffee shop for a snack on my way to the inn."

"You could order room service at least until one. Then you could nap while you waited," I offered.

"Nah, I hate room service. Never use it." A lopsided grin spread across his lips. "I guess I'd better opt for the nap." He chuckled. "Getting old is hard work, and I need the rest."

"Oh, of course." I agreed. "But can I ask you one more question? Something I'm sure the police won't share with me."

His grin widened. "You mean that cop you date? He won't help you to clear Jimmy?"

"Well … I mean … It's like this."

"Spit it out, child. I'm aging with each word."

"There is only so much help he can give me," I said.

He nodded his understanding. "Go ahead."

"What was Reverend Boggs' name before he went into WITSEC?"

"That, young lady, I'll tell you. The rat's name was Robert LaRocca. He worked at the accounting firm of Dearman and Fisher who handled some of our more delicate business transactions. He wasn't our regular accountant, but he worked on our accounts from time to time."

"Do you know if he had any family? A wife or children?"

"Yes, I do know, but I've given you more than enough to point you in the right direction. I'll leave the rest for you and your young cop friend to figure out." He stood and stepped in front of me. Taking my hand, he lifted it to his lips and placed a simple kiss on the back of it.

Too stunned to react, I sat wide-eyed with my hand in his.

"Oh, to be young." He tsked. "It was lovely to see you again, my dear."

Letting go of my hand, he reached for the cane hooked to the back of the bench. He made his way to the sidewalk. Stepping off the grass onto the concrete, he hobbled hunched at the shoulders to the corner, never looking back.

My mind swirled, trying to sort the information Gramps had given me. At least now, I had a name to go on, Robert LaRocca. Why did that name sound so familiar?

~

Mrs. Culpepper entered the bookstore carrying a large cardboard box filled with bundles of handmade cards. Her card-making class at the senior citizens center kept us well supplied. And though they weren't my style, I had to admit they were a big hit with my customers.

Ada Culpepper had sweet-talked me into carrying the cards in the bookstore by playing on my sympathies for the elderly. She insisted I'd be giving them a purpose in their lives, and seeing their artwork displayed in my store would give them a sense of fulfillment. I swear the woman could convince a Cuban to buy a wool coat.

She slid the box onto the counter and turned to face me.

I stood by one of the display tables, rearranging the books on it and making space for the new release from Tom Perkins. "How are you today, Ada?"

She sighed. "As well as can be expected, I suppose. I mean, with everything in an uproar over the reverend."

Leaning over, I picked up four more copies of the book and added three to the stack. I placed the fourth one in a stand facing the front of the store, so it could be seen through the window from the sidewalk. "Yes, it is a shame about Reverend Boggs." I figured if I acted disinterested, she'd push the point, and maybe she'd tell me about the building committee.

Walking over to me, she touched the top book of the stack. "Oh, I see Tom Perkins has a new one out. Wasn't it wonderful the way he came to your humble bookstore back in January? I mean, he basically single-handedly saved your business."

I positioned the book on the stand and nudged it a little to the left before I turned to give her my full attention. "You're right. It was a tremendous blessing, and his coming did help my store make it through a tough time." Shifting from defense to offense, I brought up the next topic. "Speaking of blessings, I've heard your bishop is coming to Pine Lake for a visit. Given what has happened with the reverend's death and all, perhaps his presence will be a comfort to the congregation."

Ada picked up the book and glanced at the back cover. "I suppose, but the visit had been planned before the events of Saturday. In fact, he came in last evening."

"Oh." I placed my hand on my chest in mock surprise. "Really? Why did the bishop come? Do you know?" I hoped she'd take the bait.

Tossing the book back onto the stack, she shrugged. "I believe it had something to do with the building committee."

"Yes, that's right. Your church has been raising funds for a new annex for some time, hasn't it?"

She clasped her hands together, allowing her purse to swing from her elbow. "I guess it depends on what you think is a long time. There were some of us who had become concerned when the quarterly financial reports didn't quite add up to what should have been in the account."

"Were you concerned someone had been stealing from the fund?" Walking to the counter, I stopped by the cardboard box to inspect what she had brought me. Inside, I found thirty bundles of six cards and envelopes. Each bundle was tied together with a beautiful blue ribbon.

She followed me to the counter. "Of course not. No one in our congregation would do such a thing, but there was a discrepancy. I agreed with the reverend that an investigation was warranted. Besides, I've never trusted the reverend's secretary, Tammy. She knows more than she should."

Pressing my lips together, I choked back a laugh. Knowing too much was Ada Culpepper's specialty.

"Well, wasn't there a treasurer or an elder or someone in charge of the account?" I moved behind the counter to make out a receipt for the merchandise. "Even my chess club in high school had a treasurer for all the money we made with our car washes."

"If you must know, the reverend and one of the committee members kept up with offerings designated for the fund." Her eyebrows drew together, and she pursed her lips.

"Oh, who was the committee member?" I jotted down the number of bundles and how many cards were in each on a receipt pad with the amount we had agreed on per bundle when she first persuaded me to carry the cards.

"Why do you want to know?"

"Curiosity, I guess, since I was at the wedding when the murder happened. I'm trying to help Julia's cousin, Betsy, the bride."

Her eyes took on a sparkle. "I had heard you were there when the police walked in, but I didn't believe it. You do have a knack for always being where you shouldn't."

"Call it my destiny." I pulled the receipt from the tablet, took the payment from the cash register, and handed it to her. "So, who was the committee member? I might know him. Pine Lake isn't that big."

"True. His name is Levi Jackson, but I doubt it's anything more than bad math. He's not that bright. I really don't understand how he got the position as treasurer."

Leaning against the counter, I nodded. "Interesting, I don't think I know him, but I did go to school with a Pearson Jackson."

"That's his younger brother." Ada glanced at the receipt and money in her hand. "Oh, by the way, supply prices have gone up, so we'll need to increase our price per card. Hope that's not a problem. After all, you're making such a difference to the seniors," she called over her shoulder as she trotted toward the door.

Once the bell rang, Flora poked her head around the corner of the small hallway. "Did I hear Ada Culpepper's voice?"

I smiled. "Yes, you did. She dropped off the cards for this month's order."

Flora let out a sigh. "Well, I'm glad I stayed in the back. That woman would try the patience of Paul."

"And the other eleven apostles. But today, I'm glad I had the chance to see her." I tucked the receipt pad under the counter where it belonged.

"Why?" Flora strolled to the counter.

"Because without knowing it, she may have given me my first lead that doesn't involve Jimmy's family."

CHAPTER TEN

Drumming my fingers on the table, I studied Gabe as he read over the menu at the Deli on the Square. Why he insisted on reading the menu every time we came here was beyond me. We'd been meeting for lunch at this same restaurant for months now—every Tuesday, so he should know the menu by heart.

Deb was our server because we always sat at the same table. I ordered the tuna melt with a side of fries, and he ordered the roast beef po' boy with a side of coleslaw. Deb would ask for our drink orders. He'd ask for coffee then change it saying he'd already had his limit of caffeine and make a lame joke about getting a ticket.

I shifted in my chair, tamping down the sense of dissatisfaction threatening to invade our time together.

Gabe glanced up from the menu. "Are you all right? You seem a little tense today. You're not still mad about the police-station thing, are you?"

"No." I leaned my forearms on the table. "Why do you always look over the menu before we order? It never changes."

"I don't know." He shrugged. "Guess I just want to be sure." Wrinkles rippled across his forehead reminding me of a dried raisin. Placing his menu on the edge of the table, he leaned forward clasping his hands together in front of him. "Okay, spill. Something is bothering you. It's written all over your face."

I shrugged one shoulder, placing my chin on my fisted hand,

and leaned my elbow on the table. "I don't know. Do you ever feel like we're in a rut?"

Gabe straightened. "A rut? With you?" A grin slid across his lips, and a twinkle of mischief played in his eyes. "You, Amy Kate Anderson, are anything but a rut."

Rolling my eyes, I huffed.

"Why? Do you think we're in a rut?" He asked.

For a detective, he sure wasn't catching a clue. "Yes, I do."

The waitress appeared with her green pad and pen and asked for our drink orders.

"I'll have an unsweet tea." I gestured toward Gabe with my hand. "Go ahead. Tell her your drink order."

He scowled and turned his attention to Deb. "I'll take a cup of coffee." She waited with her hand hovering above her pad. Even she knew.

The words flew out before I could stop them. "No, wait. Make it water. I've already had my caffeine for today. I wouldn't want to get a ticket for exceeding the limit."

Deb's eyes widened, and I pressed my lips together, forgetting to breathe.

Realizing I had a death wish, Deb said, "I'll be back with those drinks in a jiffy." And she dashed away to the safety of the waitress station.

Gabe sat back and crossed his arms. "Okay, what brought this on?"

"What do you mean? Did something have to happen for me to notice we're stuck?"

"All I know is last week when we met for lunch on Tuesday, you were perfectly happy with our routine. Now, out of the blue, you're ..." He hesitated.

"See even you admit we're in a routine." I sat straight. "Our lives are planned out to the nth degree." I stabbed my finger on the surface of the table. "There's no spontaneity. We've become so accustomed to one another we're taking each other for granted."

"What do you mean I take you for granted? I call. We go out on dates. I've even become a regular at your dad's Sunday family dinners. What more do you want?" He flopped back in his chair with his arms open.

Leaning forward, I hissed, "I want to know that one Tuesday you might order a chicken sandwich with a side of baked beans. For heaven's sake."

"Fine. That's what I'll have today. Okay? Happy?"

"That's not the point," I snapped.

Deb reappeared with the drink orders and set them on the table. Looking from me to Gabe, she asked, "the usual?"

If looks could kill, Gabe would soon be doing twenty to life. His warm brown eyes changed to rock-solid steel. "No. Not the usual." He picked up the menu and placed it in front of him. Closing his eyes, he waved his finger in the air and let it fall onto the plastic-covered sheet. "I'll have the fruit platter. No cottage cheese."

Deb stood motionless for two breaths, unsure what to do. She looked at me with an expression of horror.

"You don't have to do this."

"No, if eating fruit will prove to you, I care about our relationship, then fruit it is." He handed the menu to Deb who had yet to say anything.

"Don't be silly." I turned toward Deb. "Bring him the roast beef po' boy and a side of coleslaw."

Deb pulled her order pad and pen from her pocket and jotted something down.

"Deb, if a roast beef po' boy shows up on this table, I won't leave you a tip for a month." Gabe crossed his arms and leaned back in his chair. "I mean it. There had better be a fruit platter in front of me and nothing else. Apparently, my relationship with this woman depends on my food choices."

"Fine. Be stubborn. But eating fruit for lunch doesn't prove that we're not in a rut."

Deb scratched out what she had written and dashed off something else. With a hint of trepidation, she met my gaze. "Do you want the usual?"

Gabe tilted his head to one side with his arms still crossed. "Yeah, you want the usual?"

Now, I was stuck. I hadn't looked at the menu in months. In fact, I had no idea what the other options were. Rats.

Sheepishly, I glanced from Gabe to Deb. "Is a grilled cheese sandwich on the menu?"

"No, but I could put in a special order." Deb shifted her weight from one leg to the other and looked over her shoulder to the kitchen.

"No, that's okay. I don't want to put you to any extra trouble," I said.

Gabe scoffed. "Really? You don't want to be any trouble." He shook his head. "Bring her a tuna melt with a side of fries and if you could, please bring a bottle of ketchup when you bring the order."

"Do you still want the fruit platter?" Deb asked.

Gabe answered never moving his gaze from mine. "No. Bring me a hamburger. I'm not sure a fruit platter can fix this relationship."

Neither one of us said much, and by the end of the meal, my stomach churned on the few bites I had swallowed.

What was I doing? This guy was one of the good ones, and here I was kicking up dust over nothing. Well, almost nothing. I mean we are in a rut. Not sure what to say and not wanting to leave things as they were, I tried to salvage the last few minutes of this disastrous lunch. "So, will I see you Thursday for coffee at the bookstore?"

He wiped his mouth with his napkin and laid it on the table. "Maybe. I don't want to be too predictable."

I smashed the breadcrumbs on my plate with my fork.

Leaning forward, Gabe placed his elbows on either side of his dish. "You never told me what brought all this on. Last week, everything was fine, and now this week everything is out of kilter. Does this have something to do with the wedding Saturday?"

"No, not the wedding. I just became painfully aware we've fallen into a rut. Maybe, I was out of line about taking each other for granted, but I do believe we've grown comfortable with each other to the point that, as a couple, we're predictable." I gazed up from my crumb smashing to find his warm brown eyes locked on me.

He reached across the table and took my hand holding the fork. "But isn't that the nice part of knowing someone so well? You become so comfortable with them you can predict what they will do or what they will say. Isn't that the kind of intimacy—most people are looking for, Amy Kate?" Gabe's phone buzzed in his suit-jacket pocket. He let go of my hand to answer it.

I already knew who it was. Floyd Simms, Gabe's partner, had also been pulled into our vortex of predictability.

When Gabe disconnected, I smiled. "Floyd?"

"Yeah." He stuffed his phone back into his pocket.

"He's going to meet you out front in five." I let the fork slip from my fingers. It clanged against the ceramic of the plate.

Nodding, he reclaimed my hand. "So, what if we are predictable? There are a lot worse things we could be as a couple. I mean, there's a lot to be said for knowing you can depend on certain things in a relationship."

"Yeah, I guess."

He stood and pushed his chair under the table. "I'll walk you out."

"No, I think I'll stay and finish my fries." I smiled up at him. "So, will I see you Thursday?"

He grinned. "You can count on it."

I followed his movement through the deli and watched as he strolled through the glass door. Why did it bother me that our relationship was predictable?

Deb swung by to pick up Gabe's dishes. I caught her eyeing the tip he'd placed under his plate. Picking it up, she slid it into her pocket and reached for the half-empty water glass. "I'll just take these."

"Um, thanks."

Holding the dishes in one hand and the glass in the other, she leaned her hip against the edge of the table. "What's wrong, hon? You guys didn't seem like yourselves today. Are you all right?"

"I'm fine." I frowned. "But my love life is dying a slow, painful death."

"Are you talking about Mister Tall, Dark, and Drives a Corvette?" She shook her head. "Some people don't know when they have it good." She cut her eyes in my direction then straightened. "Hon, take some advice from somebody who's been around the block a couple of times. Men like him are rare gems. A lot of women can't tell the real article from paste. That one there, he's the genuine article. I'd keep him somewhere safe if I were you."

~

My van groaned when I shifted into park settling her in my space in the garage. I could sympathize with the old girl. What a day.

Gathering my purse and the half-dozen articles I had printed off the internet about Frank Morelli, I climbed out of the passenger seat and followed the sidewalk to my apartment's front door. A sigh escaped my lips when it came into view. Home at last.

Between my chat with Jimmy's mobster grandpa and my lunch with Gabe, all I wanted to do was to jump into some sweatpants, don my favorite Snoopy tee-shirt, and curl up on the sofa to binge-watch *Father Brown*, one of my all-time favorite British crime shows.

I sorted through the keys on my keyring and found the one I needed. Pinching it between my pointer finger and thumb, I leaned forward to jiggle the key into the lock, but before I could get it into the keyhole, the door flew open.

"Amy Kate, you're home." Julia's wide-eyed expression didn't give me much hope for a quiet evening of relaxation and bingeing a show. She took my elbow and escorted me into the living room. "Here, let me take that." She pulled the stack of articles from my hand and tossed them onto the coffee table.

"What's going on? I thought you'd be at the inn working." Turning toward the coat stand in the corner behind the door, I shoved my keys into my purse and hung it on one of the hooks.

Julia stepped closer to me and placed her hand on my forearm. Leaning in, she said, "It's Betsy."

I scanned the living room and what I could see of the kitchen but no Betsy. "Where is she?"

"She's in my room." Julia shook her head. The corners of her mouth pulled down. "It's not good. She went to see Jimmy today. The DA wants to bring formal charges."

"I figured that would happen. To be honest, I'm surprised they waited this long before pressing charges, considering all the circumstantial evidence." I patted Julia's hand resting on my arm and moved toward the couch.

Letting her hand fall to her side, she followed me into the living room.

I needed to sit down and take off my shoes. "Did Betsy call Elizabeth to see what she had to say?"

"I don't think so, but I didn't even think about Elizabeth. Betsy called me in tears, threatening to go to Jimmy's grandfather for help since she wasn't getting any satisfaction from the police." Julia sat beside me on the couch and tucked her bare feet under her bottom. "I came right home. Pulling his family into this any further isn't going to help Jimmy. The police already think he's up to his neck in the family business. Involving Gramps would make matters worse."

"Funny you should say that." I peeled off my high-heeled sandals and propped my feet up on the coffee table. "Guess who I chatted with this morning?"

Julia tilted her head. "Really, you went to interview Frank Morelli? A man who's been connected to over twenty deaths?"

I leaned forward and picked up the pile of articles from the coffee table, shaking them for effect. "Forty, according to one article in the *Atlantic Times*." Placing the pile in my lap, I leaned back against the soft cushions.

A twinkle played in Julia's eyes. "I have to hand it to you. Most people would've put it off for as long as possible or skipped it altogether, but not you. Fearless, that's what you are."

"Or in Gabe's opinion, careless." The thought of telling him about my conversation with Frank Morelli didn't thrill me. Maybe that's why I'd picked a fight with him over something less volatile, like our dating life being in a big muddy rut. Another sigh rose from within me.

"You, okay?" Julia asked.

"Yeah, I'll be fine." Or at least I hoped I would.

"So, what'd you find out?" Julia hugged one of the throw pillows to her chest and gave me her full attention, not even trying to hide her enthusiasm.

"Well, for starters, Reverend Boggs wasn't always Reverend Boggs. His real name was Robert LaRocca, and he worked for an accounting firm called Dearman and Fisher."

"Not Reverend Boggs?" Julia shook her head. "He seemed so nice. Always friendly."

"I know. And get this, he's the one who testified against Tony Morelli in the case which sent him to prison. A few months after he'd been incarcerated, Tony was killed in a fight." I sat up, the excitement of recounting the story reviving me. "At first, I thought

Gramps might have wanted retribution for the reverend sending his brother to jail. But he says he didn't have anything to do with Boggs' death. Made it sound like it benefited him to have his brother in jail. He hinted Tony had wanted more than his fair share of the power and responsibility in the family, and he wasn't above taking it if he thought he could."

"Wow." Julia's eyes widened another inch.

"I know, right? He basically said it had saved him from doing something that would've torn his family apart and gave him the opportunity to handle it quietly. From what he said and the way he acted, I think Frank Morelli had his brother killed while in jail."

Julia's mouth gaped open. "No way."

"And as pretty as you please, he named off a few Bible brothers who had their own sibling problems."

"Really, brother's from the Bible? How unexpected." Her brows formed a sharp V.

"I know, right? Which is why I believe he dealt honestly with me."

"Umm, an honest murderer?" Julia squinted and puckered her lips. "I don't think there is such a thing."

"I'm not planning on giving him the Nobel Peace Prize, but I just don't think he did this." I handed her the articles. "Not after talking to him and reading these."

"What did the articles tell you?"

"That Frank Morelli never killed anyone where it could be traced back to him. To kill the reverend while attending the wedding—for a man of his reputation—would have been sloppy. Too many questions would be asked. It's not his style."

"True, and he would be the number-one suspect."

"Unless you find the groom holding a bloody cake knife." I crisscrossed my legs and sat Indian-style, facing Julia. "Plus, he said he'd never ruin Jimmy's big day. If he'd wanted to kill the reverend, he'd have done it after the celebration and when the rest of the family was safe in Atlanta."

A sharp bark caught my attention. Gizmo jumped up into my empty lap, his whole-body wiggling. Placing his paws on my shoulders, he licked me on the chin. "Where did you come from?"

"He was with me." Betsy walked down the hall toward the living room.

"Hi," I called trying to put a little extra pep into my voice.

"Hi." Her answer sounded as dry as burnt toast.

"I heard you went to see Jimmy. How did it go?" I ran my hand along Gizmo's back, and he calmed down, relaxing beside me on the couch as I petted him.

"They're charging him." Betsy plopped into one of the overstuffed chairs. "But I've decided I'm done crying over it. It's not helping, and if I want my husband—" She paused, her bottom lip quivering. "—my fiancé back, I need to do something more productive than keeping the tissue companies in business."

"Good girl. I need all the help I can get if we're going to figure out who did this." I stood. "What we need, ladies, is a plan." Turning to Julia, I asked, "do we still have the bulletin board we used in Matt's case?"

Julia smiled and hopped up. "Yes, I slid it under my bed. Do you want me to go get it?"

"Please and bring some notecards and pushpins. Let's create a crime board and see if we can sort out all these facts." I pointed toward the pile of articles.

Thirty minutes later, we sat in the kitchen staring at the blank board lying in the middle of the table, not sure where to start.

"Okay, let's put on what we know for a fact. And we'll add our opinions later," Julia suggested.

"Well, we know Frank Morelli is a killer and my Jimmy isn't." Betsy lifted her chin.

I didn't want to squabble over what was fact and what was opinion in her statement, so I scribbled Frank's name on a card and stuck it on the board, positive he wasn't our killer.

"We also know Reverend Boggs was Robert LaRocca." I wrote his name on a card and stuck it next to Frank's.

"Did you say, LaRocca?" Betsy leaned forward propping her elbow on the table. "Wait, that sounds familiar." She straightened and wiggled her fingers over the board. "Give me a minute." She closed her eyes. Then she hopped up and darted to the living room, returning with the laptop, which she handed to Julia. "I want to say Mark's last name is LaRocca."

"The groomsman with the great hair?" Julia took the laptop from Betsy and, pushing the board out of the way, tapped the screen for the photo of the first page of the guest book. "I'm looking for the page where the wedding party signed their names during the rehearsal dinner. Here it is. LaRocca is Mark's last name. Do you think he and the reverend are related?"

I dashed to the living room and grabbed the articles from the couch. Returning to the kitchen, I thumbed through the stack and found the copy I needed. "According to this news article, Robert LaRocca left a wife and a twelve-year-old son behind when he went into WITSEC."

"That's weird, isn't it? Don't they send the entire family into the program?" Julia peered at me over the screen.

"Usually, but the article said the wife had a booming business in the Atlanta fashion industry and didn't want to give up her success." I flipped over a few sheets and found a second article with a photo of his wife winning an award. "Here's a picture of her."

"She's pretty," Julia commented.

"Yeah, she is. I also found several articles about the Morelli family. Car bombs, robberies, money laundering, trafficking—it was a pretty long list. They're not a nice bunch."

"Wow, these people are serious." The color drained from Betsy's face as she eyed the thick stack of articles. "What have I done? I've married into a mob family."

"No, you've married a wonderful guy whose extended family is, well, questionable," Julia offered.

Betsy shot her a look. "Really?"

"Jimmy's great. He just picked a bad situation to walk into." Julia shook her head.

Betsy's eyes filled with tears, but she bit her lip and blinked them back.

Grabbing another notecard, I wrote Mark's name on it and pinned it to the middle of the board. "We need to find out if Mark is Boggs' son, and if he recognized his father."

"Even if he is his son, what reason would Mark have to kill his father?" Julia asked.

"Maybe he felt betrayed for being left behind or angry toward his father for not contacting him after all these years. Who knows?"

"Yeah, but he wouldn't have known about Reverend Boggs until he was already here." Julia folded her arms on the table in front of the laptop.

"True, if Mark did it, he improvised the whole thing." I leaned back in my chair with a thousand thoughts shuffling through my brain. Then one floated to the top. "Betsy, where did you get your cake knife?" I picked up a blank card and wrote 'cake knife' on it.

"I found it in the little shop across from your bookstore, Junk in the Trunk. They had several. Originally, I had hoped to receive one as a shower gift, but I didn't. So, I picked one up when I got into town. Why?"

"Well, the murder weapon was a dead ringer for the one you used. I know because I had a good look at the two of them lying side by side on the desk in Reverend Boggs office. Remember, Gabe made me leave yours."

"That's right." Betsy tilted her head. "And they looked alike?"

"No, they were identical. It was the same exact knife." My heart pounded. This had to mean something. "Was anyone with you when you bought the serving set with the knife in it?"

Betsy bit her bottom lip as a wave of horror passed across her face. "Jimmy was with me."

"Anyone else?" I prompted before she had the chance to melt into a puddle of emotional goo.

"My mother and my friend, Kristin." She sniffled.

Julia grabbed two cards from the stack and wrote something on each one. She pushed a pin through one and then the other. The cards read *groomsmen* and *bridesmaids*.

"You're right. We need to check out the wedding party. Here's one groomsman possibly related to the deceased who could be carrying a nasty grudge and a bridesmaid who was with Betsy when she bought the murder weapon."

"Not the murder weapon," Betsy snapped. "Don't go around saying I bought the murder weapon. Jeepers, don't I have enough to deal with?"

"Sorry. I meant the cake knife." Picking up the card with those words on it, I stuck it to the board right under Mark's name. "Okay, so Julia, since the wedding party is staying at the Whispering Pines, why don't you nose around and see what you can find out. Maybe sift through a few of their rooms. You'll need to do it soon though, because if they charge Jimmy, everyone else will be free to leave town. And if that happens, we may never find out the truth."

"Okay, I'll see what I can find out tomorrow, and I'll call with an update," Julia said.

"Perfect, I'll go talk with the person who sold Betsy the cake knife. See if anyone else came in and purchased one. I'm also going to talk with Reverend Boggs' secretary to see if she can shed any light on whom he met with this week. I want to know if Mark LaRocca paid the reverend a visit. Besides, I'd like to know why she was at the wedding reception."

Julia placed another card on the board with Tammy McNair's name on it.

"What about me? I can't sit around here anymore feeling sorry for myself and worrying about Jimmy. Give me something to do." Betsy wrung her hands. "Let me help."

Julia glanced at me, waiting for me to give her cousin an assignment.

I shrugged.

"Oh, you can go talk to the DJ and ask him about the guy we couldn't ID. He's our last unidentified wedding guest," Julia said.

"I'm pretty sure he worked with the DJ as part of the setup crew." Betsy sighed.

"Maybe, but it's better if we make sure," I offered. "Besides, the DJ may have some useful information. He had a great spot to see everyone's movements. So, be sure and ask him who he saw go down the hallway."

"Will do." Betsy's stomach growled.

I took her hunger as a good sign. "We'd better order some dinner. How about a pizza? With everything?"

"Yum," Julia chimed in.

"That does sound pretty good." Betsy gave a lopsided grin.

My heart gladdened to see a smile on her face. There hadn't been many since finding Jimmy hovering over the body. I took it as a good sign, as well.

While Julia placed the pizza order, my mind focused on Mark LaRocca, the handsome guy who kept bumping into me. So, he was the reverend's son. Thinking about it, I could see a slight resemblance.

A son left behind could have reason to resent his father, but would it be enough of a reason to kill him? Maybe, and he was near the hallway leading to the reverend's office, according to what Jimmy had told me. But did Mark have enough time to kill the reverend and then return to the fellowship hall to chat with Jimmy before the body was discovered?

CHAPTER ELEVEN

The late morning sun streamed in through the long glass windows of Junk in the Trunk Antique store and made the silver tea setting in the display twinkle. Wednesdays were never busy on the town square, but two male customers mulled around in the back looking at an old wooden side table, and one woman lingered at the register.

Lilly Murphy stood behind the counter, finishing up the sale. She'd been involved with my first case, and I counted on her gratitude for my help back then to give me some answers now. Glancing up, she spotted me and gave a quick nod.

I waved and moved toward her.

The checkout counter held a large old-fashioned key register. They didn't use it, but it gave the shop an air of authenticity.

"How can I help you today, Amy Kate?" Lilly leaned her elbow on the wooden surface and placed her chin in her hand.

"Oh, I had a few questions about a customer who came in here last week."

"Does this have anything to do with what happened Saturday at the Methodist Church?" Lilly straightened.

"It does. Do you have somewhere we can talk privately?"

"Wait here and let me call Wendy. In case the gentlemen need any help with the table." Lilly glided from behind the counter and moved with poise toward a door I assumed led to a back storage area. She disappeared behind it, and a few minutes later reappeared with Wendy.

Motioning for me to join her in the back, Wendy and I swapped places. I'd never been in the belly of the antique shop before, and it gave me the impression of what a cargo hold on a ship would be like—dark, damp, and full of unknown treasures.

Lilly shut the door, and the low florescent lights flickered. To my left, I saw a room with a sign beside the entrance which read *Employees Only*. The woman strolled in, and I followed. "So, what is this all about?" She pulled out one of the four chairs sitting around a small wooden table marred with white rings and gashes.

I pulled out one of the others and slid into the seat. "The bride, Betsy Jacobs, said she bought her cake knife from you. Is that true?"

"Yes, she said she needed one, and I had a white ivory-handled set she loved. It came with the knife and a server. She snatched it right up." Lilly tucked her foot under her other leg. "But that still doesn't tell me why you're here." A smile swept across her lips. "What aren't you telling me?"

Not sure how much I should say, I ignored the question. "Was it the only set you had?"

Lilly's lips ticked up another notch, and she nodded. "I see how this is going to be. Fine. Let me think." She let out a sigh. "We had four sets. I ordered them from one of my vendors. They're some of my best sellers. Betsy bought one, and I believe Reverend Boggs' secretary bought the other three."

"Reverend Boggs's secretary bought three sets identical to the one Betsy bought?" I groaned and slumped back in my chair. "Do you know why she'd buy so many?"

"It's not unusual for Tammy to come in every few months and stock up on wedding cake serving sets. She told me it's one of the items people forget most often on their big day. They don't even miss the set until they need it."

"So, you're sure Tammy, Reverend Boggs' secretary, bought all the others?"

"Sure as the grass is green." Lilly leaned forward across the table and lowered her voice. "Now, why are you so interested in those wedding-cake serving sets? You're not here out of mild curiosity."

I squirmed in my seat, fighting the urge to tell her the whole story. "I can't say. And if Gabe finds out I told you more than what was in the papers, there will be another murder reported in Pine Lake."

Lilly grinned and straightened in her chair. "Okay, I won't press you, but I'll take it the serving sets are important to the case."

"Let's say they're a primary part of the whole thing."

"Oh? Ohh …" Lilly's eyes widened. "I see."

I stood pushing my chair back under the table. "Thanks, Lilly, for the information. It's a big help."

"No problem. And when you reach a place where you can share, please come back and fill me in on the details. I have a feeling I'd be very interested in how everything turns out."

~

The sun had risen another notch in the sky, spreading its rays over the sidewalk outside of Twisted Plots, pushing the heat index up another five degrees. If it heated up anymore, I predicted by two o'clock we'd all be puddles of sweat.

The cool air rushed around me, sending a slight chill up my spine as I entered the bookstore.

"So, what did she say?" Flora's eyes widened as she leaned against the counter, watching me move toward her.

"Lilly said Boggs' secretary did in fact buy three sets of the same cake server Betsy had purchased." I tossed my purse under the counter unwilling to make the trip to my desk in the back. "Another dead end. I had hoped someone had made a single purchase, and we'd have another lead. Of course, Tammy was at the wedding reception."

Flora straightened. Her mouth gaped open. "What do you mean Tammy was at the reception? Why would she be there?"

"I don't know, but she showed up in one of the photos I took of the crowd when the police were doing interviews."

Flora tilted her head. "So, she came to the reception, and she had access to a knife identical to the one Betsy bought. Don't you think that's a lead?"

"Maybe. She didn't have any motive to kill the reverend. What did he do? Forget Secretary's Day?" I slumped over the counter. "It doesn't feel right."

"Well, *I* think that's a solid lead." Flora shrugged. Then her eyes lit up and a smile brightened her face as her attention turned to something behind me.

I peered over my shoulder and found Alexia standing in the doorway wrestling with Grant's stroller as one of her friends from her Wednesdays moms' group held the door.

Alexia lifted the front wheels slightly, rolled the stroller forward, and lifted the back wheels.

The friend laughed. "I can't tell you how thankful I was once Ben outgrew the stroller stage. They make those things so big now you can't fit through the average-sized door."

Parking the stroller near the kid's corner, Alexia unstrapped Grant and set him on the floor on his hands and knees. Ben and his mother moved to the display of children's books.

I squatted and held out my arms to Grant. "How's my favorite sweetie pie?" The sing-song lilt in my voice sent him giggling and crawling my way. I scooped him up and swung him around in circles, finishing with a raspberry on the cheek.

"He's good. Better now that he has his aunt's attention." Alexia smiled. "Wow, beautiful flowers. Gabe?" She nodded toward the vase sitting on the counter near the computer.

"Yeah." I beamed, grateful we had worked out our differences. Well, for the moment.

Flora laughed turning toward the little toddler. "My, how he's grown. Reminds me of my own grandsons. They shoot up when you're not looking." She reached across the counter and tweaked his cheek. "Aren't babies one of God's most wonderful miracles?" Her face glowed. And she had that over-the-top bubbly lilt in her voice again.

Setting Grant on my hip, I met Alexia's gaze. "What brings you by? Needed to see your old sis?"

"Mostly. Karen wanted to check to see if you had *Goodnight Moon*, so I tagged along."

"Great." Turning to Flora, I nodded in Karen's direction. "Do you mind helping her?"

"Not at all." Flora walked from behind the counter over to the children's books.

Alexia reached for Grant who leaned toward her holding out his hands. "Honestly, I guess curiosity got the better of me, and I wanted to find out what had happened with Jimmy and Betsy. Any progress?"

A sigh escaped my lips. "Not yet. I'm chasing down all the obvious leads. The mobster family, the wedding party, but something doesn't feel right."

"What do you mean?"

"I don't know. It was something Jimmy said when I talked with him at the police station. He said he heard a door shut somewhere out in the hall when he entered the office. But then he found the body, and chaos ensued."

"Do you think he heard the killer hiding?"

"Possibly, but it could've been one of the guests looking for a restroom or the wedding coordinator looking for Jimmy," I said.

"True but why hide? If the door shut after Jimmy entered the office, that person didn't want to be seen. They could've watched Jimmy as he entered and slipped out later." Alexia shifted Grant from one hip to the other. He pushed against her with his chubby legs.

Possibilities whirled in my mind. "I hate to say it, but they could've slipped out after Betsy screamed and came to find me. The hallway would've been empty at that moment. Wonder if there is another way out of that part of the building?"

"So, you think Betsy screamed, ran to get you, and the killer took the opportunity to slip out another exit? But wouldn't they be missed at the reception? They'd have to go around and back into the fellowship hall without being seen."

"True."

"That seems a little risky to me. Too easy to be caught." Grant wiggled in his mother's arms and leaned over wanting down onto the floor.

"You can let him down, Alexia. Ben and I will watch him." Karen sat in one of the rocking chairs in the kid's corner with Ben in her lap, reading *Goodnight Moon* to him.

Flora reclaimed her spot behind the counter as Alexia released her son and watched him crawl over to the end table by one of the leather chairs.

"Have you solved the case?" Flora joked.

"No, all we've done is stir up more questions," I said.

Three other moms from Alexia's group entered the bookstore with kids of varying ages in tow. Their chatter floated into the space.

Grant rolled to his bottom and clapped his hands, letting out a stream of squeals. He took off in the direction of the children and the open door. Alexia hurried over and picked him up before he could travel too far.

The theme song from *Law and Order* pierced through the noise of the group. Realizing I had a call, I skirted around the counter and grabbed my purse from the lower shelf. Tossing the monstrosity on top of the wooden surface, I sifted through the lipsticks and wallet and tissues, searching for my phone.

"Hey, Elizabeth. Guess who's here visiting his favorite aunt?"

"You're not his favorite aunt. I am." She chuckled then cleared her throat. "Listen, I'm calling in an official capacity as Jimmy Williams' lawyer. I wanted you to know the DA has decided to move forward with their case against him and press charges. There will be a hearing to set bail next Monday, but with his family's connections to the mob and the fact he's not from here, I'm not counting on him being released on bail."

"Rats." Betsy wasn't going to like this.

"There's also the matter of the U.S. marshals. They're making their rounds interviewing the witnesses from the wedding. Your name is at the top of their list. So, be ready."

"Okay, thanks for letting me know."

"Hold on, I'm not finished. I also received the autopsy report on Reverend Boggs today, and you're not going to believe what it showed."

CHAPTER TWELVE

Tammy McNair, Reverend Boggs' secretary, stood by a large gray four-drawer filing cabinet. She hunched over the open drawer thumbing through the files, mumbling under her breath. The words *bishop* and *iced tea* mixed with other words I couldn't make out.

The large, carpeted office held her desk, several filing cabinets, and a credenza running along the side wall. Metal chairs with green cushions made a daisy chain against the wall opposite her desk, providing the congregants a comfy place to wait.

Several bouquets dotted the room's landscape. Most of the vases held white roses in some form mixed with other seasonal flowers, but a few vases contained bunches of peace lilies, marking the passing of their beloved shepherd.

Not wanting to startle Tammy, I cleared my throat and waited in the doorway.

She whipped around, a scowl etched on her face. Her nose appeared red and her eyes puffy.

Aware I had waited until the end of the workday to come speak with her, I plastered on a smile that would rival the brightest spotlight in Vegas and walked into her office as if I owned the place. "I hope I'm not intruding, but I had a few questions for you about Reverend Boggs."

"Are you with the marshal's office or the police?"

"Neither."

She rolled her eyes and huffed. "A reporter?" Slamming the metal drawer, she carried the found file to her desk. "Who do you work for? Let me guess. *The Memphis Courier* or is it one of those magazines that do those tacky exposes? I know you're not from the *Pine Lake Daily* because they sent over Chet Baker earlier, thinking he could charm information out of me." She threw the file on her desk and pulled a tissue from the box sitting on the corner of her desk. Swiping beneath her eyes, she clutched the tissue and dropped into the chair behind her. "Doesn't anyone have any respect for the deceased anymore?"

I moved to the center of the room, pulling the straps of my purse back onto my shoulder. "I don't work for any of the papers. You see, I've been asked to help prove Jimmy Williams is innocent."

Tammy raised her eyes to meet mine. Her whole body stiffened. "I'm sorry, but I don't have anything to say to you." Opening the folder she'd thrown onto the desk, she proceeded to scan the material.

"But I need your help." Lame as it sounded, it was true.

"Well, you're not getting it." She peered up from the file. "I won't help to free *that* man. Don't you know who he is? According to the newspaper, he's related to some notorious mob boss." A whimper escaped from her lips as her chin trembled. "I won't help."

I stifled the groan rising in me. The irony of her use of the newspaper article against Jimmy in light of her tirade did not escape me. I needed to know if she had any information that could help even if I had to pry it out of her with a crowbar. Figuratively speaking. My mind raced. How could I win her over?

The sobs came in earnest now. "How could anybody do that to Reverend Boggs? He was such a devout believer. He always knew what to say, no matter the situation. He'd pull a scripture out of thin air to fit the need perfectly." Looking toward me, dabbing at the tears, she asked, "What would a mobster have against a man like that?"

The tears and the comments attested to the fact she'd adored the reverend. Softening my tone, I edged closer to her desk. "I'm so sorry for your loss. You must've been very close to the reverend. How long had you worked for him?"

"Two years, but he always said I was like a daughter to him." Tears pooled in her eyes, and a few trickled down her cheeks. She wiped them with the crumpled tissue. "He was so kindhearted."

I rounded the desk and squeezed her shoulder. "I know this must be hard. It tore my heart out when my mother died six years ago."

She grabbed two more tissues out of the box and held them to her eyes.

As I comforted her, I scanned the piles on her desk. On top of the corner pile sat a black accounting book labeled, Building Fund.

Tammy sighed and sat back in her chair forcing me to remove my hand from her shoulder. Blowing her nose, she threw the tissues in the trash under her desk.

"Are you going to be all right?"

"Yes, I just thought the world of him." She shook her head. "He's gone, really gone. I keep expecting him to walk through the door any minute with a coffee for me or a new joke to share."

"It takes a while, months even, to get used to someone you see every day being gone." I met her gaze.

"I guess you know from experience."

"I do." Leaning my hip against the side of her desk, I pushed my larger-than-life, knock-off purse to the other side of my body. "Look, I'm not here to make trouble. I only want to find the truth about what happened. If Jimmy is guilty—"

"He is." Her brows pulled together forming a tight knot.

"If he is, then I want justice. That's all I'm after. Justice for Reverend Boggs," I said.

My words must've struck a chord with her because the tension drained from her shoulders. "Fine. How can I help you?"

I dug in my purse and pulled out my notebook, which held my list and a pen. Flipping to the earmarked page, I chose the first topic: Meetings. "Who did the reverend meet with last week?" My pen was poised above the paper ready to take it all down.

"I'd love to tell you, but the police took my datebook."

Surprised, I asked, "You don't keep the information digitally?"

"No, the reverend liked it old school." Tammy allowed a slight smile to lift the corners of her lips. "He hated technology.

The only reason he had a cell phone was for emergencies."

"Well, tell me what you can remember," I coaxed.

"Okay, let's see. Monday, he met with the Women's Auxiliary Club. They're working on a mission trip for next spring to Honduras. On Wednesday, he met with a young couple he was supposed to marry in two weeks." She stopped and scribbled something on a sticky note. "Wednesday evening, he met with two members of the building committee."

"Is that why the ledger is out?" I pointed to the black binder.

Tilting her head, she looked from the binder to me. Her face wore a wary look as if she'd caught me doing something wrong. "No, I collected the binders at the bishop's request."

"Oh, he's here? I'd heard he was supposed to pay the congregation a visit."

"Yes, he was expected on Sunday, and with everything that happened Saturday, I'm glad he came when he did." Tammy nodded. "He'll be doing the reverend's service once the body is released for burial."

"Of course, that makes sense. He'd want to be here for the church in its time of sorrow." I waited a tick of the clock out of respect then asked, "Can you recall anything else about the reverend's week? Anything out of the ordinary?"

She leaned her elbow on her desk and set her chin on her fist, her eyebrows furrowed. "Of course, he held the wedding rehearsal for the Williams' party on Thursday afternoon and joined them for dinner. Then on Friday, the whole place was taken over by the wedding preparations. People were coming and going. It was a madhouse. I couldn't tell you whom he—" She straightened in her chair. "Wait a minute, I did see him speaking with a young man from the wedding party in the fellowship hall on Thursday evening. It was after the rehearsal but before everyone left for dinner. I wouldn't have paid any attention to it except they both looked very upset. Mad, almost."

"What happened?"

"They talked for a few minutes. I could tell the reverend was uncomfortable, then they headed down the hall towards his office. But I figured they needed some privacy." She leaned back in her chair. "At the time, I was in the fellowship hall showing the bride and groom, her mother, and the maid of honor around the facility.

I like to show the brides the kitchen and where everything is located."

I jotted down the information about the young man. "So, how did Friday go? You said it was a madhouse."

"Yes, the DJ arrived late. He'd left some of his equipment at his house and didn't have time to make another trip. So, I showed him where all the extension cords were kept. It seemed easier to let him use the ones we have. So, everything would be ready for Saturday."

"Couldn't he get his assistant to run by his house and grab them?"

She shook her head. "I don't think he had an assistant."

I made a note about the DJ not having an assistant. "Can you describe the young man for me?"

She grinned. "Sure, he's kind of hard to forget. Tall, dark haired, very handsome."

I wrote down her description, but there was no need. It was Mark LaRocca. Who else? "Can I ask you about the cake-serving sets you bought from Junk in the Trunk? Have you seen them lately?"

"Again, the police took them all."

"Well, did you have a chance to look at them before the police took them? Do you know if one of the sets was missing a knife?" I flipped the page in my notebook and shifted from one foot to the other, wishing my monster of a purse were a few pounds lighter.

"One of the detectives, Floyd Simms, came by to update me. He asked me the same thing—if I had done anything with the cake-server sets once I'd put them away. I told him, no. I'd put them where I always do in the top drawer to the left of the sink in the kitchen off the fellowship hall. But he did allude to the fact one of the knives was missing."

"Really?" I jotted the information down onto my page. "Did you always keep them there?"

"Yeah, that way the reverend knew where to look if a couple needed one for the reception, and I hadn't been able to show the bride. It's surprising how often couples forget about the serving set." Tammy smiled. "We go through several each year."

"Which brings me to another question. I took some photos of

the crowd while the police were here doing their interviews. You were in one of the photos."

Tammy raised her chin. "If you must know, I came in to prepare for the bishop's arrival on Sunday. I didn't want to have to do it after the service, so I popped in to find the files he'd requested." She bit her bottom lip, her eyes filled with worry.

"It's okay. Take your time. What happened next? How did you wind up in the fellowship hall?"

"I went over to the reverend's office during the ceremony to retrieve the building-fund ledgers. There were supposed to be two of them." She sighed. "But I couldn't find them on the reverend's desk. So, I panicked and came back to my office to search for them. I found this one right before the police arrived, so I didn't have time to leave. As a result, they had me wait with everyone else to give a statement."

"Thanks for telling me, I appreciate it." Standing straight, I gestured toward the door. "Now, would you mind showing me where you keep the serving sets?"

"I guess not." Tammy rose from her chair and led me into the fellowship hall. "But I don't see the point. Like I said, the police have them."

"Knowing where they were kept might give me an idea of how hard it would've been for someone to swipe one without being noticed. Also, while we're looking around, could I check out the offices down the hallway near the reverend's?"

Tammy shrugged. "Sure, why not? But remember, I'm doing this for Reverend Boggs, not for Jimmy Williams."

~

Gizmo's dark eyes watched me from where he lay on the bed. I sat beside him on the edge of the mattress and extended my legs. Using the big toe on my right foot, I pushed off the sandal strap from around my left ankle and kicked the shoe toward the wall with the window. Clunk. Then I repeated the action.

Ah, sweet relief. I closed my eyes and wiggled my toes, letting them breathe for a moment before fishing out my slippers from under the bed where I kept them. The soft fur lining squished under my feet as I slipped them on.

The knot on the fashionable sandals I'd chosen to wear had been digging into the tops of my feet since lunch. It hadn't helped walking through the church and fellowship hall twice in search of anything that might clear Jimmy. But the second trip through had paid off.

I'd rushed home to tell Betsy and Julia what I'd found, but no one was home for me to tell. Rising from the bed, I moved to the door. My purse sat on the chair at my vanity dresser with the clue from the church packed inside. I patted the monstrosity as I walked past it. Surely it wasn't a sin to 'borrow' something from a church if it could prove a man's innocence. Besides, it was more like garbage that hadn't made it to the dumpster.

I sent up a silent prayer. *Please Lord, forgive me if I've overstepped the boundaries, but you know what's at stake. I'd appreciate your mercy on this one.*

When I placed my hand on the doorknob, Gizmo hopped to attention not wanting to be left behind. He jumped off the bed and darted for the door before I could open it.

Once in the kitchen, I gave him a scoop of his favorite kibble and went to dig a cola out of the refrigerator for myself. That's when I found the note from Julia attached to the stainless-steel door with a magnet.

A.K.

Gone to pick up Chinese. Betsy is with me. Won't be long.
Julia

My mouth watered at the thought of Chinese takeout. Julia knew it was one of my favorites. Mr. Wong of Wrong's Palace made the best eggrolls I've ever put in my mouth. I could've sworn a waft of fried rice floated under my nose.

Then the front door swung open, and Julia entered holding a cardboard carrier containing three medium soft drinks, followed by Betsy who carried two large brown paper bags. Forgetting the cola, I hurried to help.

Gizmo dashed over to Betsy and barked an excited welcome. She squatted down and tried to pet him, but her hands were too full. "Sorry sweetie, you'll have to wait." He jumped up, placed his paws on her lap, and licked her face before making a stab at the eggroll sitting near the top of the bag.

While Betsy greeted Gizmo, Julia caught my attention and nodded toward her.

Uh-oh, what was wrong? Then I remembered Elizabeth's call

earlier today. Not sure if Betsy had heard Jimmy had been officially charged for the murder, I tried to read her mood.

She stood forcing Gizmo to let her up, and I walked over and took one of the bags from her. "Gosh, this smells so good. I'm starved."

By the redness around the rims of her eyes and the red veins crawling across them, I'd wager she knew about Jimmy.

"Me too," Betsy said. "When Julia suggested we order takeout, I wholeheartedly agreed." Her lips quivering, she headed toward the kitchen with her bag, and Julia and I followed. Gizmo raced ahead of us.

Julia opened the cabinet to the left of the sink and pulled out some paper plates. "So how did your investigation go today?" Separating the plates, she dealt three of them out onto the kitchen counter.

"Not bad. In fact, I think I found our first real clue." I fished out the white containers with the Wrong's Palace logo on them and lined them up on one end of the counter for easy access.

Betsy froze. "Really, you think you've found something?"

The hope I heard in her voice scared me. What if I was wrong? What if the shredded pieces of paper meant nothing? "Well, maybe I'm being a little too dramatic. People shred documents every day."

"Shredded documents? What kind of documents?" Julia freed the sodas from the carrier and placed one in front of each seat at the table.

"I'm not sure. I found them in the shredder in one of the offices near the reverend's. So, I dumped them into my purse and brought them home with me to examine. They might be pieces of a missing ledger."

"You stole documents from a church?" Julia's eyebrows crinkled and her lips puckered. "I believe there's a commandment against that. Something like 'Thou shalt not steal.'"

"Don't be so uptight. It's not stealing. It's garbage." I shrugged. "Besides, if it does wind up being important, then it's evidence. Not stealing."

"Except Gabe's not going to like the fact you tampered with evidence. Again, I think there's a law or something against that." Julia dug into one of the bags and pulled out three sets of chopsticks. "Just saying."

"So, what do you think it is? You must've thought it was important, or you wouldn't have stuffed it in your purse." Betsy filled her plate and sat at the small kitchen table.

I followed suit. "From what I could make out when I examined a few strips in the car, I think it's some kind of financial statement. It had lots of numbers and some symbols I didn't recognize. Besides, Tammy, the reverend's secretary, said she'd misplaced a financial ledger. There are supposed to be two, but she's only been able to find one of them. This may be part of the missing one."

"Financial ledger. Does that mean anything to you?" Julia slipped into the chair across from me, her plate full of sweet-and-sour chicken.

"Just that Carter told me the bishop was coming into town to meet with the building committee. He said the church had been collecting funds for the new fellowship hall for some time. But I don't see how it connects to a mob boss like Frank Morelli."

"Do you still think it's mob related?" Betsy asked.

"I do. It's too convenient he was here for your wedding, and the man who had his brother put in jail winds up dead. Besides, here's the kicker. Elizabeth called me today and said she'd seen the autopsy report on Reverend Boggs." I hesitated, waiting to have their full attention.

"And?" Julia prompted.

"And Reverend Boggs was dying of lung cancer."

"Really? No." Betsy held her chopsticks midair.

"It's true." I leaned forward. "Which begs the question, who would want to kill a dying man?"

CHAPTER THIRTEEN

After dinner, I left Julia and Betsy cleaning up the kitchen and took Gizmo for a walk. We'd decided once everyone was settled for the evening, we'd pull out the shredded papers and try to piece them back together.

When I returned, Betsy and Julia had donned their comfy clothes and were lounging in the living room scrolling through the movies on the streaming service, looking for a nice movie that wouldn't cause a cascade of tears or a flare of anger from our wounded bride. Something to act as background noise while we worked on our mystery puzzle.

I dashed down the hall and returned in my own 'in for the night' hangout wear carrying my purse. Clearing the coffee table, I dumped out the contents of my bag. Mascara, pens, notebook, wallet, and piles of green curlicue papers flooded onto the tabletop. A few items rolled to the edge and dropped to the carpet.

As we worked to separate the odds and ends of my life from the shredded paper, I asked Betsy if she'd had a chance to go see the DJ.

"Yes, I did, but it was a bust. He doesn't have an assistant. And when I showed him the picture, he didn't recognize the guy." Betsy scooched off the couch onto the floor and picked up two pieces of paper.

"We'll need tape." Julia stood and sprinted to her room. The sound of drawers opening and closing drifted down the hall.

With my purse repacked, I carried it to the coatrack standing in the corner behind the front door. "Did he remember anything unusual or off about the reception or the guests?"

"He said he was so busy trying to keep people on the dance floor he didn't notice much of anything else." Betsy picked up two different pieces of paper and tried to fit them together.

I joined her on the carpet in front of the coffee table. From the amount of paper ringlets spread across the top of the glass, I figured once the pieces were reassembled, we'd be looking at five or six sheets of paper.

Julia returned with a tape dispenser. "I knew I had one somewhere." Looking at the pile on the table, she sighed. "This may take a while." Sitting beside me, she crisscrossed her legs and grabbed a handful of the curlicues.

"I think you're right." My heart faltered. Could we ever assemble all these strands back together into something legible? What if this exercise turned out to be a complete waste of time? There was no guarantee these documents had anything to do with the reverend's murder or the missing ledger.

As my doubts grew, Dad's words came to mind. *You follow every lead.* I'd heard him say that to both uniformed officers and detectives alike. Follow every lead. Yes, that's what I'd do. Shoving aside the doubt, I picked up my own pile and began to match the strands, working piece by piece.

The movie we'd selected played in the background with the volume low as we worked for the better part of two hours. Close to nine, we hadn't made much headway and needed a break to keep from going cross-eyed.

Julia offered to make everyone a cup of tea and some popcorn. While we were waiting, Betsy and I turned up the volume on the movie and watched the scene where the young man and woman are trapped in an elevator and wind up falling in love. It's a classic trope, but it gets me every time.

"So, how did you and Jimmy meet? Was it anything like the movies?" I grinned.

A warm glow spread across Betsy's countenance and a faraway look invaded her eyes. "It was so romantic. I'd just broken up with this total jerk, Ed. A friend from college, Kristin, kept telling me she knew this guy who would be perfect for me."

Betsy peered down at her left hand and played with the rings on her finger. "She was right." A sweet smile lifted her lips. "Anyway, she invited him to a Halloween party we were attending and before she could even introduce us, we bumped into each other by the food table and started talking. And everything fell into place. We danced all night, and the next day, he called to ask me for a date."

"Wow, love at first sight."

Betsy giggled. "We like to say, 'Love at first bite' since we met by the food table."

"That's so sweet." Julia entered from the kitchen carrying a big plastic bowl full of popcorn and set it on the couch between Betsy and me. "I'll be right back with the tea."

"I'll help," I offered.

"No need. I pulled out my wooden tray, so I could bring the sugar and honey as well." Julia trotted off into the kitchen.

"Good idea," I called over my shoulder before grabbing a handful of popcorn from the bowl. Glancing at Betsy who still glowed from telling her story, I asked, "So, Kristin Pike is the one who introduced you guys?"

"Yeah, she's Jimmy's cousin." Betsy dipped her hand into the bowl, but before she could bring it to her mouth, I grabbed her arm.

"Kristin Pike is Jimmy's cousin? So, that makes her Tony Morelli's daughter, right?" My mind raced, trying to remember what Gramps had said about her.

"Yeah, that's right." Betsy's head tilted.

Julia carried the tray into the living room, and I pushed the green paper ringlets to one side so she could set it on the coffee table. "Did you know Kristin Pike is Jimmy's cousin and Tony Morelli's daughter?"

She sat in one of the overstuffed white chairs with her cup of tea in hand. "No, I didn't realize they were related. I thought Kristin was your friend from college."

"Well, she is, but she's also one of Jimmy's relatives. I don't see why it's a big deal." Betsy leaned forward and claimed one of the mugs of tea.

"It's a big deal because she's part of the wedding party and the Morelli family. She could've recognized Reverend Boggs the night of the rehearsal dinner. And she had motive to want him dead." Excitement rushed through me.

Betsy scowled. "Dead? What are you talking about? Kristin wouldn't hurt anyone. She graduated *summa cum laude*."

"What? You don't think a killer can be well-educated?" Stunned by her response, I reminded her we needed a viable suspect to move the attention away from Jimmy. "We have to give Gabe and the DA someone else to look at, or Jimmy's going to go to jail for a very long time."

"Well, Kristin couldn't hurt anyone any more than Mark LaRocca or Kent Fry or any of the wedding party. No, it has to be Jimmy's grandfather. We just need to prove it." Betsy shook her head and let her shoulders slump. "I hate this."

"I thought you wanted to find the truth. To find out who killed the reverend." Julia held her mug between her hands, her gaze locked on Betsy. "Well, this is how it's done. We look at everything and everyone. Sooner or later, Amy Kate finds the key that unlocks the mystery, but until she does, we leave nothing undone."

"I guess you're right. Jimmy's innocent, so we keep looking until we find the real killer," Betsy said.

"Even if it leads to someone else close to you or Jimmy?" I tilted my head.

"Even if it leads to someone else close to us," Betsy said.

"Then we'd better get back to work on this lead." Julia nodded toward the pile of shredded paper on the coffee table.

Another hour passed and we'd pieced together half of two pages, enough to confirm these were financial statements of some sort. Numbers and squiggly symbols intermingled across the lined paper.

The sound of a revving car engine came from my purse hanging on the coatrack breaking my concentration. Surprised, I glanced at the time on the TV screen. It was after ten o'clock on a Wednesday night. Worried, I scurried to grab my phone.

"Hey, what's up? Is everything all right?" Gabe spent Wednesday evenings with his mom and dad and twin brother, Michael, and normally he didn't call me because he returned home late. "Did you have a nice time with your family?"

"Yeah, it was nice. We caught up on the latest high school

gossip since Michael is teaching tenth and eleventh grade literature this year.”

“Umm, sounds thrilling. Can’t imagine you being interested in who got asked out to homecoming or who broke up last week.” I giggled remembering all the horrible drama of high school, thankful I no longer taught school for a living.

“It’s better than reality TV.” He chuckled. “Michael always has a great story to share.”

“I bet.” I scurried down the hall toward my bedroom and shut the door for privacy.

He went silent and when he spoke again, his tone held a serious note. “Look, I called to give you a heads-up. The DA has pressed charges against Jimmy, so we’ll be letting the guests know they are free to leave town tomorrow afternoon. When Betsy came by today, I told her the news. I just wanted to check in on her and make sure she’s all right. She was pretty upset when she left.”

“Yeah, Elizabeth called to let me know, so I half expected Betsy to be in tears tonight. But she seems to be doing okay. We haven’t talked about it yet, but I figured she knew.” I sat in the chair in front of my vanity dresser.

“Well, I’m glad she’s doing all right. You never know what people will do when they’re shaken.”

“That’s so true. You don’t know what people will do when they’re upset.” An image of Mark LaRocca emerged in my mind. “On a different note, did you know Mark LaRocca was Reverend Boggs’ son?”

“We figured it out after we read the marshal’s report on Boggs. How did you know?”

“I have my sources.” There was no way I was telling Gabe I’d talked to Frank Morelli. “Does Mark have a motive? I mean, his dad did leave him and his mother when he entered witness protection. Do you think he might have resented being left behind?”

“When we talked with him, he seemed genuinely upset and disappointed at having found his father and then losing him again so soon.”

“Did he mention going to see his father?” I asked.

“Amy Kate, you know I can’t discuss this case with you. We’re not even the lead agency on the investigation.”

"I'm just curious. If I were given the chance to talk to my mom again, I'd take it in a heartbeat."

"I know." His voice tender and soft. "I hate your mom's not here. You must miss her."

"Every day. And that's knowing she's with the Lord. I can't imagine if you knew your father was still alive and you couldn't see him or talk to him. That had to be hard."

"I think Mark understood his father's life would be in danger if he tried to make contact," Gabe said. "His mother chose to end the marriage and stay for the sake of her career. But Mark said they moved a year later due to threats. He was a kid so he couldn't do much about it."

"I suppose not, but what a shock it must've been when he recognized his father at the rehearsal dinner."

"Why do you think Mark recognized Reverend Boggs as his dad?" Gabe asked.

"Oh, just something the church secretary told me." I crossed my ankles and inspected my slippers wondering how much to share with him.

"So, you've been doing some digging on your own? I thought we were working together."

"We are, but I have to do my part, don't I?"

"Fine, I won't waste my breath asking you to let me tag along. I'll simply ask you to be safe and call me if you need me."

"Sure, I put you on my favorites list, one button-push away."

Gabe's voice, a mix of tension and concern, rumbled low. "I'm serious. If you need me, call."

"Will do. I promise." Straightening in my seat, I said, "I'd better get back to Julia and Betsy. We're work … watching something, and I don't want them to have to wait on me."

"Sounds good. See ya tomorrow."

Tomorrow. My mind whirled. All the suspects would be heading out of town after tomorrow, and my chance to free Jimmy would be lost. What I needed was a plan. I had to find out more about Mark LaRocca. Was he bitter toward his father? Enough to kill him? Then there was Kristin Pike, Tony Morelli's daughter. Did she want revenge for her father's imprisonment and death? Frank Morelli didn't think so. And if what Betsy said was true, just because Frank denied having anything to do with the reverend's murder it didn't mean he wasn't involved.

And how on earth, did any of them connect to those green curlicues littering my coffee table?

I popped out of my chair and hustled down the hallway. "Julia, did you have a chance to check out Mark LaRocca's room?"

"No, but I found out he's staying in room 223 and has plans with some of the other guys from the wedding party to go to the lake tomorrow. Why?"

CHAPTER FOURTEEN

The keys to the rooms at the Whispering Pines Bed and Breakfast hung from a wooden board behind the desk in the foyer making them easily accessible. Thank goodness.

Before Betsy and I arrived, Julia had scouted out who was staying in which room. She'd already told us Mark LaRocca had room 223.

Betsy had stopped by the bookstore around ten to give me a ride. And when Flora discovered what we were up to, she offered to keep an eye on the bookstore, thrilled to be a part of the plot. She was still acting overly joyful, bubbly almost. Weird.

Glancing over my shoulder, I stepped behind the counter and pulled the keys from the board as Julia called out the numbers we needed. Betsy kept a lookout for the receptionist, Sue. Taking the duplicates left the board looking bare. We'd need to be quick and return the keys before anyone noticed.

Hiding our purses behind the fake potted trees at the end of the entry near a bench, we made sure to take our phones with us. We took the stairs two at a time. Reaching the landing of the second floor, I divided up the keys—three for Betsy, three for Julia, and four for me. Some of the rooms were on the third floor, but I made sure to take Kristin's and Mark's as well as Gramps' on the second floor. No way would I let either one of my friends take on Gramps. I could only imagine what he'd do if he caught someone in his room. Betsy had the keys for the rooms on the third floor which included her almost in-laws.

"Okay, be as quick as you can, but be sure to look in the drawers, closet, and trash can. Note anything that seems out of place or strange to you."

"Copy that." Betsy's eyes widened. "I feel like I'm in one of those action-spy movies."

"I've said that myself several times since living with Amy Kate." Julia smiled.

"Let's go." I turned but stopped. "Oh, and if someone catches you, act like you're in the wrong room or something, and get out as fast as you can. No sense taking chances."

Julia and Betsy exchanged a look, but I didn't bother to acknowledge it. I headed to Kristin Pike's room first.

The key slid into the lock and with a slight jiggle and a hard push to the old door, it opened. Sunlight bathed the room giving it a welcoming feel, and the handwoven carpet next to the bed added warmth. On the bedside table sat a small stack of books, all aligned at a right angle.

Her laptop stood opened and fired up on a small table in the corner. The computer carrying case leaned against the leg of the desk with the strap wrapped and tucked inside.

I took the opportunity to scroll through a few of her emails and check her social media postings. Not that I expected to find anything. She'd have to be crazy to post a picture or brag about killing the man who sent her pops to prison, but these days you never know. Everything looked normal—no rants or violent threats. She'd posted a few pictures from the wedding before all the chaos had ensued.

Moving to the dresser, I opened the drawers one at a time. Her clothes and unmentionables were folded; even her socks were tucked together in a layered, organized pile. A neatnik.

I poked my head into the bathroom and found there were no used towels lying on the floor. From the made bed, missing linens, and complete display of bathroom products, she'd asked for the cleaning service.

Sitting on the bed, mostly for spite, I surveyed the room. If there had been any evidence in here, it was long gone now. Empty trash, spotless bathroom, no dirty clothes. From what I saw, the Whispering Pines cleaning and laundry services did a top-notch job for their guests.

Sighing, I moved on to Monica Young's room. Now, she could've used the cleaning service. I hadn't expected to find anything, but I didn't want to leave anyone out. After all, they'd all be gone by tomorrow, and I needed to be sure.

Mark LaRocca's room was at the end of the hall. The door squeaked as I pushed it open. Not wanting anyone to see me, I closed the door the instant I stepped inside. Before I could turn around, I heard a bang behind me.

I froze.

"Shut up," A male voice called.

My heart pounded against my ribs. Boom. Boom. The beat pulsed in my ears. Clutching my chest, I waited. How would I explain this?

"Don't tell me to shut up," came a female voice. "Who do you think you are? My husband?" A round of canned laughter floated across the room.

A TV sitcom. Relief flooded over me.

Turning, I spotted an old RCA sitting on a stand along the opposite wall. From the outfits the actors wore, the sitcom had aired in the late eighties. Mark must've left it on.

My heart constricted. Oh no, what if he was back from the lake?

Hugging the wall, I glanced toward the bathroom. The door was closed, but I couldn't see any light coming from under it.

Tiptoeing closer, I stood outside the bathroom door, listening for any sound of life. Nothing. No water running, no buzz of an electric shaver, no noise whatsoever.

I thought about opening the door, but decided if I was wrong, the outcome could be a whole lot worse than being caught in his room.

Feeling confident that I was alone, I searched the room but kept an eye on the bathroom door in case.

Neither Mark nor any evidence made an appearance, and by the time the sitcom ended, I was ready to move on to the next room. I'd saved the most promising one for last. Gramps' room.

Tapping on the door, I pressed my ear close to the wood to see if anyone would answer. Nothing. I jiggled the knob. Locked. Again I knocked. Inserting the key, I turned the lock and cracked open the door. "Mr. Morelli? Mr. Morelli, are you in here?" I removed the key from the lock and moved further into the room. The bed was made and the walker he'd used at the wedding was nowhere in sight.

Breathe, Amy Kate. Breathe. With my heart racing in my ears, I pulled out the top dresser drawer and worked my way down. Nothing out of the ordinary caught my eye. Not even a gun. Which I had expected to find stashed somewhere in one of the drawers. I mean, all mobsters have guns, right?

Moving to the bedside table, I opened the two drawers. Again, nothing out of the ordinary. I leaned over the bed and ran my hands over the covers and under the pillows. I even patted down the decorative shams. Zilch.

Mystified, I strolled to the closet. I didn't figure there would be anything of any importance in it, but to be thorough, I checked. It was small and had one shelf above the hanging bar. Three shoe boxes sat on the wooden shelf. I flipped the top off each box. One pair of black dress lace-ups and two pairs of loafers.

I headed into the bathroom and rifled through his travel bag. A stick of Old Spice deodorant, some Brylcreem, and the other usual items filled the bag. Remembering my words to Betsy and Julia, I checked the trash can.

Apparently, Gramps believed in flossing. The tangles of white string filling half the can testified to it.

Disappointment washed over me. I'd bet my last dollar Gramps knew something about the reverend's death, even if he wasn't directly involved. He didn't strike me as the type to sit around waiting for the police to prove Jimmy's innocence.

Standing in the middle of the room with my hands on my hips, I tried to imagine where a known mobster would hide something important.

Annoyed, I decided to look under the bed so I could say without a doubt I'd looked everywhere before calling the whole exercise a bust. Maybe Betsy and Julia were having better luck. I knelt between the wall and the side of the bed and held the bed skirt out of the way. Hunching down and leaning on my forearm, I scanned beneath the iron frame.

I couldn't see a thing, so I sat back on my heels and pulled my phone from my pocket. Clicking a button on the screen, I turned the flashlight on to the brightest setting. Again, I hunched back over and moved the light a few inches at a time around the area. Not a dust bunny in sight. Swinging the light up, I examined the wooden slats holding up the mattress. There pushed between one of the slats and the mattress hung a wad of green papers.

I recognized them instantly. They looked a lot like the green swirly curlicues we'd worked on late into the night. Lying flat, I crawled under the mattress trying to reach the papers.

Realizing I could grab them easier from the other side, I pushed to a standing position. Then the door eased open.

I dropped to the floor and froze, my palms sweating and my heart in my throat. Pressing my lips together to keep from screaming, I squeezed my eyes shut hoping he'd go away.

"It's no use hiding," The old man croaked. "I know you're here. I always put a piece of floss between the door and the doorjamb when I leave. So, if anyone comes into my room, the floss on the floor warns me."

Well, that explains that.

"Come on out."

I raised my head. First, I spotted the open door and then I saw the older gentleman standing in the middle of the room where I had stood moments earlier.

Frank Morelli leaned on his walker and watched me with a grin on his face. "So it's you, Amy Kate. You surprise me."

Pushing against the mattress, I found my feet. "There are times, Mr. Morelli, I surprise myself."

"I imagine so." He chuckled and moved toward an antique chair covered with an intricate embroidered pattern. Sitting, he pushed his walker to the side, the yellow tennis balls sliding across the wood. Something heavy hung in his Hello Kitty pouch. "I don't mean to complain. Finding a beautiful young woman in my bedroom is usually something I love. But what are you doing here?"

Moving to the foot of the bed, I leaned against the white iron railing. "I'm looking for evidence to help Jimmy."

"I like your candor. Have you found anything interesting?" He crossed his arms and his legs at the ankles at the same time.

I stood and gestured toward the bed. "If I may?"

"Go ahead." He shrugged. Cocking his head to one side, he

followed me with his eyes.

I knelt and reached under the bed, pulling out the green pages. "Can you tell me what these are?" Standing, I slipped my phone into my front pocket and waited for his answer.

"Just some evidence of my own."

Thumbing through them, I realized they used the same symbols as the two half pages we had managed to put together the previous evening. "A budget of some sort?"

"Possibly, but I have my own theory."

Sitting on the side of the bed, I said, "I'd like to hear your theory."

A half grin propped up one corner of his mouth. "I bet you would. But let's take care of the matter at hand. Should I call the police and press charges, or should I overlook your foolhardiness and let you walk out of here with a warning? After all, you are trying to help my grandson."

"I'd call the cops if I were you." Gabe entered the room holding a coffee cup wrapped in a sleeve from the Beans and Leaves coffee shop. Frown lines formed a deep pair of parentheses around his mouth, and his jaw muscles pulled taut. He looked from Frank to me.

I popped up from the bed hiding the papers behind my back. "Gabe, you're here. With coffee?"

"Yes, as you've pointed out, we do have a routine, so when I stopped by the bookstore with your Vanilla Mud Latte in tow, imagine my surprise to find you were out."

"Guess Flora told you where to find me." I made a mental note to have a long chat with her about loyalty.

"After I threatened to make sure she received a parking ticket every day for the next week or two, she hinted you might be here. When I ran into Julia and Betsy downstairs in the foyer, they seemed concerned you were still up here." Gabe glanced toward the older man. "So, I thought I'd better come find you."

I smiled and tightened my grip on the papers I held behind my back. "Well, as you can see, I'm fine."

"This is all very touching, but I'd like to have my room back now. I have things to do." Frank grabbed his walker and pulled himself out of the chair to a standing position.

"Sure, no problem." I plastered on my hundred-watt smile,

nodded to him, and turned toward Gabe as I hugged the papers I'd found under the bed to my chest.

"Hold up. I'll need those papers back." Frank held out his hand.

"Oh, yeah. Right." Forcing a laugh, I walked over and gave them to him. "Sorry."

His dark eyes met mine. "Be sure to stay out of trouble, Amy Kate. I'd hate to see anything happen to someone so young and vibrant."

A shiver ran down my spine. My grave had been stepped on, and I didn't even own a plot. I gulped. "Yes sir. I'll be more careful."

"Good."

"Come on. I think we'd better leave Mr. Morelli to his packing."

"Oh, not to worry, copper, I'm not going anywhere. Not until my grandson is free and clear." Frank laughed. "You can't get rid of me that easy. Not when one of my own has been wrongfully accused."

CHAPTER FIFTEEN

Gabe escorted me down the stairs to the receptionist's counter where Betsy and Julia waited.

"Thank the Lord you're all right." The words strung together as Julia exhaled them all in one breath. "I was so worried."

"Yeah, we thought you might've been caught and didn't know how to talk your way out of it."

Gabe's eyes landed on me, and his brow puckered into a sharp V.

"No, I'm fine. I was chatting with Frank."

"So, how did it go?" Betsy leaned an elbow on the counter and placed her chin on her fisted hand. I spotted one of the room keys poking out of her tight fist.

Julia's eyes widened. "Anything we can use?"

"That wasn't a chat," Gabe interrupted. The concern in his voice caught my attention. "That was a warning. To stay out of his way. Come to think of it, how did you wind up in his room?" Turning to Julia and Betsy, he crossed his arms over his broad chest, still holding the coffee. "And how did you two know where I could find her?"

"It's a long story." I nodded at the coffee cup in his hand. "But thank you for my treat."

Gabe handed the foam cup to me. "Why don't you finish up here, and I'll give you a ride back to the bookstore. It'll give you a chance to fill me in on what you've been up to." He cocked one eyebrow. "Since we're working together and all."

"That's not necessary. Betsy can give me a ride, or I can walk. It's not far. A few blocks. That way I won't cause you any more trouble." I looked at Betsy for help. "You don't mind, right?"

Betsy's arms dropped to the counter. The key in her hand clanked against the wood. "No, I'd be glad to do it."

Gabe scowled and took Betsy's hand. He flipped it over, palm side up.

"Keys?" He eyed Betsy then turned to me. "Do all of you have keys in your possession?"

"Of course, we do. I have my car keys and the key to my apartment," I rattled off.

"Yeah, and I have keys to the back door here and my apartment key," Julia added with a forced laugh.

Gabe shook his head. "That's not what I mean, and you know it."

I exchanged a look with Julia and Betsy, praying Gabe wouldn't ask too many questions. Or we might all be spending the night in the jail cell next to Jimmy.

Throwing up his hands, he huffed, "You know what? I don't want to know. So, this is what's going to happen. I'm going to go wait for Amy Kate in the car. Y'all handle whatever needs to happen in here." Whipping around, he headed toward the front door but stopped with his hand on the knob. Pointing with his other hand, he looked me straight in the eye. "And don't go back upstairs."

The instant the door closed, we piled all the keys we'd borrowed onto the counter. Julia scurried behind the wooden registration desk, and with lightning speed, she replaced each key on its hook while Betsy and I kept watch for Sue, the lady who did the scheduling for the inn.

Sue emerged as Julia hung the last key. "Oh, can I help you with anything?" Her face clouded with confusion when she saw Julia behind the desk.

"No, no, there were some keys on the counter, so I went ahead and replaced them where they belonged. Thought I'd help." The smile that appeared on Julia's face would've caused any toothpaste model to cringe with envy.

Seeing we wouldn't be able to discuss our recent adventure with Sue in the room, we agreed to order a pizza and run over what we'd all learned later that evening. I couldn't wait to tell them about the papers under Frank's bed.

"I guess I'd better go. Gabe's waiting." But as I turned to retrieve my purse from behind the fake Ficca plant, Mark, Kent, Kristin, and Monica bounded through the front door, chatting with one another, their skin blotchy and red from their time at the lake. I threw Julia a conspiring glance. A few minutes more and our geese would've been cooked.

Sue greeted them with a warm hello before bustling off to see about extra towels for one of the guests. Spying us, the group moved our way.

"Hey, we were hoping we'd see you today," Kent directed his words toward Betsy. He had a beach towel draped around his neck and wore a pair of swim trunks.

I didn't hear Betsy's answer because Kristin started talking to me. "I think your boyfriend is waiting for you in that sweet ride of his," she cooed tugging at the brim of her floppy hat.

"Yeah, I know. I was on my way out." I moved toward the plants at the end of the foyer and withdrew mine and Betsy's purses placing hers on the nearby bench. No one paid any attention to me, they were all focused on Betsy. Rejoining the group, I slung my purse over my shoulder and took a few steps, not wanting to go now that some of my prime suspects were here.

Monica faced Betsy. "Hey, we want you to know how sorry we are for all you and Jimmy are going through. I know it must be a nightmare."

"Yeah, Detective Simms came by to let us know they were charging him. Man, that's too bad." Kent shook his head.

Mark stepped forward. "He told us we could leave at any time, but most of us are staying. At least for a while. We don't want you to go through this alone."

"Definitely not." Kristin scowled. Pulling off her sunglasses, she stepped to Betsy's side and wrapped her in a one-arm embrace. "I got in touch with my husband to let him know I wouldn't be home, yet. No way am I abandoning you, my sweet friend. Not at a time like this."

"Everyone is staying at least through the weekend. The hope

is the real killer will be caught soon." Kent pushed his hands into the pockets of his swim trunks and turned to me. "Any progress?"

"Well, I can honestly say I've been working on it all morning." I grinned as Julia smothered a giggle.

Kristin released Betsy. "Glad to hear it." She looked around the foyer then lowered her voice. "I'm sure you're looking at Jimmy's grandfather. If it were me, that's where I'd start."

"Isn't he your uncle?" Julia asked.

"Yes, he is, but like Jimmy, I'm not part of the family business, either."

My eyes fell on the five-carat engagement ring on her left hand and the pair of Gucci sunglasses she dangled from her fingertips. She followed my gaze. "I don't have to be. I married well. My husband, Randy Pike, is the CEO of Pike Industries." She lifted her chin. "I'm grateful for what Uncle Frank did for me when I was younger. When I needed help, he stood by me, but I don't have any illusions about what sort of man he is. You'd be wise, Amy Kate, to keep your eye on him."

"I'll take that under advisement." From what I'd seen of Frank Morelli, it'd be in my best interest to keep both my eyes on him. Turning to Julia and Betsy, I gestured toward the door. "I'd better go. Gabe's probably getting anxious. I'll see you two tonight."

Gabe, true to his word, waited for me in his Corvette parked in one of the front spaces. His head was turned toward an older woman walking her dog, which gave me a great view of his profile with his chiseled jawline and Roman nose. He leaned his elbow out the window as he tapped his thumb on the steering wheel to the beat of the music playing from the radio.

I rounded the back end of the car and opened the passenger door. Sliding onto the leather upholstery, I placed my coffee in the cupholder and before fastening my seat belt, I dropped my purse to the floorboard at my feet. "Thanks for waiting. You didn't have too though. I could've caught a ride with Betsy."

Gabe leaned forward and turned off the music. "And miss the chance to find out what you and your *crew* have been up to this morning? No way." He put the car into reverse and pulled out of the parking lot. "After all, as long as I keep driving, you're a captive audience." A grin appeared on his lips making the corners of his eyes crinkle.

"Really, you'd hold me captive in your car? For my information? With these fuel prices?" I played along.

"If I have to." He shifted and turned down a street headed in the opposite direction of the bookstore. "Okay, spill."

Since I didn't have all day to let him chauffeur me around, it would be prudent to tell him what he wanted to know. Besides, it might help him when he looked further into the case, even if the official version claimed they had the killer.

"I talked Julia into doing some snooping for me while she worked. She overheard several members of the wedding party making plans to take a trip to the lake today. You know, one last hurrah before everyone left town." I squirmed in my seat, my legs sticking to the leather where my skorts stopped. Not wanting to incriminate the others, I kept my confession of the search of the rooms to my actions only. "So, I took the opportunity to, you know…" I shrugged.

The grin on Gabe's face faded. "Tell me you didn't take anything. It's bad enough you broke into their rooms."

"Well, technically I didn't break in." The deep crease that appeared on Gabe's brow let me know he didn't appreciate my misplaced attempt at levity.

"No, you lifted the room keys. Did you take anything?" One of his eyebrows shot up.

"No, I didn't take anything." I crossed my arms, tamping down the irritation stirring in me. Counting to ten, I kept my focus on the road rolling past me out the windshield.

"Good. At least that's something." Gabe shook his head, downshifted, and turned right. Pulling over to the curb, he parallel parked near the Methodist church. Turning in his seat, he faced me. "Look, Amy Kate, you're not making my job any easier. With the marshals taking point for this investigation, I can't keep you from being charged if they find you snooping."

Lifting one shoulder, I turn my head to look out the passenger window.

He leaned toward me. "I find you in a room with one of the most ruthless crime bosses in the United States, holding papers belonging to him that can connect him to the investigation, and you expect me to be okay with that? I can't look for the killer and keep my eye on you. And what if one of the marshals had caught you?" Touching my chin, he turned my face toward him. "If anything should happen to you on my watch, I'd never forgive myself."

The concern shining from his eyes melted my heart.

"I agree with you and Elizabeth. The whole setup is too convenient. And Jimmy strikes me as a smart guy—maybe not good under pressure but smart enough to know if you're going to kill someone, don't do it at your own wedding." Gabe's smile reappeared, and he intertwined his fingers with mine.

"You're not going to arrest me for borrowing the keys at the inn, are you?" I asked.

"Not today." He gave me a half-grin. "So, what did you find out?"

"To be honest, not much. But those papers you saw—I discovered those under the bed, stashed between the mattress and the slats of the bedframe."

"He didn't want those found."

"Right. And here's the thing. I went to the church yesterday and spoke with the secretary. She let me look around in the reverend's office and in the offices along his hallway."

"Yeah, Jimmy's never wavered from his claim he heard a door shut right as he entered the reverend's office that afternoon." Gabe rubbed the back of my hand with his thumb, but his eyes settled on something out the windshield. "I went back to search but didn't find anything helpful."

"Well, I did. And guess what it was?"

His attention pivoted back to me. "What?"

"Some shredded papers that looked remarkably similar to those in Frank's room, green with a lot of numbers and symbols on them."

"Were they pages from a financial ledger? That's what they looked like from the quick glimpse I had when you gave them back to Morelli," Gabe said.

"That's what Julia and Betsy and I believe them to be."

He tilted his head to the side. "When did they see them?"

"We might have started a jigsaw puzzle of sorts on our coffee table." I pressed my lips together not sure how Gabe would respond to this new information. "It's slow going, but we've been able to piece together two halves of two different pages."

"I'd like to drop by and see those tonight if that'd be okay." Winking, he added, "Notice I'm not asking how you acquired them."

"Thanks for that." I patted the back of his hand holding mine. Looking around, I noticed the church.

Gabe let go of my hand, turned off the engine, and opened his door.

"What are you doing?" I asked.

"Going to the church to see about a break-in they reported. Apparently, someone smashed in a window and ransacked the reverend's office as well as the secretary's."

"Wow," I said. "Sounds like they were looking for something."

"I know. You coming? Or do I get to have all the fun myself?"

Tammy, the reverend's secretary, stood behind her desk with several stacks of files in front of her.

Gabe tapped on the door and waited for her to acknowledge us.

Glancing up, she nodded. "Come in. I suppose you're here about the break-in." Her mouth pulled tight into a pencil-thin line. "I've already spoken with one of the uniform officers earlier this morning." She waved at the files littering the floor near the filing cabinet and the papers that had winged their way to spots not suited for notes and memos.

"As you can see, they made quite the mess. It's going to take me the next few days to put everything back in order. Then there are all the items I need to deal with because of what happened to the reverend. This is not what I need with the bishop here and—" Tears sprang to her eyes, but she sniffled them into submission.

"I won't keep you long." Gabe scanned the office. Turning his attention back to the dark haired, forty-something woman, he pulled a notebook from his suitcoat pocket. "Have you been able to figure out if anything is missing? A file or perhaps something more personal?"

She sighed and caught a stack of files midair that slipped toward the edge of the desk, stopping them before they hit the ground. "Not really. So far, the only thing I'm sure is gone is one of the building committee's financial ledgers. Like I told you, yesterday—" She turned toward me. "I'd pulled it out of the safe Saturday in preparation for the bishop's visit Sunday. They're supposed to be two, but I lost one and haven't been able to find it. So, I gave him the one I had. He returned it yesterday morning before you came by. Now this." Exasperated, she let go of the wayward pile and gestured toward the messy room. "What am I supposed to tell the bishop? Both ledgers are gone."

"I'm sure he'll understand," I offered.

"What did the ledgers look like?" Gabe stepped over a few papers that had drifted to the space between the door and Tammy's desk during the break-in.

"They were thick black binders that held green lined paper. Nothing special. The building committee kept their records in them. You know, like who gave what and when, as well as when it had been deposited into their account."

"So, the building committee had a separate account from the church?" I followed Gabe closer to where Tammy stood.

"Yes, it seemed prudent at the time for the committee to keep the fund separate from the regular tithes. So, none of it would be mistakenly used for a different purpose." She placed her hand on her hip and tilted her head, a far-off look in her eye. "You know, come to think of it, an elderly gentleman did happen in here yesterday. Not long after you'd left. He'd seemed in a bit of a panic, clutched at his chest, and asked for a glass of water."

"What happened?" Gabe asked.

"I picked up the phone to call 9-1-1, but he reassured me all he needed was a glass of water. But when I returned from the kitchen, he'd gone, and the ledger had been moved. I'd put it on the corner of my desk, so I would remember to put it back in the safe. But when I returned, it sat in the middle of my desk." She shook her head. "I don't know what I was thinking. I should've put the ledger back in the safe right then. The bishop will probably fire me."

Not wanting her to become too distracted, I interrupted, "Did this elderly gentleman have a walker with a Hello Kitty pouch on the front and tennis balls on the feet?" My brow furrowed, realizing this was where Frank acquired the pages I'd found under his bed. He'd used his age to his advantage and snatched a few pages from the ledger.

"Yes, how did you know?" Tammy's eyes widened in surprise.

"I've met him." With a huff, I crossed my arms. How low can one person go? "I guess he thought those documents might help his grandson, Jimmy."

"Oh, so he's related to the groom. I hope that young man rots in jail." Tammy pursed her lips and lifted her chin. "Do you think he did this?"

"No, I don't." Gabe shifted his weight and changed the topic. "It's obvious you cared for the reverend."

"Very much. Before he came to Pine Lake, our church was dying. God's Spirit seemed to have dried up and vanished from this place." She shifted her weight and redistributed the pile under her hand to make it more stable. "Then he showed up and his sermons were full of life and faith and hope. We were like seedlings in desperate need of water, and every Sunday he poured out God's Word on us. Without him, this church would've closed years ago." She looked down at the stacks of papers and shook her head.

I couldn't imagine someone in the WITSEC who had connections to the mob saving a church. Unless … "Do you think the reverend's faith was genuine?" I meant the question for Gabe, but Tammy snapped at the chance to answer.

"Definitely. He was the most wholehearted believer I had ever met. Reverend Boggs often reminded me God has a plan for us, and there is a reason for everything that happens." Her lips trembled, and she blinked back the tears threatening to dampen her lashes. "He'd be the first to say what's happened here is part of the Lord's plan." Plopping into the black leather chair behind her, she added. "But I don't see how."

I rounded the desk and threaded my arm around her shoulders. "It's going to be all right. Detective Cooper and I will get to the bottom of this. Reverend Boggs' killer will be brought to justice."

She fished a tissue from her front slacks' pocket and dabbed under her eyes. "He'd probably ask for leniency for the soul."

Gabe cleared his throat. "I hate to get back to business, but those binders you say have been stolen, do you have any idea why someone would want them?"

She shrugged. "A few weeks ago, the reverend asked the committee to go over the books in preparation for the quarterly report for the congregation. But that was routine." She bit her bottom lip and met Gabe's gaze. "So, one of the committee members, the treasurer, Levi Jackson, brought in the binders. Everything seemed normal until later in the week when Reverend Boggs asked me to call the bishop. Said he needed to talk to him, and it couldn't wait."

"Did he say what it was about?" Gabe asked.

"Something about wanting to invite him for a visit to look over the books. That's how the reverend had put it." Tammy shook her head. "But I don't see what that has to do with the reverend's death."

I leaned my hip against the edge of the desk. "Oh, I hate to bring this up, but did you know about his diagnosis?"

She nodded. "He told me a few months ago."

"Did he share the news with the whole congregation? Or just a few people?"

"No, he wanted to keep it to himself. He didn't want anyone to treat him any different. It would come out eventually anyway."

"It's so odd to me." I crossed my arms, letting my mind wander. "Why would someone want to kill a man who was going to die anyway?"

Gabe snapped his fingers then pointed at me. "To shut him up."

"What?" Tammy scowled. "What do you mean?"

"The killer couldn't wait for the reverend to die of natural causes. He needed him out of the way now." Gabe glanced at me then turned his attention to Tammy. "Are you sure nothing else is missing? The financial ledger is the only thing gone?"

She nodded. "Yes, I misplaced the one, and the other has been stolen. Why?"

I didn't have the heart to tell her one of them had been shredded and now lay on my coffee table like puzzle pieces.

"Because my gut is telling me this isn't mob-related at all. This has to do with the building committee. Who else has seen those ledgers?" Gabe leaned forward, planting his hands on the desk bringing him face-to-face with Tammy.

She furrowed her brow in thought. "The members of the committee, myself, and the bishop saw the one."

"The bishop." I glanced at Gabe who nodded.

"Where is the bishop staying?" Gabe asked.

"In the reverend's home. It's owned by the church, so of course, when other church clergymen come to visit, they stay there."

"Then we'd better go check in with him. See if he can shed any light on those financial books."

"Oh, I'm sorry. He's not in town today. The bishop had some business to attend to in Boaz and won't be back until late." She opened one of the drawers in her desk and pulled out a sticky note and a pen. "Would you like me to leave him a message?"

"No, I'll swing by tomorrow," Gabe said.

Outside on the sidewalk, I stopped Gabe by his car. "So, you don't think this is mob-related?"

"No, I don't. It seems to me everything revolves around those ledgers. How many pages did you say y'all have put together?"

"About half of two different ones. But I'll see how much progress Betsy's made tonight when I get home," I said.

"Great. I'd like to look at them. Maybe have someone from the marshal's office in the white-collar crime division give them a once-over for me."

"Okay. But what are you thinking?" I asked. "How are the financial pages connected to the reverend's murder?"

"I'm not sure. But I do find it suspicious the reverend was killed after he asked the bishop to pay him a visit. And from what I've heard from some of the members of the congregation, the bishop was here to audit the building committee's accounts."

I grinned at his reference to members of the congregation. After all, I'd asked the same source he had—his father, Carter Cooper. He was right, though. It was odd the reverend was killed soon after the announcement of the bishop's visit.

Besides, with all these pieces of green-lined paper floating around, it couldn't be a coincidence that both myself and Frank Morelli came to the same conclusion—something didn't add up. But what, I still didn't know.

Looking at the time on my phone, I moved to the passenger side door. "Speaking of the marshals, I need to hurry back to the bookstore. One of them is meeting me there at four to interview me."

Gabe hustled to his side of the car and stared at me over the top of his Corvette, a wide grin on his lips. "Just remember, go easy on them. It's their first time with a home-grown detective."

CHAPTER SIXTEEN

"Okay, so what did we find out about the wedding party?" I stood in the kitchen of our apartment looking at my roommate and her cousin, Betsy, who sat across from me at the table. Holding the bulletin board up so we could all see it, I pointed to the card marked groomsmen.

Betsy rolled her eyes and huffed.

Julia had called me at work to warn me about Betsy's foul mood. Apparently, she'd done a google search on unsigned marriage certificates and found that in the grand state of Alabama, even with the ceremony completed, she and Jimmy were indeed not married.

"I discovered Kent, the redheaded groomsmen, loves peanuts. He had bags of roasted peanuts all over his room." Julia nodded toward the board where his name hung on the list with the others from the wedding party. "A complete slob. He's doomed to be forever a groomsman and never a groom."

"Funny, Kristin Pike's room was the exact opposite. It was spotless," I said.

"Really?" Betsy leaned her elbows on the table. "I find that hard to believe."

"Why?" Julia asked.

"When we were in college, her room looked like a train wreck. She never cleaned unless she was stressed. Her room looked its best right before finals." Betsy tilted her head and squinted her eyes, focusing on the list of names.

"I guess some people eat when they're stressed and others clean." Julia pointed to the bulletin board. "What about Mark LaRocca? What did you find in his room?"

"Just the TV on. Scared me out of my skin. But nothing to incriminate him. But I've saved the best for last."

"Ooh, do tell." Julia's eyebrows winged up as a sparkle of interest danced in her eyes.

"I found some pages from a financial ledger stuffed between the slats and the mattress of Frank Morelli's bed." I laid the bulletin board down and picked up a note card. After writing 'financial pages' on it, I added it to the board. "And get this, the ledgers have been stolen from the church office."

"Really?" Julia sounded surprised. "a break-in at the Methodist church?"

"Yeah, and when Gabe and I went to speak with Tammy, the church secretary, she told us an older man had dropped by the other day in need of some help, clutching his chest and asking for a glass of water."

"What did she do?" Julia's eyes widened.

"She wanted to call for an ambulance, but he insisted he just needed a moment to rest, and the water. So, she went to get him a glass, and when she returned, he'd gone."

"Do you think it was Frank Morelli?" Julia's voice filled with excitement.

"From the description she gave Gabe, I do. And get this, she said the ledger sat on the corner of her desk before she left to go to the kitchen, but when she returned, she found it sitting in the center of her desk. It had been moved. That must've been when he took the pages I found stuffed under his bed."

"Well, that's it then. He's the killer." Betsy straightened in her seat. Her lips pulled tight.

I shook my head. "Based on that line of thought, we're the killers. We're following the same theory as Frank. That someone from the church is involved. From what I'm seeing, he's trying to help his grandson."

Betsy popped out of her seat. "I can't believe you." She slapped her hand against the tabletop. "You're defending a known killer. And why hasn't Gabe arrested him instead of putting my poor Jimmy through this horrific nightmare? If Frank has pages from the ledger, then he's probably the one who stole it. He must've hired one of his goons to go back and lift it after he saw it there."

"He's not the killer, Betsy. I don't know what he's done in the past, but this time it's not him. Sure, he may have stolen the ledger, but it doesn't make him the murderer." My voice trembled as I fought to keep it steady. "Now, what did you find in the rooms you searched?" I turned my attention back to the board.

Betsy shot me a look, but the anger in her eyes had dissipated before her backside hit the seat of the chair. She plopped back with an air of surrender. "I didn't find anything out of the ordinary. How about you, Julia?"

"Nothing."

"Then the financial pages are our best clue." Biting my lip, I weighed our options. "Tomorrow, I'll try to talk with the bishop, since he's seen one of the actual ledgers. Maybe he can tell us what's so important about them." I spotted the note card that read 'unidentified man' and looked to Betsy. "Have you been able to find out anything about the man in the picture?"

"No, but I'll work on it tomorrow."

"Maybe try Flora. The woman's always saying she's related to half the town. She might have a name for you." I thought about offering to talk to Flora myself, but Betsy needed something to do to keep her mind off her misfortunate nuptials.

"And what about the cake knife? Betsy, you said Kristin and your mom and Jimmy were with you when you picked it out at Junk in the Trunk. Lilly told me Tammy had bought the last three serving sets she had. Did you show anyone else the cake knife?"

"I showed the other bridesmaids the set while we were getting ready for the rehearsal and the dinner afterward."

"So, all the bridesmaids knew what your set looked like on Thursday." I drummed my fingers on the table. "Did any of them know where the serving sets were kept in the church?"

Betsy closed her eyes. Her brows pulled into a knot.

Julia and I waited.

"Hmm, let me think. Before we left the church, the secretary showed us to the bridal suite down the opposite hall from the reverend's office. She took us to the stage where the DJ would set up Friday morning. We poked our heads into the restrooms to see how many occupants it would handle, and yes, she took us to the kitchen." Betsy opened her eyes.

"Who was with you?" Julia asked.

"Pretty much the whole wedding party. We all sort of fanned out in the fellowship hall. Kent went to hold the reservation for us at the restaurant. But everyone else was there."

"But who was in the kitchen?" I asked.

"All the women." Betsy shrugged. "Jimmy, my mom. Then everyone left but Mark."

"Did Tammy show you where the extra cake servers were kept?" I pressed.

"Umm, she didn't show them to us, but she did mention they were in the top drawer to the left of the sink. Why? Do you think this is important?"

"Well, if the killer didn't buy their cake knife from Junk in the Trunk, they had to get it from somewhere."

"But why bother? Why not use any kind of knife?" Betsy bit her lip.

"I believe the killer planned to take your cake knife after the fact, leaving just the one to make it look like your knife had been the one used to end the reverend's life. Which would leave the pool of suspects to those at the wedding. Maybe they wanted to incriminate Gramps. I don't think the murderer counted on Jimmy coming into the office when he did to sign the marriage certificate. Jimmy probably scared him off. And since I carried the cake knife with me when you came to get me, they had to leave it like it was. Two cake knives."

"Oh my, what a mess this could've been if you'd left the cake knife on the table in the fellowship hall and someone had swiped it." Betsy bit her lip, fighting to stay calm. "There'd be no hope at all for Jimmy. At least with a second knife, we have a chance to prove someone else nabbed it from the kitchen."

"Yeah, we would've never realized a different knife was used. Everyone would've assumed it was the one you bought," I said.

"Wait a minute." Julia shifted in her chair and pulled her left knee up under her, leaning on her elbow. "When I put the keys back on their hooks this afternoon, I noticed a bag in the trash under the front desk from Beautiful Weddings.”

“The boutique near the highway?” Betsy asked.

“That’s the one. You said the second knife had to come from somewhere. What if it came from a different shop? Maybe Beautiful Weddings.”

“Yes, that has to be it. Nice job, Julia.” I grinned at my friend. “Now, Betsy, can I ask you to call around tomorrow to all the wedding and trinket shops in the area that might carry wedding items? See if you can find out who in town sells those cake-serving sets. And I’d start with Beautiful Weddings if I were you.”

“Sure, but couldn’t the killer have bought the server set online?” Betsy asked.

“Nope, the killer wanted one identical to yours, and you didn’t have yours until you arrived here. So, they wouldn’t have time to order one. It had to be purchased here and after you’d picked up yours.” I paused letting my words sink in. Setting down the bulletin board, I paced from the table to the wall and back. “Floyd Simms told Tammy one of the knives from the church-serving sets was missing. That means it could be someone from the church.”

“Yeah, I’m sure everyone who’s ever used the Methodist fellowship hall for a function knows where to find the serving sets,” Julia said.

I pivoted, took four steps, and pivoted again. “I also need to talk with Levi Jackson, the treasurer for the building committee and the bishop. Maybe they can shed some light on what’s going on with these crazy ledgers. Ada Culpepper did say there were some discrepancies in the numbers. But she chalked it up to bad math.”

“Maybe another chat with Mrs. Culpepper might be in order.” Julia’s smile climbed all the way to her eyes which glowed with a hint of mischief. “You do know how much Gizmo loves an early-morning walk. You could catch her when she’s walking Alvin.”

Even Betsy giggled at Julia’s suggestion. “Yeah, we all know how much you and Gizmo love anything that happens before eight.”

“Fine, but I’ll need a super grand Vanilla Mud Latte tomorrow to make it through the day.”

"Speaking of coffee, how about a nice cup now? We might need one to rev up our brains." Julia rose and opened the cabinet where the coffee filters were kept. The instant she lifted the lid from the coffee canister the air filled with the rich aroma.

Turning back to the bulletin board, I replayed the scene in my mind of the reverend's office the day of the murder. Jimmy had stated he'd moved the chair. It had been facing toward the window which meant that the reverend had his back to the killer. I'd made that observation then but hadn't added it to the other facts.

"What is it?" Betsy asked. "You're about to stare a hole into that bulletin board."

I grabbed a new note card and jotted down my thoughts. "Jimmy said he'd swiveled the chair to face him. That it had been facing the window and not the door."

"Yeah, that's what he said." Betsy nodded, leaning forward and examining the board herself as I pushed a pin through the card onto the board. *Knew Killer* sat next to *Mark LaRocca.*

"Well, it strikes me that if the reverend had his back to the killer, it would mean the killer either snuck up on him, you know, or …" I pushed my hair behind my ear. "He knew the killer and felt comfortable enough to turn his back on him."

"Or her," Betsy corrected.

Julia gasped. "So, you're saying the reverend was killed by someone he knew and trusted?" She flipped the button on the coffee maker, and the machine gurgled to life.

I met Betsy's gaze. "Or her," I repeated as I plopped into the chair behind me, allowing new thoughts to form in my mind. I'd been running on a male-only theory—mobsters, gunmen—that sort of thing. But now an odd but plausible idea occurred to me. Could Ada Culpepper be an embezzler? A murderer? I laughed at the thought, but still…

"What's so funny?" Julia asked.

"Oh, nothing." I giggled.

Gabe called around nine to say something had come up and he couldn't make it by to see the pages. Or lack of them. We'd worked on them until frustration and exhaustion had set in.

Later that night, I tossed and turned in bed not sure if it was the coffee or the strange thoughts about Ada keeping me awake.

~

Okay, so six o'clock in the morning wasn't my best time of day on any day, but add to it that it was Friday after a topsy-turvy week, and all I could think about was coffee. I stared at my reflection wondering if I could improve on the ponytail and baseball-cap look I had going on.

Gizmo lay on the end of my bed watching me poke my earrings through the holes in my ears.

"Come on, boy. We'd better hit the trail, or we'll miss our intended target."

People set their clocks by Ada Culpepper's routine. By a quarter past six, she'd be headed back towards her house which led her right past my apartments, The Heartlands. Sure enough, as I rounded the building to the sidewalk, Ada was leaning over with a doggie bag in hand, cleaning up a small mess Alvin, her white stubby bulldog, had made.

"Ada, you're sure up early. Did you have a nice walk in the square?"

She straightened and did a quick assessment of me before tying a knot in the bag she held. "I'd say you're the one who's up early for a change. As I'm sure you know, I walk Alvin every morning." Her shoulders stiffened as she spoke. "We begin *our day* at half past five with a few brisk laps around the town square, then we slow the pace down a bit so Alvin can finish any business he might have to do before we go home for a breakfast of eggs and yogurt."

Alvin wagged his thin tail at the mention of his name.

Gizmo sat on the patch of grass in front of the apartments between Ada and me, with his head tilted to the right, listening to the conversation with great interest.

Seeing Ada in the light of day vanquished all the weird and unsettling thoughts I'd had about her the previous night. She certainly wasn't a murderer and probably would've needed to schedule the crime in her datebook if she were. *How's a week from Tuesday for that strangulation?* No, I couldn't see it. "Ada, I'm glad I ran into you."

Her face scrunched into a web of lines, and a glint of skepticism seeped into her eyes. "Why? You haven't taken on a side job to the bookstore, have you?"

"No, no, I'm not selling anything. I hoped to enlist your help with my inquiries into the reverend's death since you're on the building committee. When I saw you the other day, you told me you had found some discrepancies in the finances."

She shifted her weight, and the stiffness in her shoulders seemed to climb down to her hips causing her whole torso to become rigid. Her crossed arms served to emphasize the fact she didn't appreciate my interruption of her routine. Even the doggie bag dangling from her hand quivered with her irritation. "What do you want to know about the committee?"

The August sun ascended another notch in the sky causing me to pull my pink baseball cap down further on my brow. I stepped a little to the left to evade the direct light, forcing Gizmo to move as well. "The names of the other members would be a big help. I know you and Levi Jackson are two of the five members."

"Don't get me started on Levi Jackson." She rolled her eyes and shook her head. "He's let us all down."

"What do you mean?" I asked.

"Well, first of all, how he came to be the treasurer, I'll never know. He has no experience, and he's only been a member of our church for a few years."

"Oh, I see." I nodded my understanding but didn't interrupt her rant.

"Basically. I knew when we elected officers, I should've been given that position, but no, they put me in as secretary, again. For the last five years I've served on the building committee, and either Pam Tisdale or myself have been placed as the secretary because…and I quote, 'we have the best handwriting for taking the minutes of the meeting.'" She tsked. "Utter nonsense."

It sounded like sour grapes to me, but it wouldn't help my cause to mention it. So, instead, I kept to the point. "So, Pam Tisdale is also a member."

"Yes. Along with Robert Green and Todd Foster." She tugged on Alvin's leash when he barked at a passing jogger.

"Thanks, Ada. I appreciate the help." Not having paper with me, I dragged Gizmo over to the hedges so he could do his morning necessities and I could hurry inside to write down the names.

Ada watched. I'd half expected her to dash away relieved to return to her precious schedule. But instead, she followed me, pulling Alvin along beside her, his short legs doing double time to keep up. "Levi wasn't even the best candidate for treasurer. At least I'd had experience keeping books when I worked for Calvin and Colbert Realty. I used to keep up with the office slush fund, and I handled all the office accounts. You know, what we spent on coffee and business cards. Those things."

"Oh, I forgot you used to work for them. So, what does Levi Jackson do? Maybe his job gives him some experience as well." Gizmo trotted to the end of the row of hedges before sniffing out a spot.

"He works for Doctor Jenkins as a nurse practitioner. The only numbers he handles are blood pressures and temperatures. I mean, really, there's no comparison."

Obviously, I'd landed on a sore topic for Ada.

"To put me as secretary and that young man as treasurer? I'm not sure what the committee could've been thinking." She dragged Alvin to where Gizmo and I stood. Alvin sat in the shade of the hedges then slumped to the ground dropping his head onto his front paws.

I pressed my lips together to keep from giggling at the dog. The poor boy wanted to go home to his eggs and yogurt. "Well, I'm sure they might consider moving everyone around again, since the bishop is here. You mentioned some bad math? Do you think Levi Jackson did something illegal?"

The lines between her brows puckered. "Well, that's why the bishop's here. To do an audit. There had been some discrepancies, and the reverend felt the bishop should be informed."

"An audit. How interesting. I thought the reverend simply wanted the bishop to take a look at the books, but he'd called for an internal audit?"

"Yes, he's the one who caught the discrepancies in the books at our monthly meeting while we were prepping for our quarterly report. Which I thought was strange since last quarter when we checked them, everything was in order. I mean, how can they be correct one time and be so off three months later?" The corners of her mouth pulled down. "It's that young man, Levi. I knew the instant they put him in charge of the purse strings, there'd be trouble."

Gizmo had joined Alvin lounging on the cool grass in the

shade of the hedges.

"What made you think that?" It was probably Ada's sour grapes talking, but I wanted to be sure.

"Things I've heard."

"Like what?" I glanced at Gizmo who lay on his side with his eyes closed.

"You know I'm not a gossip. I leave that for people like Flora."

Now, I remembered why Ada Culpepper and I didn't get along well. She always put herself in a different class from everyone else. But she was talking again—

"But if it'll help catch the reverend's killer, I heard Mr. Jackson had a little gambling problem. About two years ago, I recall he came to church with a black eye. Swore he ran into a doorframe in the middle of the night. Not long after that incident, we had to change the night we held our monthly meetings from Wednesdays to Thursdays because he said it interfered with another activity."

"So what? That doesn't prove anything. He could've joined a bowling league or something."

"Don't be a simpleton. We all know Gambler's Anonymous meets on Wednesday nights in the basement of the Episcopal church." Ada's gaze dropped to where Alvin napped. "I'd better take him home. He gets so upset when his schedule is thrown off."

I smothered a giggle as the sound of Alvin's soft snores greeted Ada's tug on his leash, testifying to his ability to chillax even in the midst of a disrupted schedule.

CHAPTER SEVENTEEN

Flora was inserting the key into the lock as I stepped out of the Beans and Leaves with my Vanilla Mud Latte. After my encounter with Ada, I needed some liquid strength.

"Good morning."

A smile spread across her lips when she spied me. "Nice of you to be on time."

I held up my empty hand, palm out. "Stop. I've already taken one for the team this morning. I met Ada Culpepper out on her walk with Alvin."

"Oh, you poor dear." Flora patted my shoulder as I crossed the threshold into the bookstore. The bell on the door jingled as the door swished shut behind us. "What a way to start a Friday."

"Tell me about it. Her one saving grace is that she is a fountain of information." I shrugged. "And she takes excellent care of Alvin. So, maybe she has two useful qualities."

"True. She does have a soft spot for her furry friends. I guess she can't be all bad." Flora moved down the short hallway to the workroom in the back. When she emerged, she had divested herself of her lunch bag and purse.

I stashed mine under the counter, knowing I wanted to find a moment sometime in the day to go speak with the bishop. Everything Betsy and Julia and I had discussed pointed us to those ledgers. Even the information I'd gleaned from Ada this morning had all but encircled Levi Jackson with red glowing arrows, identifying him as the prime suspect.

But how to prove it. With the ledgers stolen and no other piece of evidence to indicate him, other than the Pine Lake grapevine, I was at a loss as to my next step.

Taking a sip of my latte, I leaned my elbows on the wooden counter and contemplated where to go from here. I needed to give the DA reasonable doubt about their case. But how?

Frank Morelli's face with his steel dark eyes popped into my mind. He still had a few of the pages from the stolen books. Maybe they could prove Levi Jackson was up to no good. If only we could finish assembling our pages; we hadn't made much headway.

"My, you're deep in thought." Flora brushed past me to pull the feather duster out from under the counter along with the glass cleaner and paper towels.

"I'm trying to put all the pieces together."

"It's a shame about Jimmy. Are you any closer to figuring it all out?"

"Not really. I have a suspect, but so far I haven't been able to put him at the scene of the crime."

The bell jingled on the door, and Elizabeth breezed into the bookstore. "Morning all."

"Well, what a nice surprise," Flora cooed, flicking invisible flecks of dust from the counter. "One of my favorite people."

Elizabeth beamed. Ever since Mom's death, she missed the attention of an older woman in her life. So, whenever Flora praised her, she ate it up like candy corn at a harvest festival.

"Hey, what are you up to?" I asked.

"I wanted to come by to give you the results of the forensic workup from Saturday's crime scene. They discovered a second print on the cake-knife handle besides Jimmy's."

I blew out a sigh of relief. "Thank goodness. So, they're going to let him go since they have another suspect, right?"

Elizabeth tucked her head, peering at the carpet. "No, they say he's still the prime suspect. There is too much circumstantial evidence not to proceed with the case against him."

"You've got to be kidding me. The fact there's another print on the murder weapon should at least be enough for reasonable doubt." I grabbed my coffee and trotted over to the brown leather chairs that sat near the long window at the front of the store.

Elizabeth followed and plopped into the chair adjacent to mine. She stashed her purse beside her in the seat. "I know this is hard to hear, but we need more."

"Has Gabe spoken to you about the stolen ledger?" Had he taken the time to talk with her since we'd interviewed the church secretary?

"He's kept me in the loop. Sounds like a viable line of inquiry. But without the ledgers, it's gonna be hard to prove they were the motive for the reverend's death."

"Well, if the information in the ledgers is the motive, it would explain why the killer needed the reverend dead now."

"What do you mean?" Elizabeth crossed her legs and let her black high-heel shoe dangle from her toes.

"According to Ada Culpepper, Boggs called for the audit. He's the reason the bishop is here. If Levi Jackson embezzled from the building fund, he'd want to make sure the reverend couldn't tell anyone. Maybe Levi didn't know the reverend had already contacted the bishop, or maybe Boggs discovered him destroying the ledgers, and Levi killed him hoping to make it look like someone at the wedding had committed the crime." I leaned forward with my forearms on my knees, holding my foam cup of coffee between both hands. "After all, why else would you kill a man who was already dying of cancer? The answer as Gabe pointed out is because you can't wait for him to die. You need him out of the way now."

"Or they didn't know the reverend was dying." She swung her foot. The loose shoe danced on the ends of her toes. A faraway look invaded her eyes, so I waited.

"Let's suppose the killer does know about Boggs' condition." She met my gaze. "Boggs is dying, but he's discovered you're embezzling money from the church. So, he asks the bishop to do an internal audit. The reverend wants to make sure he's not mistaken."

"But knowing what we do about Reverend Boggs' old life as an accountant, he must've recognized the inconsistencies the minute he saw them. So, the question is—why did he notice them this time? I mean, the committee went over the books quarterly. What was different about them this time?"

Elizabeth shot straight up from her chair. "The books. The

books were different this time.”

I shook my head and held up my palms. “That’s what I just said.”

“No, Amy Kate, there were two sets of books. Levi Jackson kept *two* sets of books.” She slipped her shoes back on her feet and rose from her seat. Bending over, she grabbed me by my shoulders. “You may have just given me enough ammunition to get Jimmy out of this mess.”

“Okay, but what if Levi has destroyed the phony set?” I hated to burst her balloon, but this was a legitimate concern. I mean, if the guy killed for them, he wouldn’t leave either set lying around.

“I’ll cross that bridge when I reach it. But if we can match his prints to the one on the cake knife, we should have enough to convince the DA to drop the charges while they continue the investigation.”

As she moved toward the door, I considered telling her about the pages Julia, Betsy, and I were putting together, but I didn’t want to muddy the water. She’d have too many questions. Besides, there was that pesky little rule about not tampering with evidence. She might have to report it, and I didn’t want to put her in that position. Instead, I veered off on another route. “Jimmy’s grandfather might have a few pages from one of the phony ledgers in his possession. You might want to check into that.”

She froze with her hand resting on the metal handle of the glass door and called over her shoulder, “I’m not even going to ask how you came by this information.” And with one swift push, she darted out the door on her way to save Jimmy.

The minute Elizabeth left, I dashed behind the counter and grabbed my purse.

“Off to save the world?” Flora grinned as she made circles with the feather duster on the stack of display books in the center of the store.

“Did you hear what Elizabeth said? If the print matches Levi Jackson’s, Jimmy should be free by this afternoon.”

“So where are you off to? To go tell Betsy?”

“No, I need to speak with Levi Jackson before Gabe gets a warrant for his arrest. I don’t want to have to go through what happened when I spoke with Jimmy again. Gabe came close to banning me from the squad room for life.”

"But if he's the guy, let the police handle it."

I shook my head. "Flora, you know that won't work for me. I need to be sure—to talk to him and see what he has to say. Besides, you know my superpower is persuading people to open up to me. Maybe he'll tell me more than he would one of the detectives."

"Oh, and here I thought your superpower was finding trouble." The smile on her lips traveled to her eyes and brought a warm glow to them.

"Ha-ha." I scoffed. "Fine. Let's say I have two known superpowers, and I try to use both for good and not evil." Smiling, I pushed open the front door, the bell clanging hard against the glass. Jogging across the street, I jumped into the driver's seat of my blue mobile. The waft of warm air in the cab of the van hit me, stifling my breath. August could be so unforgiving with its heat. By the time I arrived at Doctor Jenkins' office, I'd be swimming in my own perspiration. Cranking up the air, I endured the hot blasts hoping the AC would cool the car before I hit the parking lot.

The air had just reached a reasonable temperature when I pulled into a front spot outside of the doctor's office. Not sure how I'd sneak past the receptionist, I swung open the door and slid out from behind the steering wheel, peeling my legs off the seat.

The woman behind the window at the front desk pointed to a clipboard as I approached. "Print your name on the schedule to the right for Dr. Moore and on the left for Dr. Jenkins. Do we have your current insurance information?"

"Umm, I'm not here to see either one of the doctors. This is more of a personal matter. I'd like to speak to Levi Jackson if that's possible."

She swiveled her chair to face one of the ladies behind her who pulled files from a massive sea of manila folders. "Rowena, did you see Levi this morning? Someone's here to see him."

Rowena turned, squinted, and shook her head. "I don't think I've seen him. But that doesn't mean anything. You want me to go check for you?"

The woman cut her eyes toward me, and I nodded.

"That'd be great, Rowena. Thanks." Swinging her chair back toward me, she said, "You can have a seat over there. I'll let you know when he's available."

I slipped into the designated chair and scanned the waiting area. Several older patients filled seats around the room. A small boy whose face turned red every time he coughed sat across from me. His mother beside him didn't look much better. Crumpled tissues poked out of her fist in her lap, and occasionally she lifted them to her nose to swipe it. The boy held tight to her other arm, his head leaning against her shoulder.

Whatever they had, I did not want it. My mind sprang to the small bottle of antibacterial gel at the bottom of my purse. Sticking my hand deep into the abyss, I scratched around until I felt the familiar shape.

A door at the back of the waiting room opened, and Rowena appeared. Smiling and nodding, she made eye contact with all the patients as she moved toward me. She reminded me of a politician running for reelection. Reaching me, she squatted to my level. "I hate to tell you this, but Levi called in sick today."

"Could I have his home address? It's important, or I wouldn't ask."

Glancing at the front desk, she sighed. "I'm not supposed to give it out, but I can tell you he lives in the Magnolia Arms apartments."

"No number?"

She shrugged one shoulder. "It's the best I can do without getting into trouble." Her eyes drifted back to the woman behind the glass.

"Got it. Thanks." Standing, I pulled my anti-bacterial gel from my purse and squirted a few drops into my hands. Slathering it all the way up to my elbows, I headed to the front door and used my hip to push it open, praying the whole time, I hadn't caught any of the bugs traveling around that room.

It took less than ten minutes to reach The Magnolia Arms apartments. They were located on the street behind the old railroad depot that had been converted into several floors of art studios and a stage for local productions.

As I drove past the dilapidated guardhouse, the sight of the dangling gates and the piles of abandoned furniture along the drive into the apartment complex caused a small flutter of concern to come alive in my stomach. Should I call for backup?

The old train depot peeked between the dilapidated building. I wasn't easily frightened, but this place gave me the creepy crawlies. Parking, I eased my way up the steps leading from the parking lot to the sidewalk, making sure to step over the broken taillight and empty takeout containers.

I stood outside the apartment complex weighing my options. There were three buildings with three floors each, which meant there were thirty-six apartment doors for me to knock on to find Levi Jackson. And the odds of me finding him before I found some other form of trouble didn't look too good.

Fishing my phone out of the side pocket of my purse, I pushed the bookstore's number. I figured I should let someone know my location in case they needed to start a manhunt for me later. And if anyone could find out Levi Jackson's apartment number, Flora could. Her contacts with the Pine Lake grapevine had served me well in the past.

"Twisted Plots bookstore. This is Flora speaking. How may I help you?"

"Flora, it's me, Amy Kate."

"What are you doing calling on the store phone?" A hint of concern sounded in her voice.

"I figured you'd hear it better than your cell phone. Besides, when you're working, you don't always carry your phone with you." Flora being in her sixties had grown up in a generation who didn't have the crazy attachment to their phones the way my generation did.

"Maybe, but when you call the store phone, it makes me worry."

"There's nothing to be concerned about." My eyes drifted over my surroundings, and I hoped I sounded convincing. "But I'm at the Magnolia Arms apartments looking for Levi Jackson. One of the nurses at the doctor's office told me he lives here, but for legal reasons, she couldn't give me the exact address. I thought I could find his apartment by simple elimination, but there are thirty-six apartments, and I don't relish the idea of knocking on each door. Alone."

CHAPTER EIGHTEEN

"For heaven's sake, don't you dare go alone." Her voice filled with concern. "I know all about the Magnolia Arms apartments. The name appears at least once a month in the *Pine Lake Daily*. Stay put in your car with the doors locked, and I'll see what I can find out." She muttered, "I swear you're worse than my two sons when they were teenagers. Always getting into one scrape or another." Then the call ended.

I retraced my steps to the car. Sliding behind the steering wheel, I pressed the lock button and settled in to wait. Not a minute later, a man with a head full of ruffled gray hair and a beard to his belly appeared out of one of the apartments on the ground floor. When he spotted me sitting in the van, he grinned.

Giving him a half-hearted wave, I tried to break eye contact, telling myself he was harmless. Just someone's grandpa. Instantly, my mind jumped to Gramps. Images of dead bodies, drug deals gone wrong, and puppies chained to trees flashed across my brain.

Gripping the steering wheel, I kept my gaze glued to the man, watching him in the side mirror once he passed my van, every nerve in my body aware of the possible dangers.

He headed to the back of the parking lot and fumbled with his keys. Before opening his door, he glanced my way again.

A revving engine sounded from the passenger seat beside me sending me into orbit. With a hand over my racing heart, I grabbed my phone, annoyed for letting myself get so wound up.

A picture of Gabe showed on the screen. I pushed the button to receive the call, but before I could say a word, he spoke. "Hey, so, I talked with the bishop this morning. He said Reverend Boggs called him here for an internal audit because he'd seen the books at the quarterly meeting and knew something was fishy."

His voice sounded so good. I took two deep breaths and made myself focus on the information instead of my thumping pulse.

"Up until then, everything had jived, but this time, the numbers were off. Boggs even told the bishop he thought Levi had been keeping two sets of books which confirms what Elizabeth and I discussed earlier. She said you had helped her figure it out."

A buzz came over the line. "Can you hold for a minute?"

"Sure."

I accepted the incoming call from Flora.

"Hey, I talked with Mary Beth, who called Tamale, who texted her son who used to live in the Magnolia Arms apartments up until two months ago. Tamale's son said Levi Jackson lives in the third building. It has a big three in the upper right-hand corner. You can't miss it. His apartment is on the second-floor, number 324."

"Thanks, Flora. I owe you."

"Actually, you owe Tamale. I offered her a free book as a reward for any information. After all, we didn't have time to play around while you sat in the parking lot."

"Agreed. But we can square up later. I gotta go. Gabe's on the other line."

"Oh, does he know where you are?"

"No, and I intend to keep it that way," I said.

"Good luck."

Grabbing my purse, I slid out of the car and jogged up the short flight of steps to the sidewalk. Making my way to the building with the giant three hanging in the corner, I clicked back onto my call with Gabe.

"Hey, Gabe, that was Flora. I need to go."

"If Flora's calling you, I take it you're not at the store." He sounded suspicious.

Shoot, he was too good at this job. "No, I'm not at the store."

"Should I even ask where you are? Because your sister thought you might go see Levi Jackson today. Tell me you're not at his apartment."

I did a pretty neat version of the Texas-two step for an Alabama girl and sidestepped his question. "Flora's given me some information I need to follow up on, and I hate to keep her waiting at the store. So, I really do need to go."

Okay, I know I gave him the impression that I wasn't here. But all that I said was true. Flora had given me information. I did need to follow up on it, and I did hate to keep her waiting at the store while I worked on Jimmy's case. The fact the three things weren't connected, I chalked up to a simple technicality.

But for some reason, my heart cringed at Gabe's next words. "All right, I'll let you get back to…whatever, but be safe." Like he knew I was up to something. Then he added, "Floyd and I are on our way over to see Levi Jackson. That's why I called. It looks like Jimmy could be released later today."

An explosion of joy rushed through me, and I knew I should share the good news with Betsy and Julia this instant. After all, it's what we'd been working for—the release of Jimmy. But something didn't feel right. I had to hear what Levi Jackson had to say to be sure we had the right guy.

Ending the call, I dashed up the metal stairs of building three to the second floor and scanned the numbers on the plaques beside the doors. Moving to the second door on the left, I balled my fist and pounded. When I didn't hear any movement inside, I gave four quick, sharp raps.

A voice from behind the door called, "Hold your horses, I'm coming." Glancing at the phone in my hand, I noted the time. It was close to lunch. Surely the guy hadn't been sleeping.

The door cracked open, and I got my first glimpse at who I assumed was Levi Jackson.

"What do you want?" He squinted against the sunlight then took a step or two back into the dimness of the apartment.

"I'm here to speak to Levi Jackson."

"What do you want with him?"

I didn't have time for a game of word ping-pong with this guy. Not with Gabe on his way. "Look, let me get straight to the point. I need to talk to Levi Jackson about the murder of Reverend Boggs."

"I thought they caught the murderer. That guy whose

grandfather is the head of some crime family or something." He leaned his arm against the door and looked down his pencil-thin nose at me.

"Yeah, they have someone in custody, but I thought you might have some information that could help the young man's case."

"Like what?"

"So, you are, in fact, Levi Jackson?" I tilted my head and watched a myriad of emotions cascade across his face—irritation slid into worry then braked at anger.

"Yes," he admitted. "I'm Levi Jackson. But I can't help you." He backed away and started to slam the door.

With lightning reflexes, I jammed my foot between the door and the frame. My red high-heel sandal collapsed squeezing my toes, as searing pain shot through every nerve in my foot. My little toe felt like it had been lopped off, only held in place by the wide strap of my sandal. I bit the inside of my cheek to keep from uttering words which should never pass through my lips.

Levi jerked the door wide and pulled me inside his apartment. "Why did you do that?" In one swift motion, he closed and locked the door.

"You left me no choice." I leaned on his arm and hobbled into the small living space, hoping my last date with Gabe wouldn't be at my funeral.

A recliner sat in the middle of the room facing a big-screen TV positioned on a table. A blanket and pillow lay beside the chair, giving me the impression, he'd been sleeping in the living room.

He deposited me on the sofa and went to the small kitchenette. Glancing over my shoulder as I massaged the injured appendage, I found Levi placing ice in a dish towel. I dropped my purse beside me on the seat and removed my shoe.

"Here." He handed me the makeshift ice bag.

I lifted my foot onto the edge of the couch and held the ice to my toes.

He plopped into the recliner, his hands tapping the armrests. "What an idiot move. You know, I could've hurt you."

"Maybe, but it was worth the risk. You don't seem to understand my need to talk to you. It may save a young man from going to prison for something he didn't do."

Levi squirmed in his chair. The brown leather creaked with his movements. "I don't know how I can help."

"Can I be candid?"

He chuckled. "You mean you've been holding back?" His unshaven cheeks plumped as a smile spread across his face.

"I know you've been embezzling money from the building fund." My eyes locked on his face to assess his reaction.

He crossed his arms, but he didn't appear to be moving for a weapon or a heavy vase or even the front door. Which with my new injury worked in my favor, since I couldn't stop him from running if I wanted to.

"And what makes you think I've been embezzling money?" His deep voice took on a sharp edge.

"For one, the two sets of books, and for another, your gambling habit."

He leaned his forearms on his knees. "Are you a cop?"

"No, I'm not a cop."

"So, I don't have to answer any of your questions, right? In fact, I could throw you out on your ear, and you couldn't do a thing about it."

"True. But the cops are on their way, and I may be your one chance. Tell me what happened the afternoon of the wedding, and I'll see what I can do to help you."

He stroked his chin with his right hand and leaned back in his chair, his shoulders sagging. Levi Jackson looked old and worn out. "I'm so ashamed of what I've done."

My heart raced. Was he about to confess?

I grabbed my purse and rummaged around in it for my notebook and pen. but Levi plunged into his story.

"I thought I had been so careful."

I held up my hand, palm side out. "Wait a minute." My notebook had fallen to the bottom of my oversized shoulder bag, and the pen from the bank I kept in a side pocket was nowhere to be found. I didn't want to miss a single word.

"Are you kidding me? I'm pouring my heart out here, and you want me to wait?"

My hand landed on my notebook. I grabbed a pen from his coffee table. "Go ahead. Please. You'd thought you'd been careful.”

He rolled his eyes but continued, “My gambling debts had mounted up, and I felt like I was drowning. My wife left me. My whole world was spinning so fast I thought I'd lose my mind. Then one evening after our quarterly meeting, I got a bright idea. Why not use the funds for the new fellowship hall to pay off my debts? No one would miss them, and I'd have the money paid back before anyone was the wiser. After all, the congregation had been collecting funds for years. It wasn't like they were in a rush to use them.”

“So, you faked a set of books and used the money to cover your losses.” My hand flew over the page, making sure not to miss a syllable.

“Yeah, I owed about thirty-thousand dollars, and the fund had close to a hundred thousand. The church wouldn't mind giving me a little loan, which I'd pay back.” He rose from his seat. “I mean, I knew it was wrong, but it didn't feel like stealing.”

I removed the ice pack and scooched to the edge of the couch, not sure what I'd do if he bolted for the door.

Opening the refrigerator, he took out a soda. “Want one?”

“No thanks.”

He retraced his steps to the recliner and popped the tab on the can as he retook his seat. “So, I paid off my debt. Started Gamblers Anonymous and worked hard to pay back the money before anyone noticed.”

“But?” There was always a ‘but’ in these sorts of stories.

“But about a year or so later, I'd had a string of bad luck and needed to blow off some steam. So, back to the poker tables I went. At first I lost a little, but it didn't take long before I lost a lot.” His chin met his chest as he let out a heavy sigh. “I sort of used the building fund as my own private bank.”

“That's when you made a mistake, right?”

“Yeah, I took the real set of books to the last meeting instead of the phony ones.” He popped out of his chair and crushed his soda can with his bare hand. Foam spewed everywhere and dripped down his arm. “I'm an idiot.” Shaking his head, he slammed the can onto the coffee table and pulled some paper towels from the kitchen counter. “Once Reverend Boggs saw those books, he knew. The other members didn't seem to catch on to what had happened. I tried to say I'd done a poor job this last quarter with the numbers, and I'd rework them, but the reverend—he didn't buy it not even for a second."

"So, how does this connect with the reverend's death?" I didn't mean to be rude, but I needed the Reader's Digest condensed version. Gabe and Floyd would be here before I found out what this meant for Jimmy, and I wanted to verify Levi was in fact our man.

"It doesn't have anything to do with the reverend's death." His eyes grew round as he stopped wiping his shirt and met my gaze.

"It didn't?" I nodded for him to continue.

"The reverend had kept the real books from the quarterly meeting, and I knew I had to get them back before the bishop showed up to do the audit. I figured no books, no proof, no prosecution. My plan was to destroy the real set and dish up the phony ones. When I'd heard there was a wedding on Saturday, I decided it'd be the perfect time to search the reverend's office for the ledgers to shred them."

"And you found one of them because I discovered the shredded pieces in the office next door to the reverend's."

"So, that's how you knew about the embezzling. Not bad for an amateur."

A blush crept up my neck to my cheeks. "How many ledgers are there?"

"Two real ones and two fake ones. Boggs confiscated the two real ones the night of the meeting. They showed what the account had in it." Levi slid into the recliner and hesitated. "But now I have the three that are left."

I was running out of time. Gabe and his partner would be here any minute. Levi needed to get to the point. "So, you stole the ledger from the secretary's office. But did you kill Reverend Boggs?"

CHAPTER NINETEEN

"No, I didn't kill the man. I heard someone coming down the hall while I was in the office next to his, so I stopped shredding. Listening, I heard voices coming from the reverend's office, then a door shutting. So, I went back into his office to look for the other ledger, but instead of the ledger, I found Boggs stabbed in the chest."

"Did you touch anything?" The fingerprint on the knife handle sprang to my mind.

"No, I thought I heard someone coming, so I hightailed it out of there. As I slipped back into the office next door, I spotted the groom coming down the hall. I closed the door before he saw me."

"Well, that explains the sound of a door shutting Jimmy said he'd heard." I moved the towel with the ice in it to the coffee table.

"After that, I went down the hall into the fellowship hall."

"Wait a minute. You were in the fellowship hall during the wedding reception?" I grabbed my phone from the side pocket of my purse and pulled up the picture of the unidentified guy by the stage. I held the picture out a bit in front of me and compared it to the man sitting in the recliner. Sure enough, our mystery man was Levi Jackson.

Scowling, he shrugged. "I hoped to leave before the cops showed up, but it didn't happen that way. The police were crawling all over the place taking statements before I knew it. So, I hung around backstage near the DJ setup and tried to remain invisible until I could leave without drawing any attention."

I crossed my arms, not convinced this guy was telling me the whole truth.

"I swear I didn't kill Reverend Boggs. Why would I? He'd already called the bishop for the audit. The evidence was all I cared about." He squirmed in the recliner. "I swear it." He held up his left hand as if he were taking an oath on the Bible.

Banging on the front door erupted through the apartment. "Police, open up."

Levi shot out of the chair; his eyes big as moon pies.

I jumped up. Where could I hide?

Before either of us could act, Gabe burst into the room. Floyd Simms and two uniformed police officers rushed past him.

Spotting me, Floyd stopped dead in his tracks and lowered the gun he held in his hands. "Looks like you were right," he called to Gabe.

Levi paled and sank to the floor.

Floyd moved toward him and helped him up by his elbow. Turning Levi to face the wall, Floyd holstered his gun and pulled his cuffs from his suit-jacket pocket. With one fluid motion, he snapped the cuffs around the frightened man's wrists.

The uniformed police officers followed Floyd's example and holstered their weapons.

Gabe strolled across the room to where I stood frozen as Floyd led Levi Jackson to the recliner and forced him to sit.

"Amy Kate, I thought you were following up on some important information Flora had given you." One brow winged up. "I figured you'd be here." Little sparks of mischief sprang to life in his brown eyes.

Floyd dug in his pocket and pulled out a dollar. "A bet's a bet." He grinned and handed the bill to Gabe.

I balled both my fists and planted them on my hips. "You placed a bet that I'd be here?"

"I did." Gabe dipped his head. "I never pass up a friendly bet on a sure thing."

Floyd shrugged. "I figured you had better sense than to talk your way into an apartment of a potential killer, but Gabe seemed pretty certain we'd find you here."

So much for my impressive Texas two-step.

"But in his defense, he did flash the blues and run every red light and stop sign from the police station to here, and it wasn't for him." His head bobbed toward Levi.

"Well thanks for the concern." I scowled, a little miffed that my almost-steady boyfriend thought he had me all figured out. Another fact proving we were in a rut. He'd bet on me being here and he'd been right. P-r-e-d-i-c-t-a-b-l-e.

Gabe shrugged. "Now, you can't be mad at me. You're the one who's in the wrong place. You led me to believe you were going back to the bookstore, but here you are. Right in the middle of the investigation, like I figured you'd be." His dark eyes filled with warmth as he held my gaze.

A warm blush rose to my cheeks, and my heart fluttered under his scrutiny.

"All right, Levi, let's have a little chat about those ledgers," Floyd said.

Gabe broke the connection and glanced around the room, aware we weren't alone. "Let me walk you out."

"Fine." I picked up my high heel and strapped it back onto my aching foot. Then I scooped up my purse, tucked my notepad in the side pocket, and tossed the pen back onto the coffee table where I had found it. "You can walk me out."

"Remember what you said, Amy Kate, about helping me." Levi Jackson called before I crossed the threshold. "I don't want to go down for murder. I'm in enough hot water as it is."

A few minutes later, I stood beside my blue Caravan waiting for Gabe to open my door, trying to remember why I had been so angry with the handsome, rugged detective. So, he knew me better than I thought. Was that so bad?

Once he'd opened the driver side door, he handed me the keys. The brush of his fingers over my skin as our hands met sent a cascade of tingles rolling up my arm, giving me a slight shiver even in the summer heat. I set my Goliath of a purse on the driver's seat before he took my other hand in his.

"So, what was that all about in there with Levi Jackson? What did he mean by you'd said you'd help him? I'm pretty sure he's the guy." As he spoke, Gabe made small circles on the back of my hands with his thumbs. "I figured you'd be pleased Jimmy's off the hook. It took a lot of convincing to coax the DA to broaden the scope of the investigation. But he couldn't ignore the existence of the ledgers. Not after I told him about what you'd found in Frank Morelli's room."

"I know. I am happy Jimmy's going to be released, and I'm sure you're right about the embezzlement. Once I got him talking, he told me all about the two sets of books and his gambling problem, but—" I squeezed his hands and stared at my red high-heel sandals.

"But what?"

"He didn't kill Reverend Boggs." I lifted my chin and met his gaze.

"Why? What did he tell you?" Gabe's thumbs stilled. His narrowed eyes locked on me.

"Well, he said he'd crashed the wedding to search for the two ledgers that proved he'd stolen the money. He figured without proof, they'd have a hard time making the charges stick."

"None of that lets him off for the murder. With the reverend dead, wouldn't it make it easier to pin the missing money on him?" Gabe dropped one of my hands and leaned against the side of the van. "Especially if he knew the truth about the reverend's past."

"I don't know. Levi sounded so sincere. He doesn't strike me as the type to kill someone." I moved next to him, still holding his hand, and leaned my hip against the van. "He's a nurse. He's supposed to save lives, not take them."

"True, but you said at the crime scene the killer knew his anatomy. As a nurse practitioner, Levi Jackson would know all about the body. Plus, he fits the profile. Desperate, in trouble, a loner with an addiction—besides the fact he had motive and opportunity." Gabe stared down at the ground, shaking his head. "Nope, this is the man who murdered Reverend Boggs."

"I guess you're right. He did have motive and opportunity. And the reverend knew him, which fits my theory."

"Yes, and I'd bet the dollar I just won from Floyd the fingerprint we found on the handle of the cake knife will be a perfect match to his."

Smiling, he turned to face me. "So, are we still on for a movie and takeout tonight? I've been wanting to stream that new comedy with the ghosts. Heard it's funny and clean if you can imagine that."

"Oh, that's right, it's Friday." Returning his smile, I levered up onto my toes and kissed his cheek. "I'll have to see what's going on at the apartment. Betsy's still staying with us, but if Jimmy is released today, there might be a celebration."

"Suppose you can't miss it, huh?" Gabe leaned forward and brushed his lips against mine. Then in a low, husky voice near my ear, he added, "I think I could use some time with my best girl after Tuesday's lunch debacle. I wanted to make it up to you and show you that ruts aren't all bad."

I lowered to my heels. As he held me by my shoulders, I met his gaze. His chocolate brown eyes glistened with humor and a depth of warmth that made my breath catch in my throat. "I'll … I'll have to let you know about tonight. Betsy and Julia will expect me to celebrate with them."

He pulled me into his arms and rested his cheek on the crown of my head. His woodsy musk swirled around me. I inhaled and melted further into his embrace wanting to stay there forever.

Footsteps sounded on the metal stairs. The echoes carried across the parking lot.

I let go of Gabe, and we turned to see two uniformed officers leading Levi Jackson down the stairs to the squad car. Floyd came out of the apartment carrying three black ledgers— the two phony ones and the one he'd stolen from the church.

Facing me, Gabe chuckled. "I can't tell you how much I don't want to go, but I must. And you need to be on your way to the bookstore. You mentioned something about not wanting to make Flora wait for you."

Tilting my head, I wiggled my brows. "Maybe she could wait a little longer."

"Amy Kate Anderson, you are going to be the death of me." Taking hold of the van door, he nodded toward the driver's seat. "In you go."

Moving the monster purse to the passenger seat, I slid behind the steering wheel, then Gabe closed the door with a bam. "I'll let you know about tonight."

He winked. "You do that. Oh, and I'll need those shredded pages from the ledger you have." Rapping on the door twice, he stepped back from the van.

"Oh sure." I waved out the open window. My heart

flipflopped when I looked in the rearview mirror and found him watching as I drove away.

~

Floating from the van to the bookstore, I hummed a little tune as I danced around the display tables and glided toward the wooden counter where Carter stood. The only thing keeping me grounded was the boulder I carried disguised as a purse.

Flora poked her head out from behind the shelves in the romance section as I passed. She rolled her eyes and tsked before continuing her task.

Two women passed me chatting as they headed out onto the sidewalk, leaving the store empty except for us worker bees.

Carter focused on the screen in front of him tapping on the computer keys. Looking up, he smiled. "I see you're in a good mood. It must be in the water. Flora's been on cloud nine since I arrived."

"Um, I am in a good mood." I let my hand fall to the surface of the counter and sweep along the edge of the wood as I continued toward the hall.

Carter chuckled. "Well, whatever the reason, I'm glad to see you happy and less worried. I take it there's been a development in your investigation?"

Stopping in mid-stride, I pivoted to face Carter. "Yes, there has."

"Okay, I'm all ears. What's happened?" He propped his arms on the counter and flashed his pearly smile which always reminded me of Gabe's.

"I'll be right back." Chucking my purse onto the floor near my desk, I checked my pants pocket for my phone then returned to the main area where Carter waited.

Flora appeared from the romance section with a stack of books tucked in her arms. She glowed brighter than a firefly in July.

"All right, Flora. Something's up with you. Give." I crossed my arms and nailed her with a cool stare.

She giggled as her smile spread from ear to ear. "I've been dying to tell you, but I was sworn to secrecy until they were through the first trimester. My son, Derek, and his wife, Kathy, are expecting their third. I can't wait. We hope it's a girl since they already have two boys.”

“Aw, that’s wonderful.” Carter clapped his hands together. “Babies are so fun.”

“Congratulations.” I offered and drew Flora in for a hug, books and all. “What a terrific blessing.”

“I know.” She sighed. Placing the books onto the counter, she leaned her elbow on the surface. “So, what happened at Levi Jackson’s place?” Her eyes widened in expectation.

“Gabe and Floyd showed up and arrested him on suspicion of Reverend Boggs’ murder.”

“What?” Flora’s hand shot to her chest right over her heart. “Oh, my. I would’ve never pegged him as a killer.”

I shook my head. “That’s the problem. I don’t think he did kill the reverend.”

“What makes you say that?” Carter asked. “Gabe wouldn’t have made an arrest if he didn’t think there was sufficient evidence to make a case for the DA.”

“I know. But it’s the way Levi insisted he hadn’t done it. He confessed to embezzling the money from the building fund without a single hesitation, but he swore he hadn’t killed the reverend.”

Carter’s brows pulled together. “And you believed him? Why?”

I shrugged. “Because he said he was at the church Saturday during the wedding, and that he heard someone with the reverend when he was in the office next door shredding papers from one of the ledgers.”

Moving around the counter, I dragged a stool closer to where Carter stood and took a seat placing my phone on the counter in front of me. “The pieces of paper I found prove he did indeed shred some of the pages. And I have a photo of him near the stage in the fellowship hall after the police arrived, verifying the rest of what he told me.”

“He could’ve been going through the reverend’s things, and Boggs caught him red-handed, so he killed him. And he made up the part about hearing someone with him.” Carter cocked his eyebrow.

“True, but Levi’s story goes along with Jimmy’s statement about hearing a door shut when he entered Boggs’ office. It was

Levi slipping into the office next door." I tapped my fingers on the hard surface of the counter. "Someone else was there. Between the time Boggs spoke with Jimmy in the fellowship hall and the time Levi found him dead in his office, somebody else got to him and killed him."

"That's not a lot of time, dear." Flora pursed her lips and moved to the center of the room surveying her surroundings. "I have an idea. Okay, Carter, you be Boggs. I'm Levi, and Amy Kate, you're Jimmy. Let's say this is the fellowship hall and your office is Boggs' office."

CHAPTER TWENTY

"Okay." Carter and I walked around the end of the counter and stood in front of Flora. "What do you want us to do?"

"I'm going to go into the workroom and pretend to shred papers. As I do so, I'll time us to see how long everything takes. You speak to Jimmy, a.k.a. Amy Kate, then head to the office and shut the door. Amy Kate, you wait the amount of time you think Jimmy waited before going to Boggs' office."

"Okay, but what are you trying to prove?" I asked Flora not sure what she was thinking.

"I don't know, but it's what they always do on those true crime shows. They reenact the crime as told to them by the witnesses."

"Well, it can't hurt." I shrugged, not sure how the killer had time to do the deed.

"I'm game," Carter added.

Flora hustled down the hall to the workroom and yelled, "I'm ready. Shred, shred, shred." Her voice carried down the hall.

Carter turned to me and in a deep somber tone said, "I'm going to my office." Breaking character, he asked, "What else should I say?"

Giggling, I told him to say something about the marriage certificate.

"Please, come sign the marriage certificate." The words rumbled out deep and rich. "Reverend Boggs had a baritone voice."

In that moment, my heart filled with admiration and love for this wonderful group of friends and employees. Not many people would go the extra mile, but my peeps always went two.

"Amy Kate, aren't you going to answer me?" Carter nudged my arm.

"I'll tell Betsy we need to sign it." I played along.

Carter turned on his heels and trotted down the hall to my office, being sure to close the door behind him.

Bam. I counted to fifteen with Mississippi whispered in between each number. With measured steps, I moved down the hall to the office. Entering, I found Carter seated in my chair with his arms flung out wide, eyes closed, looking the part of a corpse.

"Time." Flora stepped out of the workroom studying her wristwatch, and Carter rose back to life.

"How long did it take?" I knew it couldn't be long.

"Maybe two minutes." Flora sighed and shook her head.

"Well, let's add five because Jimmy told me he waited for Betsy and talked with both Mark, his groomsman, and the wedding coordinator before going to Reverend Boggs' office."

"So, seven minutes. But what does it prove—Our reenactment?" Carter stood and leaned his hip against my desk.

"Oh, my stars, of course." I gasped. "That's it."

"What?" Flora gestured with her hands. "Tell us. Don't keep us in suspense."

"The killer was already in the office waiting for the reverend." I plopped into the chair Carter had vacated moments earlier. Disbelief washed over me. "That's why Levi Jackson heard the voices so well. When the reverend entered the office, he left the door open for Jimmy and Betsy to come sign the marriage certificate. Someone was there waiting for him."

"If Levi heard the killer leaving, who did Jimmy hear?" Flora leaned her shoulder against the door jamb.

"Jimmy heard Levi going back into the office next door after he'd found the reverend's body." Flora had missed it when I'd told Carter about Levi. "He'd heard Jimmy coming down the hall and didn't want to get caught." My mind spun in circles. I needed to see a map of the church.

Five minutes later, we were back up-front sitting in the club chairs near the floor-length windows. Carter hovered over a legal pad on the coffee table in the middle of the cluster of chairs, sketching the fellowship hall and the hallways leading to both Boggs' office and Tammy's for me.

"So, sometime after Levi lifted the ledger from the reverend's office and returned to search for the second ledger, someone slipped into Boggs' office and killed him," I said.

"There are three offices along the hallway leading from the fellowship hall before Reverend Boggs'." Carter placed slashes on his sketch where the doors would be.

"This hallway runs into another hallway. Are there any exits?" I rested my forearm on my knee as I studied the drawing.

"Yes, there is one to the right past the reverend's door, here." He made the top of the T connecting the long hallway to a shorter one. Then he placed slashes to indicate the exit at the end of the right section.

"Are there any offices between the exit and the reverend's office?" Flora pointed to the paper.

Carter's brows wrinkled as his gaze drifted off into the distance. Nodding, he added a slash between the reverend's door and the exit. "There is an office next to the reverend's. It's for the children's minister, but we haven't had one since we moved here last year."

I picked up the pad and leaned back in the brown leather chair, letting all this info ping around in my brain. "So, Reverend Boggs comes into the fellowship hall to tell the couple they need to sign the marriage certificate. During this time, Levi Jackson is in the office next door to the reverend's, shredding pages from a ledger he'd taken from the reverend's office, unable to locate both.

"When footsteps approach, he stops shredding, so he won't be discovered. He waits. A moment later a door shuts. Realizing shredding the document there is too risky, he goes into the reverend's office to look for the other ledger so he can leave. But instead, he discovers the reverend dead and panics. A minute later, he hears Jimmy coming down the hall and slips back into the other office."

"But how did Levi get away?" Flora's brow furrowed.

"He joined the guests in the fellowship hall hoping to go to Tammy's office to search for the second ledger. Which he did about the same time the police arrived. So, he hung around the stage with the DJ and slipped out when everyone was busy."

"Did you see him?" Flora asked.

"No, I didn't. But there were a lot of people and distractions." I bit my lip, trying to recall what had happened moments before Betsy fainted and the police arrived.

Carter took up the tale. "Then according to what Jimmy told you, he found Betsy and told her about the marriage certificate. She went to the bride's suite, so Jimmy went on to the reverend's office without her, figuring he'd sign it, and she could sign after they threw the boutique and garter."

"Right. And as he entered the room, he heard a door close somewhere nearby before he closed the door to the reverend's office. Which means, he wouldn't have seen anyone go past," I said.

"And if Jimmy heard that door close, then they could hear the reverend's close, giving them the opportunity to slip out the exit." Flora sat on the edge of her seat.

"Yeah, but Levi went to the fellowship hall, and no one said they heard a third door shut. And heavy metal exit doors make a lot of noise when they close." I studied the exit near Boggs' office marked on Carter's map.

Flora nodded. "Even when you're trying to be quiet. They're impossible." She rolled her eyes.

"Sounds like you speak from experience," Carter teased.

A pink hue rose on Flora's cheeks. "I tried sneaking out of a funeral once. Let's just say I learned a valuable lesson." The corners of her lips tilted upward.

Studying the sketch in my hand, I focused on the sound of the two doors shutting. Flora had a point. If an exit door had been used, Jimmy would've heard it. "So, if neither Levi nor Jimmy heard another door shut, the killer had to be in the fellowship hall." Meeting Carter's gaze, my eyes grew wide. "The killer did what Levi Jackson did. He rejoined the wedding."

A smile swept across Carter's lips. "And if the killer was a guest at the wedding, why run? It'd be safer to slip back into the crowd. Disappearing would've been the tip-off."

"Exactly," I said.

As I wrapped my mind around our new conclusions about the

killer's connection to the wedding, my phone on the counter rang out with a hearty chorus of the wedding march, the ring tone I'd assigned to Betsy when all this started.

I jumped up and dashed to the counter to answer it, wondering what she needed. She'd gone through gallons of chocolate ice cream and so many cookies I'd lost count since this began. The bakery could pay their electric bill twice over with the money from our purchases. But I was determined to be there for her. "Hey, Betsy."

A customer entered, so I took the phone and headed to my office, leaving Carter and Flora to help him.

"What can I do for you?" I figured she'd called to tell me the good news about Jimmy, so I settled into my swivel chair ready to act surprised.

"Oh, Amy Kate, Gabe called to let me know they've arrested Levi Jackson for the murder. And Jimmy should be out later this afternoon."

"That's great news. I know how relieved you must be." A rush of delight flooded my heart for my friend.

"Yes, I am. That's part of the reason I'm calling. We're celebrating tonight at the Whispering Pines in the café around eight, and I wanted to invite you to be there. So many of the wedding party stuck around for moral support, I thought it would only be right to throw some sort of celebration."

"I wouldn't miss it." The thought of the happy couple being reunited made me smile.

Betsy grew quiet, and when she spoke, her voice quivered. "But there's something else." She hesitated.

"What is it?" I leaned forward and placed my elbows on my desk holding my cell phone tight against my ear. "What's the matter?"

"I just left the Beautiful Wedding Boutique following up on the bag we spotted at the bed and breakfast like you asked, and guess what? The owner remembered someone buying a serving set like mine on Friday afternoon. I showed her a picture of it to make sure."

"That's wonderful." Maybe Levi Jackson had purchased it. "Did she remember who the customer was?" Hope flooded my heart. Maybe my gut had been wrong about Levi.

"No, she said she didn't recognize the buyer and didn't catch a name."

"That's too bad. Did you have her look through her receipts? Maybe they used a credit card, and we could pull the name off it." A hopeful lilt stained my tone.

"She looked. They paid with cash. But she does remember one very definite detail about the buyer." Betsy paused, and her tone grew somber. "The person who purchased the serving set was a woman."

"A woman?" I sat straight in my chair. "You're sure she said the customer was a woman?"

"Yes, I'm positive. In fact, I asked her the same thing. And she said men so rarely come into the shop that she'd have remembered it. So, she was certain the customer was a woman."

"I should learn to trust my gut," I muttered more to myself than to Betsy.

"What do you mean?"

"Levi Jackson. He's not the killer."

"Did you talk to Levi Jackson?" Her voice edged up to a shriek. "You're not helping him, are you? If he's cleared, they might not release Jimmy."

"Betsy, if Jimmy is innocent, which he is, then finding out the truth can't hurt him."

"Please, don't do anything to mess this up," She begged.

"How can finding the truth mess anything up?" The minute those words left my mouth, I knew I'd said the wrong thing.

"Really? You're asking me how things could go wrong? Haven't you been paying attention?" She hissed.

I held the phone away from my ear.

"My whole world has been messed up. My fiancé or husband, who knows, is in jail for murder. My whole wedding party is stuck in town, their lives investigated like insects under a magnifying glass. And let's not forget I was married by a known felon." Punctuating the last word, she took a deep breath. The sound of sniffling floated across the line. "And now, I'm part of a notorious mob family. So yeah, I know absolutely nothing about how things can go wrong."

My heart broke. She'd been through so much, and now here I was, tossing on more. Betsy didn't care who killed the reverend.

She cared about Jimmy and being with him, like any normal woman in love.

"I'm sorry. I shouldn't have said that. You've been through so much. The two of you deserve all the happiness in the world."

Another sniffle. "If we're even married."

"Jimmy will see to it you two are properly wed. In the meantime, I'll be at Whispering Pines tonight with bells on. In fact, I'll bring the whole orchestra."

Betsy giggled then sniffed. "That won't be necessary. I'll be all right once Jimmy is out and by my side."

"Well, I'll see you this evening."

"Hey, Amy Kate, thanks. I wouldn't have made it without you and Julia."

"No need to thank me. That's what friends do." I pushed the disconnect button and tossed my phone onto my desk. Now, what was I supposed to do with this new piece of the puzzle? All along, I had figured the killer to be a man. Even Betsy had suggested it could be a woman, but I'd dismissed the possibility.

Sure, it could've been a coincidence a woman bought the exact serving set as Betsy last Friday—the day before the murder—but all my inner alarms were ringing at once.

It was fine for Betsy not to worry about who had murdered the reverend. Once they released Jimmy, they'd be on their way to happily-ever-after. But I needed to know the right person was behind bars. I needed to know for me, I needed to know for my community, but more importantly, I needed to know for Reverend Boggs.

CHAPTER TWENTY-ONE

Kirk arrived right on time for his five o'clock shift with Carter. Before leaving, I finished restocking the children's section with the new arrivals that had come in on Thursday. After giving the two a few instructions, I pushed opened the glass door and let it swish closed behind me, leaving in its wake the nagging feeling about Levi Jackson.

The sun hung low in the horizon. The squeals of the children in the park drifted past me on the hot breeze. The rich blue expanse of the sky with its lazy clouds placed just so, took my breath away.

Tilting my face up toward the sky, I let the warmth of the breeze melt away the events of the week. I stood breathing in the late afternoon fragrance until the delivery van from the Cracked Flowerpot Florist roared past with its faulty muffler, breaking the spell. "Perfect," I grumbled and stuck my hand in my purse to fish out my keys.

My blue caravan sat in the parking lot across the street from the store. I dashed across the pavement continuing to rummage in my purse for the keys, not paying attention to my surroundings.

A loud bark close to my ear startled me. Clutching my purse to my pounding chest, I scanned the vehicles. A poodle in the car nearest me jumped and snarled, pressing his face against the window.

A sharp pang of irritation replaced my terror, and I wagged

my finger at him through the glass. "You should be ashamed of yourself, you little Attila the Hun."

Ignoring the small nuisance, I propped my purse on my leg to do a deep dive into the caverns of the beast. Where in heaven's name were my keys?

The white ball of fluff stuck his nose out the crack at the top of the window to get a better whiff of me. At least with his muzzle stuck in the crack, he couldn't bark.

My fingers curled around the shape of a metal flower. Pulling the key ring out, I sighed and found the silver one which would open my van door. Rounding the back of the vehicle to the driver's side, I pushed the key into the lock and turned it.

What a day. I tossed my purse into the passenger seat and stepped on the running board. Grabbing the handle to the side, I hoisted myself into the driver's seat.

A piece of yellow paper folded in half flapped under my left windshield wiper. Standing on the running board, I reached around the edge of the front glass and snatched the paper from under the wiper. No doubt an advertisement, I'd toss it at the house. Not reading it, I took my seat, shut the door, and fanned myself with the yellow flyer before stuffing it in the seat beside my purse.

Cranking the car, I flipped the air conditioner to high and rolled down the windows to let all the hot air blow out to make way for the cool. I unfastened the top button of my shirt and pulled at the collar.

Reaching into the side pocket of my purse, I pulled out my phone to check the time. Almost six. That gave me enough time to make dinner and change for the festivities at eight. I figured Julia would be at the Whispering Pines baking something delicious for the reunited couple.

As I sat waiting for the air conditioner to start pumping cold air, I contemplated whether to invite Gabe to the shindig. After all, Friday was our date night. And there's nothing better than a solid rut. I mean routine.

But—and this was a doozie of a but—I didn't know how Betsy and Jimmy would feel about me inviting the cop who had arrested Jimmy in the first place to the celebration.

I put my phone in the phone holder attached to one of the air vents and shifted the van into reverse before I drizzled into a puddle.

Parking in the garage, I grabbed my belongings along with the flyer and an empty foam coffee cup from the cup holder and made my way to the apartment.

The cold air swooshed around me like a favorite song when I swung open the front door. Gizmo ran to greet me, wiggling his whole body from nose to tail.

"Hey, boy. Give me a minute and I'll take you out." Closing the door with my foot, I latched my purse across a hook on the coatrack to keep it from toppling over and stuffed my keys into my pants pocket. I pulled my phone from my back pocket and pushed Gabe's number.

"Hey there, did you decide about tonight?" Gabe asked.

"That's why I'm calling." I put my phone against my ear and held it in place with my shoulder so I could carry the empty coffee cup and the yellow flyer to the trash while pulling off my shoes. "Betsy invited me to a little celebration tonight at the Whispering Pines and …" I hesitated not wanting to hurt his feelings.

"And you don't think they'd appreciate it if I escorted you." Gabe chuckled. "I can see that."

"I'm sorry. But I do think it's important to Betsy I be there. And after all she's been through, I'd hoped you wouldn't mind this one-time skipping date night."

"No, I get it. Maybe we can do something Sunday evening. The two of us alone."

"That sounds great." Opening the trash can, I threw in the foam coffee cup. Then I opened the flyer to read it before tossing it. "Oh dear."

"What is it?" Gabe asked.

"A note. It says 'Leave it alone. Rats wind up dead.' Can you believe that?" I dropped my shoes to the floor and leaned against the kitchen island holding the yellow sheet of paper. "Gabe, who could've done this?"

"Where did you find the note?"

"Under the windshield wipers when I left work this evening. I didn't read it. Thought it was an advertisement. It's printed on yellow paper and everything."

"When did you last use the van?" Gabe asked.

"Well, after I left Levi Jackson's this morning, I didn't use it again until I made a lunch run for Flora and me around two. Your dad had already arrived for his shift." My mind whirled, sorting through what I had seen on my way to my van. The poodle, the kids in the park, the florist van. "I didn't notice anyone around in the gravel parking lot when I went to the van."

"And when was that?" Gabe sounded like a full-on detective now.

"Around six. I know because I checked the time on my phone." I bit my lip. "So, sometime between two and six someone placed the note on my van." Straightening, , a shot of energy coursed through me. "That means Levi Jackson isn't the killer. There's no way he could've left this note. He was in custody."

"Amy Kate, the note doesn't prove anything. We know Levi Jackson embezzled the money from the building fund, so he had motive. The threat of exposure to the bishop fits the timeline. Jackson had to do something. He couldn't wait for the reverend to die from his cancer; he had to protect himself. And there's the fact he's a nurse practitioner. Like you pointed out at the crime scene, the murderer knew his anatomy. It's all there."

"I don't know. My gut still says he's not the guy." I walked to the table and pulled out a chair. Plopping into the hard seat, I laid the note on the table and studied it. The handwriting, neat block letters, didn't match the feel of the message. "Something's not right. Why would someone who wasn't the killer leave me this note?"

"I don't know. Maybe Levi had someone do it for him to throw us off his track. Or maybe someone wanted some attention, their fifteen minutes of fame. This case has been all over the news this week with the Morelli crime family at its center. Or maybe in some way someone thought they were helping Jimmy. You know, trying to redirect suspicion, not knowing we already had another suspect." Gabe sighed. "I'm not sure. But I do know Levi Jackson had the means, the motive, and the know-how to pull it off."

"Yeah, you're right." I leaned back in the chair willing my inner voice to shut up.

"And thanks to your photo, we have conclusive proof he was there during the wedding. Add the fingerprint we pulled from the knife, and it's airtight. Levi's the killer."

"So, the prints were a match?"

"I won't get the results until tomorrow, but I'm confident they'll match."

CHAPTER TWENTY-TWO

I arrived a little late to the Whispering Pines Bed and Breakfast and had to make my own parking spot. Hoping Officer Pete wouldn't notice my creativity when he made his rounds at nine, I locked the doors and circled the old house to the front. Since I parked under a tree in the back away from the lights, I figured I had a fifty-fifty shot of not receiving a ticket.

As I entered the cafe at the front of the house, a splendid display of pink and green balloons floating up along the ceiling greeted me. The tables were adorned in pink and green tablecloths to match the couple's wedding colors, and sparkling confetti covered the flat surfaces reflecting the light and giving the room a disco feel. The DJ who had worked Betsy's wedding occupied the tables near the back wall and had the music thumping at an obnoxious volume.

Jimmy and Betsy stood behind a table in the center of the room that held a chocolate sheet cake with the words "New Beginnings" scrolled across it. Appropriate, after everything the couple had been through this week.

A crowd of about thirty friends and family holding glasses of champagne surrounded the happy pair. By everyone's gaiety, I concluded the toasts had already begun.

"Well, there's our hero. Or should I say, heroine." Jimmy shouted above the beat of the music when he spotted me joining the crowd.

Everyone turned in my direction. Not sure what to do, I

waved, not a full-out prom queen wave, but more like an honorable mention for a science fair.

Betsy rounded the table and headed my way. Everyone parted giving her clear access. She grabbed my hand and pulled me to where Jimmy waited.

"How can I ever thank you? If you hadn't kept the police looking for someone else, I truly believe I'd be locked away without anyone digging any further," Jimmy said.

Gramps held up his glass. "Here's to Amy Kate, detective extraordinaire." His Italian accent washed over the long English word giving it an old-world feel.

"I didn't do much. If it hadn't been for Betsy's belief in your innocence, none of this would've—"

"If it had been left up to me, poor Jimmy would still be in jail." Betsy clutched Jimmy's hand and brought it to her lips, pecking out several kisses then grinning up at him. Turning to me she added, "And let's not forget how you spent all week propping me up emotionally. You and Julia—" she turned and looked toward Julia, who stood on the right side of the crowd between the cake table and the DJ. "The two of you together saved me. Y'all kept me busy, and more importantly you gave me hope."

"To Julia and Amy Kate," sang out Mark LaRocca who held up his glass.

Everyone else followed suit.

"So, when do you guys leave for the honeymoon?" Julia asked.

"Tomorrow afternoon." Jimmy pulled Betsy close to his side and gazed down upon her face. "I have a little surprise for you."

Betsy tilted her head, her eyes narrowing. "What have you done now?" Her tone cautious as she pulled away from his embrace.

Jimmy let go of her, raising his hands in surrender. "Nothing that'll land me in jail, I swear. I've learned my lesson." He made a comical face causing a gentle wave of giggles and chuckles to run through the group. "No, I've asked the local justice of the peace to marry us." Gathering Betsy back into his arms, he leaned down, and planted a big smooch on her lips. When he broke the kiss, he added, "Our appointment is tomorrow at ten. This way we'll know for sure we're married. No guessing about it."

The look in Jimmy's eyes spoke volumes. Ten times louder than any music a DJ could play. It was the way Carter looked at his wife, Maureen, and it was the way my dad had looked at my mom throughout their marriage.

"To the happy couple," called out Jimmy's mother, Aurora.

Kristin, the maid of honor, yelled, "Here, here."

The sound of clanking glasses and "at-a-boy's" rang out from the circle.

"Let's eat. Cut the cake already," Eric, one of the groomsmen, called.

Betsy released Jimmy and turned toward the cake. Her hand froze in midair when she went to pick up the knife. She gasped as all the blood drained from her complexion.

Instantly, Julia noticed her cousin's strange behavior and moved closer to the table.

Standing beside the couple, I spotted the knife the moment Betsy hesitated. Someone had put an exact copy of the ivory-handled knife that had killed Reverend Boggs on the table. Moving around the stunned couple, I grabbed it. Julia saw the blade in my hand before I tucked it out of sight.

"I'll go get something to cut the cake. Why don't you two open the presents from the wedding. You never had a chance to see what everyone brought. And Jimmy's mom has been dying to share what she gave you for your honeymoon trip," Julia said.

Aurora, seeing the pained look on the couple's faces, stepped forward and caught Betsy's hand. "That's a great idea, Julia." She led the two to the tables by the row of windows where the presents and cards from the reception had been displayed.

Julia grabbed me by my elbow and hauled me into the kitchen. "I swear this is not the knife I set out when I moved the cake to the table." She released my arm.

"You know I've grown to hate this knife, all versions of it. I can only imagine how Jimmy and Betsy feel about the stupid thing." With disgust, I dropped the offending cutlery onto the metal table in the middle of the kitchen with a clang.

Moving towards a prep station, Julia reached toward a magnetic strip hanging along the side wall that held several black-handled knives.

"Their faces said it all." She shook her head, pulling a knife from the strip. "What a disaster."

"Maybe not."

Julia cut me a glance as she walked to the sink to rinse the knife in her hand.

"What do you mean?"

Leaning her hip against the industrial-grade basin, she studied me letting the water run over the blade. "I know that look, Amy Kate. What's whirling around in your head?"

"I haven't had a chance to tell you what happened this evening when I went to leave work."

"Okay, I'm all ears." She turned off the water and faced me.

"I had to park in the gravel lot next to Twisted Plots. All the spaces out front were taken when I came back from the lunch run for me and Flora. Which isn't a bad thing."

Julia nodded.

"Anyway, when I reached my van around six, I found a threatening note on the windshield. It said, 'Leave it alone. Rats wind up dead.'"

Julia gasped. "Did you tell Gabe about the note?"

"He was on the phone with me when I read it. But he didn't seem worried about it. Gabe thinks he has the right man in custody. But with the note and now this stunt, there's no way Levi Jackson killed the reverend. I didn't think he was guilty when I talked to him this morning, and with these new developments, I'm even more convinced he didn't do it."

"But if the killer knows the murder has been pinned on someone else, why risk being discovered? I mean, they literally got away with it." Julia reached for a white dish towel to dry the blade. She ran the cloth over the sharp edge. Laying the knife on the clean surface of the metal table, she pulled open the drawer beneath its edges.

"I don't know. At first, I thought the note was left by someone who didn't know they had arrested Levi Jackson. But this, it's a deliberate message."

"I agree. But what does it mean?" Julia dug around in the drawer for a minute before pulling out a server. "Found it." Looking up, she met my gaze and froze. "What?

Julia knew me too well for me to hide my feelings, so I didn't try to disguise the wave of fear rushing through my body. "I think one of the guests may be in danger.”

"Who?” She shut the drawer and picked up the black-handled knife.

“I’m not sure. But I know one thing for certain. That message was for someone here. Tonight.”

CHAPTER TWENTY-THREE

Throughout the next hour, I kept my eye on the various guests wondering if the intended victim had understood the message. Then another thought hit me. The killer could be here with us.

Julia had suggested I contact Gabe to let him know what had happened. But what had happened? A knife appeared. So what? And after our conversation earlier, I didn't want to call him until I had something substantial to tell him. Besides, what if the knife had been placed there by mistake, and the culprit was too ashamed of his mistake to say anything?

After the gifts had been opened and the cards read, Julia wove through the group passing out slices of cake while Mark LaRocca refilled everyone's glass with their beverage of choice—champagne, water, or soda. He made a big show of it, adding to the lightheartedness of the evening.

When Jimmy spotted Julia's mom about to leave, he kicked a pile of wrapping paper out of the way and turned a chair around to where he could stand on it. Stepping up onto the seat, he called to her to stay for a minute. Turning, he motioned for the DJ to cut the music. "Before you all go, Betsy and I want to take this opportunity to thank you for staying with us through this ordeal and giving us so much encouragement and moral support." Jimmy beamed and stretched out his hand to Betsy who rose from her seat and stood next to the chair where he was perched. "We never would've made it without you guys. I know how much it meant to

Betsy to have her parents and Kristin here this week."

Betsy bobbed her head and blew a kiss towards her maid of honor. "Love you, girl."

"Back at you," Kristin said.

Then she pointed to her three bridesmaids all clustered around Eric, who by the way, looked a little like a statue of a Greek god. "Ladies, you're the best ever."

Monica, Lara, and Regina all cooed in unison at the attention.

"And Mark, you and Eric and Kent being here, coming to see me in the worst possible circumstances." Jimmy hung his head and cleared his throat. "It meant a lot to me. And, Gramps, you take the cake. Those lawyers you sent." Jimmy gave the older man two thumbs-up.

"You're my grandson. What else could I do?" A gleam of pride shone in his eyes as he leaned heavily against his walker. Kristin who stood next to him patted his shoulder.

"Enough mush." Kent yelled. "Are we going to celebrate or what?"

"Wait a minute. It's not every day a man regains his freedom."

A few chuckles skittered around the semicircle of friends and family.

"Though I can't invite all of you to the wedding tomorrow morning at the courthouse, I do want to invite all of you to meet us here at two for a real *just married* send-off. It'd mean so much to us. So, no pressure." A half grin played on his lips. "But if you can, we'd love it." Jimmy nodded to the DJ before stepping down from the chair. The seventies music resumed, and Abba's "Dancing Queen" filled the space. Jimmy pulled Betsy into a warm embrace.

Gramps headed toward the door along with Julia's mom. With the party breaking up, I didn't feel right about leaving Julia alone to clean up, not with a killer nearby. So, I decided to hang around until the end.

Scanning the dwindling crowd, I spotted Mark seated in a remote corner away from the DJ.

I slid into the seat next to his with my red plastic party cup in hand.

"Need another refill?" He reached for the two liters of soda sitting on the table between us.

"No, I'm fine."

He shrugged. "Have it your way." Turning his attention back to the group, he pointed to Betsy and Jimmy. "They sure look happy, don't they?"

"Yeah, they do." Reaching out, I laid my hand on top of Mark's hand on the table. "I wanted to tell you how sorry I am about your father. It has to be hard to lose him all over again."

He placed his other hand over mine. "Yes, but I am so grateful I had the chance to talk to him one last time."

"Oh, when was that?" I asked.

He leaned in closer, so I could hear him better. "Thursday night after the rehearsal, I went to confront him." Mark peered down at our hands. "But once we started talking, all the anger I'd had toward him about leaving us drained away."

"Did he tell you about the cancer?"

He nodded. "Said he had at best six months, and if I'd let him, he'd like to be a part of my life during the time he had left." Mark leaned back in the chair and released my hand. Pressing his fingers against his eyelids, he let a few wayward tears fall. "I must admit I fell apart. When I calmed down, we talked about what had happened." With the back of his hand, he swiped the tears away and reached for the drink napkin under his cup.

I leaned closer at this new revelation.

Mark took a minute to regain his composure before he continued. "He told me the hardest thing he'd ever done was to leave my mom and me behind. But he knew if he brought me along, it'd be a miserable life for a kid. And he knew as long as Tony was in jail, we'd be safe. Frank Morelli didn't have any interest in seeing his brother cleared."

"Why didn't Frank want Tony out of prison?" I wrapped my hands around my cup of soda and rattled my melted ice. The water droplets on the outside of it cooled my palms.

"Maybe because his brother had ambitions of his own that didn't include Frank being around."

Wide-eyed, I recalled what Frank had said about this subject. "Is that what your dad told you the other night? That Frank had wanted Tony incarcerated?"

"Yep. Then he talked about how he'd found his calling. How

being a reverend had changed everything. At first, he'd played along, treating it like a role, but in the privacy of his own home, he did whatever he pleased. But the more he studied the Bible to prepare for sermons, the more it sank in and stuck." Mark's lips lifted. "He told me he was truly happy here. That in Pine Lake he'd found God, and funnier still, God had found him."

"Are you leaving tomorrow, or can you stay? For the funeral." I drank a sip of the watered-down soda trying to fight my own emotions about losing a parent. Whenever I came across someone else experiencing this kind of pain, I couldn't help reliving a little of my own.

"I'll be leaving. Work and all, but both my mom and I intend to be here for the funeral." His eyes softened. "My mom couldn't believe I'd found him. I called her straightaway Thursday night, but when I called again Saturday, the shock of it all sent her into a spiral of emotions. I'm going back to help prepare her. The marshal said they'd contact me when the body was released to the funeral home." He shrugged. "He didn't think it'd be long."

"Well, that's good. And I'm so glad you had some time with him. At least you were able to settle things between the two of you before he died."

"Yes, but it could've been so much more." A flash of regret shown in his eyes. "But at least the police have the right man in custody now. The killer will pay for his crime against my dad, and justice will be served."

Before I could say I didn't think they had the right man, Jimmy approached from the far side of the room and stopped in front of the table. "I hate to break this up, but we wanted to get a group picture before anyone else leaves."

"Sure." I popped up from my chair and left my cup on the table wiping my palms on one of the drink napkins littering the surface.

"If you two could go over to where the DJ is set up, I'll go find Tom and Regina who seem to have wandered off." He winked, a sly grin growing across his lips. "Facts show weddings are one of the top ten places to meet your future spouse."

"After this wedding, I'm considering avoiding them at all costs," I muttered.

Later that night, when Betsy, Julia, and I were safe and sound back at our apartment, I couldn't erase the thought of the ivory cake knife out of my head.

I thought about it while I brushed my teeth before bed, and it continued to plague me when I turned out my lamp on my bedside table. The rascal wouldn't leave me alone.

Gizmo yelped when I turned over for the fifth time and pushed him to the edge of the bed. Aggravated he gave a little doggy huff and jumped down in favor of sleeping on the floor near the window.

Somewhere close to two, I gave up the fight and slid my feet into my pair of fuzzy pink slippers. Grabbing my robe off the chair in front of my vanity, I shoved my arms through the sleeves. My door gave a low creak as I inched it open and shuffled down the dark hallway to the kitchen trying not to wake Betsy asleep on the sofa.

If I had to be awake, I might as well make some hot chocolate and nab a slice of cake Julia had brought home from the party. It was times like these I was thankful for Julia's passion for baking. I heated a cup of hot water in the microwave and pulled the plate with the leftover cake from the refrigerator. Placing it on the kitchen table, I shuffled over to the cabinet where we kept the packets of hot chocolate, then I opened the drawer below it to grab a spoon and a fork and took the cup from the microwave.

Before settling at the table with all my goodies, I pulled the magnetic pad from the front of the fridge and found a pen in the junk drawer. I needed to write down all these crazy thoughts bouncing around in my head. The bulletin board in the living room hadn't been updated in the past three days, and I needed to see it all laid out. Besides, Betsy was snoring with gusto.

I tore the paper on the hot-chocolate mix and dumped the powder into the cup, stirring to make sure it dissolved.

Picking up the pen, I jotted down the word, *knife*.

An image of it popped into my brain. How many were there? I had one in my hand when I went to the reverend's office the day of the wedding. Jimmy held one in his hand, covered in blood. Both were in evidence. Now, tonight another one appeared. Had it been a message from the killer? And who was the message for?

When I heard someone had bought a knife at Beautiful Weddings, I believed it to be the one used to kill the reverend, but then Tammy had said one was missing from their stash in the kitchen. So, were there three knives or four?

Levi Jackson didn't place the knife by the cake tonight since he had an airtight alibi by being in jail. And he most certainly didn't leave the threatening note on my van. Sure, he could've had someone else do it, but did he? And if so, who? There was no avoiding the fact he embezzled the money from the church, but was he a cold-blooded killer?

Blowing on my hot chocolate, I debated how to proceed. Let's see. Jimmy didn't do it. I wrote down, *No Jimmy*. And since I didn't believe Levi was the killer either, I wrote down, *No Levi*.

Thumping the pen on the pad, I growled in frustration. "Think, girl. Think." My time was running out. After tomorrow afternoon, everyone would be on their way home. And the wrong man would be prosecuted for the reverend's death. For the sake of his congregation and his son, the reverend deserved justice.

I had to be missing something.

So, who had a motive to kill Reverend Boggs, or for that matter, who had a motive to kill Robert LaRocca, his real identity? It seemed more likely Boggs' past had caught up to him than someone in town having a beef with the reverend. Most churchgoers don't solve their issues with violence.

Gramps, maybe. His lingo fit the note. But what message would he be sending by placing the cake knife at the gathering and to whom? And no one in the wedding party had the medical background to push the knife into the right spot between the fourth and fifth ribs.

Only Levi Jackson.

Tearing the sheet from the pad, I crumpled it up and tossed it toward the garbage can.

"Is this what you do in the middle of the night? No wonder you're such a grump in the mornings." Julia headed to the cabinet where we kept the plates for a saucer. Pulling out the silverware drawer, she grabbed a fork before joining me at the table. Sliding the cake toward her, she cut a thick slice and plopped it onto the saucer. "So, what's on the paper you tossed?"

"Nothing but scribbles. I can't figure this out. We know Jimmy didn't do it. Levi isn't the guy. So, what am I missing?"

Julia dug her fork into the cake and scooped a bite into her mouth. Her eyes closed in delight. "Yum. Even if I do say so myself."

I giggled. "Tell me about it. I could've eaten the whole thing. You're lucky I left you any."

Tucking her feet under her in her chair, she leaned her elbow on the table. "So, what do you have so far?"

"Well, if what we know is true, then there are three knives involved in this case."

"Okay?" She nodded.

"The one Betsy bought, the one missing from the church kitchen, and the one a woman bought at Beautiful Weddings boutique." I took a sip of my hot chocolate and cradled the mug between my hands. "Now, we know the knife from Beautiful Weddings was purchased on Friday, and we have no idea when the knife went missing from the church kitchen. It might not be connected at all." I groaned.

"Let's say that all the knives are part of the case. That would mean the killer has two identical knives. He used one to kill the reverend. Was the other one just to send a message like you suggested earlier, or does it hold some other kind of significance?"

"Like what?" I dug my fork into the cake and lifted a bite to my mouth. An explosion of sheer sweetness melted on my tongue, and I dragged my fork through my lips so I wouldn't miss one delicate burst of flavor.

Julia grinned. A twinkle of pleasure danced in her eyes at my antics.

Her smile faded as she returned her focus to our conversation. "Well, I don't know. Maybe it's some weird mob thing. You know, a secret code." She rose and padded over to the sink. Reaching to the left, she opened the cabinet holding the glasses and grabbed one. She put the glass under the tap and turned on the water. "A ceremony or a ritual?"

"You know as much as I do about that stuff. But the note left on my van sure sounded like Gramps. It gave off a mob vibe."

Julia slipped back into her chair at the table with the glass of water in her hand. "True. Do you think he could be the killer?"

"He could've placed the note on my van and maybe the cake knife at the party tonight. But there's no way he could've gone down the hallway to the reverend's office during the reception without someone noticing. Not with that walker of his."

"Maybe he ditched the walker." She took a sip and placed the glass on the table.

I hesitated. "Thinking about it, I haven't seen him once without either a cane or the walker. No, I'm pretty sure he's dependent on it."

"All right, what about the woman who bought the serving set from the boutique? How does she fit into all this?"

Leaning back in my chair, I let one pink fluffy slipper dangle from my toes. "I'm not sure."

Frustration surged through me with this admission. I was no closer to the answer than I was an hour earlier.

The way Mark had spoken about his father and the changes in his father's life made me want to see the killer caught. It wasn't about helping a friend anymore. Now, it was about helping a whole community who had lost the reverend they'd come to love.

Sure, the man had worked for the mob, but God was in the business of forgiveness. In fact, it was his family business. And Robert LaRocca, a.k.a. George Boggs, had found his way into God's family. I chuckled at the thought. Boggs had traded one family business for another. He deserved justice. Those who loved him deserved to know the truth. If only I could fit all the pieces together before time ran out.

CHAPTER TWENTY-FOUR

Saturday morning found me sliding out of bed well after nine. Thank goodness, Kirk and Flora had the morning shift today. I planned to let Kirk go home early since he had an exam Monday in Calculus three and had asked for time off to meet with his study group. Hopefully, Flora wouldn't mind me running over to the Whispering Pines to participate in the bride and groom's farewell. It shouldn't take too long to throw a few bird seeds and blow a few bubbles.

Sighing, I pushed myself up to a sitting position noticing Gizmo was nowhere in sight.

The little scoundrel must've scratched when he heard Julia moving around this morning getting ready to go to the bed and breakfast. Knowing her, she'd probably taken him to the grassy area out front of the apartments and brought him in and fed him, so I could grab a few extra hours of shut eye. How Julia could get up at five after our late night was beyond me.

My tongue ran across my teeth. The chocolate icing from the cake last night left a weird feeling in my mouth. I hunted for my pink fluffy slippers and leaned over to pick up my robe from the floor where I'd tossed it sometime around four.

Julia and I had played around with a few possibilities about the knives, but nothing came from it except a few extra calories around my hips. We'd finished off every crumb.

Shuffling across the carpet to the door, I made my way to the bathroom in the middle of the hallway. First order of business, I needed to take care of this cake breath.

Gizmo barked from the couch to let me know he didn't appreciate my pink footwear. No matter how often I wore these fluffy balls of comfort, Gizmo acted like it was the first time he'd seen them and had to investigate them.

Forty-five minutes later, dressed and in the kitchen, I stirred two spoonful's of sugar into a cup of much-needed coffee. I blew on the warm liquid and watched the steam rise. Grabbing my phone from the charger, I saw I had a missed call from Gabe.

I hesitated. After last night's debate about the guilt of Levi Jackson, I wasn't sure I wanted to chat with Gabe yet. In the wee hours of the morning as I gobbled down the last of the moist cake, I told Julia I wanted to go visit the bishop this morning to see if he could shed any light on the embezzling or maybe on Levi.

Spotting the time, I realized I had about an hour before I needed to be at Twisted Plots. Pouring my coffee into a travel mug, I hurried to the coat rack and pulled my purse from the hook. The weight of it made my knees sag. When this was all over, I desperately needed to downsize this thing. The local chiropractor had spotted me coming out of Elizabeth's law office a few weeks back and warned me an overstuffed purse could cause permanent damage to my shoulders.

I guess being lopsided wasn't trendy anymore.

Passing the First Methodist Church of Pine Lake, I pulled into the driveway of the late reverend's house. I rang the doorbell and his housekeeper, Joan Clark, answered the door. Tammy had given me the housekeeper's name.

"Good morning, how can I help you?" Her scowl negated the pleasantness of her words.

"I would like to speak with the bishop. It concerns the reverend's case."

"I see. You're that girl who's worked some of the other cases in town. The daughter of a retired detective if I remember correctly. I've seen your picture in the papers." She ran her eyes down my figure—sizing me up, I'm sure. "Now, I guess you fancy yourself a detective."

Having lost control of the conversation, I took back the reins and brought this runaway horse to a full-and-complete stop. "Is the bishop here?"

Joan hesitated. "He's busy. But I'll let him know you came—
"

"Oh, who's here, Joan?" A short man with gray hair that shot out in all directions stepped around the housekeeper. His dimples rippled up his cheeks. "Well, hello there. You're the young lady who helps people with their unique problems. The reverend spoke of your exploits in his monthly reports to me. So much so I feel as if I know you."

The bishop's disposition was contagious. Unfortunately, Joan appeared immune. "If you don't have need of me, sir, I have a bit of ironing to do to get you ready for tomorrow. And of course, I'll have lunch ready at noon."

"Aw, would you care to join me for lunch? Joan won't mind setting a second place. Would you, dear?" He glanced toward Joan who squinted and puckered her lips as if she'd eaten something tart.

"No, that's all right. I need to be at work by noon. I stopped by to see if I could ask you a few questions about Levi Jackson."

The smile on the bishop's lips fell, and a hardness entered his eyes. "You mean that devil of a man who has stolen from the church? What could you want to know about him?"

"If we could sit, maybe I can explain my interest in him." I dragged my gaze across the foyer as the bishop shut the door behind me.

"Let's go into the study. It's the second door on the left." Turning to Joan, he added, "I'd appreciate not being disturbed. Thank you."

The study held wall-to-wall bookcases filled with thick tomes. The smell of the old, musty volumes brought back fond childhood memories of spending hours in the old bookstore—the one I'd bought and redesigned into Twisted Plots.

I sauntered over to the dark brown leather couch across from two matching wing chairs and set my purse on one end of the couch while I sat in the middle. The bishop entered and shut the door before taking a seat in one of the wing chairs.

"I must admit you do have my curiosity up. What could I tell you about Levi Jackson?"

"Well, because of certain circumstances that have happened since his arrest, I'm wondering what sort of fellow Mr. Jackson is?"

"What sort of fellow?" The bishop crossed his ankle over his knee and rubbed his chin. "I guess I'd say he's likable. But deceitful. I mean, he had me fooled. The few times I'd met him over the years, he seemed like a decent person."

"You mean you didn't suspect him of embezzling money or think he might be involved in anything else suspicious?"

"No, but then I pondered the scriptures on Judas."

"Judas?" My mind whirled trying to recall the stories from the New Testament. "He was one of Jesus' disciples, right?"

The bishop's smile lit up his face. "That's right. And he too oversaw the coin bag." Shaking his head, he met my gaze. "And he too sold out his teacher."

Well, that pretty much told me what the bishop thought of Levi Jackson. A thief and a liar. But was he a killer?

"Do you think Levi is capable of murder? I mean, it's one thing to steal and lie, but could he have stabbed the reverend? A man he worked with so closely?"

The bishop leaned forward with his forearms on his knees. "I can't say either way. It's a far piece between stealing money to pay off gambling debts and killing a man." Sitting up, he sighed. "But if a man is desperate, he will do almost anything."

I bit my lip to keep from expressing my own opinion. From the bishop's words, he wouldn't agree. "So, you think they have the right man in jail. You believe Levi Jackson killed Reverend Boggs in order to hide his secret."

"When you put it that way, it sounds a little farfetched. I was already aware of the discrepancies in the books. Killing the reverend wouldn't change that."

"Did Levi know you already had the information?"

"I'm not sure. You'd have to ask him."

Yeah, I didn't see Gabe letting me interrogate another one of his prisoners. Not after how I had acted with Jimmy. "I don't think that's an option."

"Well, if you don't think Levi is the killer, who do you think took the reverend's life?"

"I'm not sure. But the fact the wedding party consists of the mob family from his past is too much of a coincidence for my taste."

"Yes, it's a nasty business about him being a part of WITSEC. But I guess he must've loved the Lord or else his acting rivaled the performances of a seasoned performer. His love for his congregation showed in everything he did for them. You can't fake that."

"His son Mark said his dad had found peace here in Pine Lake."

The bishop nodded and rested his arms on the chair. "I'm glad to know his faith was genuine. I'd hate to think of him ending up … well, you know."

Catching sight of the clock on the wall behind the bishop, I stood. "Oh, the time. I'd better go. My assistant, Flora, will be expecting me at the bookshop." I moved toward the door leading to the foyer. "Thank you, though, for seeing me. I'm so very sorry for your loss. It's never easy losing someone you worked with so closely."

"No, but you have given me comfort knowing he found God. After the U.S. marshals became involved, I'd wondered about the state of his soul. But now you've confirmed that for me, and I appreciate it."

I took my leave of the bishop. Hoisting my bag into the passenger seat, I pointed the van in the direction of the bookstore, hoping I wouldn't be late. Today I didn't have the heart to listen to one of Flora's speeches on being dependable and on time. Not today. Not with a killer about to leave town and get away with murder. Two hours left before the bride and groom's big send-off. And nothing connected.

I hated when puzzles had leftover pieces because it meant I got it wrong. And no matter how I put this puzzle together, there were always pieces lying to the side.

CHAPTER TWENTY-FIVE

A crowd stood waiting in the foyer of the Whispering Pines Bed and Breakfast at a little past two. Glancing around, I spotted the three groomsmen and the best man who stood next to Gramps and Jimmy's mom and dad. The maid of honor, Kristin, and the three bridesmaids were also in attendance along with a few other family members like Julia's mom and dad, and of course, Julia.

Everyone had been given a little pink bag of birdseed and a small green bottle of bubbles to use when the happy couple made their appearance.

Betsy's mom had gone upstairs to help her daughter prepare for her grand entrance as Mrs. Jimmy Williams.

Her father, on the other hand, paced behind the crowd like a caged lion. I watched him as he made his trek from one end of the foyer to the other. Every few steps, he'd dab at his eyes with his handkerchief, looking rather distraught.

I had to admit I was relieved Jimmy had arranged for the justice of the peace to marry them. Now, there'd be no doubts about the legitimacy of their vows.

Several of the waitresses from the café stood in the doorway waiting to see the bride's outfit.

Footsteps echoed from the top of the stairs, and everyone turned to see Betsy descending. She glowed as she floated down one step at a time dressed in a light green suit with scalloped edging. Beneath the suitcoat, she wore a sweet pink laced blouse adding enough color against her face to highlight her rosy complexion. The pink pillbox hat, reminiscent of a past era, completed the look. The word stunning didn't cover it.

Jimmy, who had been chatting with Gramps, froze once he caught sight of her. His eyes never left Betsy.

Blinking back happy tears, I couldn't help but cheer. "Woo, woo!" I clapped even though my hands were full, and my purse pulled on my shoulder with the motion. Looking at Betsy now, I couldn't imagine her as the zombie bride who had cried herself to sleep a week ago. She looked so fresh, so beautiful.

I glanced over toward Julia who struggled to fight back tears and gave her a thumbs-up.

When Betsy's feet touched the wooden floor of the foyer, Jimmy rushed to her and wrapped his arms around her. "You look beautiful, my darling."

Betsy smiled up at him and rose to her tiptoes. "Kiss me, you idiot."

Beaming, he did as she commanded.

The waterworks started in earnest. Not one single person had a dry eye—not even the waitresses or the tough mob don.

The crowd, sniffling and swiping at their eyes, followed the couple out the front door onto the sidewalk. Stopping to say a proper goodbye, they split up. Betsy took one side of the semicircle comprised of friends and family, and Jimmy took the other.

"Thank you so much for being here." Jimmy shook hands with one of the groomsmen. He stepped closer to the door where his grandfather stood and patted Gramps on the shoulder. "I can't tell you how much I owe you. Thanks for being in my corner."

"Where else would I be?" The older man grinned. He reached into his suitcoat pocket and pulled out an envelope. "Here's a little something to make your honeymoon a little sweeter."

Jimmy shook his head. "No. You've done enough." Gently, he pushed the man's hand away. Leaning down, he kissed him on his forehead.

Gramps chuckled. "On that note, I think I'll head up and start packing." He turned his walker to the side. "Be safe, kiddo." And with that, Frank Morelli pushed open the doors to the foyer and disappeared inside.

Turning my attention back to the group, I found Julia standing beside me. I smiled and was going to make a comment about how nice she looked, but before I could get the words out, Betsy laid her hand on my shoulder. "I can't leave without getting a hug." She leaned into me, avoiding my monster purse, and squeezed me tight.

I thought I might lose my breath.

When she let go, she captured my hand holding the birdseed and clutched it to her. "If it weren't for you and Julia—" she cleared her throat, blinking back tears. "I don't know what I would've done. How lucky can a girl get to have three of the best friends in the world."

Julia shrugged. "Aw, no biggie."

Stepping around me, she grabbed Julia. "You are just the best cousin ever," Betsy cooed. Looking around, she spotted Kristin and waved for her to join us. "Kristin, thank you so much for staying with me this horrible week. You have gone above and beyond the duty of a maid of honor."

"My pleasure." Kristin smiled, looking uncomfortable at being placed in the spotlight.

"Did I ever tell you two it was Kristin who introduced me to Jimmy?"

"You told us you met him at a Halloween party," Julia said.

"That's right. Kristin and I knew each other in college. Even though she was studying nursing and I was an education major, we were in the same sorority. Isn't that crazy? She told me all about her cousin Jimmy and thought we'd be perfect together." Betsy sighed and gazed down at the wedding band on her left hand. Nudging Kristin, she said, "I guess you were right. That party changed my life."

"Darling, let's go." Turning, Betsy spotted Jimmy standing by the car parked by the curb decked out in white streamers with a sign attached to the back that read 'Just Married.' Releasing my hand, she dashed to his side.

Realizing they were about to leave, I struggled to open my birdseed. By the time I'd unknotted the ribbon, people were flinging the small pellets at Betsy and Jimmy who stood by the car wrestling with the door.

"Try the key," Mark yelled. "Someone might have locked the

doors."

Laughter flitted through the group.

Meanwhile, some of the guests opened the little green bottles of bubble juice. I followed suit but spilled half the bottle on the sidewalk. Blowing through the wand, the bubbles lifted into the air. The hot August temperature didn't allow them to last too long, but they made a nice display around the bride and groom as Jimmy wrestled with the key.

Opening the door for his new bride, Jimmy helped Betsy slide into the passenger seat then ran around to the driver's side door. Rolling down the window, Betsy hung out and waved as Jimmy eased the car forward sending the streamers dancing.

Relief flooded over me as I watched the car turn the corner headed to the highway. I spun around to look for Julia and Kristin, but I only saw Julia talking with her parents. So, I went to join them in the shade of the awning.

"Hey, Amy Kate. It's good to see you." Mr. Jacobs, Julia's dad, greeted me.

"It's good to see you too." I glanced around trying to locate Kristin.

"Are you looking for someone, my dear?" Mrs. Jacobs asked.

"I thought I might say goodbye to Kristin before I left. I need to get back to the bookstore to help Flora."

Julia shrugged. "I think I saw her go inside. She's probably ready to hit the road like everyone else." Turning toward her mom, she said, "Did you know Kristin introduced Betsy and Jimmy?"

"No, I had no idea." Mrs. Jacobs smiled. "I mean I knew Jimmy and Kristin were related, but I didn't know she had started this whole thing." Laughing, she swept her hand toward the guests mingling on the sidewalk.

"Betsy told us even though she was an education major and Kristin was studying nursing—"

"What did you say?" I tilted my head and watched as the puzzle pieces in my mind fell into place. It clicked. "Kristin has a nursing degree?"

Julia's eyes widened. "I guess so. What is it, Amy Kate?"

"Kristin has a nursing degree. And she was present when the church secretary told them about the serving sets."

"Are you talking about the serving sets with the ivory-handled knives?” A sharp V formed on Julia’s brow.

“Yes, and she had motive.” I shoved my hand into my purse fishing for my phone. When would I learn not to carry everything and the kitchen sink? “She wanted revenge. For her father being sent to jail because of Reverend Boggs’ testimony.”

“So, she killed the reverend for revenge? For sending her father to jail where he died?” Julia asked. “Is that what you’re thinking?”

Sliding my hand around in the depths of my purse, I touched each item. No phone. “Yes. This wedding was her perfect opportunity. When she recognized the reverend at the rehearsal dinner, she devised a plan. All she had to do was catch him alone on the big day. Everyone would be so busy they wouldn’t miss him until later.”

“Okay, but what about the third knife?” Julia asked.

Gasping, I froze. “The third knife. Oh no!” I sprinted toward the door of the bed and breakfast.

“What’s wrong?” Julia shouted over the chatter of the group on the sidewalk.

“She’s going to kill Frank Morelli.”

The crowd stilled and glanced my way.

“The third knife was for him. For leaving her father in prison. For his death.” Stopping at the door, I turned. “She blames Frank for it all.”

Grabbing the knob, I flung open the door and shouted over my shoulder. “Call Gabe.” I took the stairs two at a time with my purse weighing me down like an anchor. Trying for the life of me to remember Frank’s room number, I shouted. “Frank. Frank, are you up here?”

No answer.

I stood at the top of the stairs, determined to find the right room. Heading down the direction I had gone the first time he caught me snooping left me with half of the eight rooms on the floor. Scanning the doors, I dismissed two of the remaining four rooms, knowing Frank didn’t order room service.

Two rooms left.

Standing outside the first one, I pressed my ear against the door. Nothing. Turning the knob, the door gave way, and I flung it open, hoping for the element of surprise.

Screams echoed into the hall from the woman standing in her robe and slippers with a towel wrapped around her head. I had indeed surprised her.

I sprinted to the other room without so much as an apology to the horrified woman. Not waiting, I placed my shoulder on the door and pushed. The door sprang open.

Frank sat on the bed with his hands held up, palms out.

Kristin stood over him, holding an ivory-handled knife in one hand, her other hand wrapped around Frank's throat.

I stopped short. "Kristin, you don't want to do this."

"Why not? He didn't hesitate to put a kill order out on my father. If it wasn't for my dear uncle here, my father would've been at *my* wedding. He would have walked *me* down the aisle and given me away." Tears streamed down her face. "But instead, I watched this dirty rotten devil play up the fact my father wasn't there and how honored he was to step in and be there for me. What a bunch of bull!"

I inched closer letting my purse slide from my shoulder into my hand.

She tightened her grip around his throat. "You swine. Acting all broken up, making that toast about how much you loved and missed him. And I sat there knowing you were the one responsible for his absence."

Frank gasped trying to draw in breath. His eyes bulged.

"Now you'll be the one missed." She pressed the knife against his chest. "I believe if I push right here." She drew back the blade.

Swinging my purse behind me, I spun around once propelling it forward with all my might. The huge black projectile whacked Kristin in the side of the head as she plunged the knife toward Frank. The impact of my overstuffed purse shoved her off balance, pushing her into the bedside table and knocking her out cold.

Frank dove off the bed toward his walker and his Hello Kitty pouch. In seconds, he spun around holding a gun. "Both of you stay right where you are."

My purse, still in motion and still attached to my hand, pulled me forward causing my feet to tangle with Kristin's legs sprawled out in front of me. With the grace of an intoxicated elephant, I stumbled, rolled, and plopped my way, face-first onto the bed. Not exactly a heroic posture.

"Drop it." A familiar voice boomed.

My heart flip-flopped. Relief rushed over me. I sat up overjoyed to see my almost exclusive, you're-the-one, not dating anyone else, boyfriend.

Floyd Simms rushed in behind Gabe and snatched the gun from Gramp's hand. He pulled Kristin up to a standing position and proceeded to read her her rights.

Officer Pete entered. Floyd handed him Gramps' gun. And the officer took Gramps by the elbow leading him out into the hall. As they left, Officer Pete asked to see his carry permit.

Gabe holstered his gun as he strode across the floor to where I sat perched on the bed still attached to my mammoth black purse I'd decided to name 'Killer.' "Are you all right?"

"Now I am. I take it Julia called you."

"She did, but not before I got the results from the fingerprints. Levi Jackson's didn't match. No surprise to you. But once I heard that, I started thinking about what you said and headed this way. I was halfway here when Julia called."

"Thank goodness. I'm not sure what would've happened if you hadn't come when you did." Untying my hand from the black strap, I let the purse nestle into the mattress.

"Hopefully, he'd have held Kristin here until we arrived, but …" He shrugged.

Floyd led Kristin out of the room.

Gabe sat beside me on the bed. "I'm guessing the print will match Kristin's."

"It should."

"How did you figure it out?" A gleam of pride shone from his eyes.

"When Betsy told us today Kristin had studied nursing in college, everything made sense. Like how the killer knew which cake-serving set to buy, and the fact a woman had been the one to buy a serving set from the Beautiful Wedding Boutique and not a man."

"What about the Beautiful Wedding Boutique?" Gabe asked.

"When Betsy, Julia, and I were here Thursday, we found a bag from the boutique in the garbage can in the foyer by the registration desk. I didn't know how it fit in until today."

"So, Kristin recognized the man who sent her father to jail and plotted to kill him while she had the chance. She thought she had a legitimate reason for being here and could avoid suspicion. And since she's married, we wouldn't put it together that she was part of the Morelli family until she was long gone. But she didn't count on you." Gabe leaned closer.

"True. Or the fact I'd bring a cop to the wedding as a date." I grinned. "Since I knew Betsy so well, I found out Kristin Pike was once Kristin Morelli, Tony Morelli's daughter and Jimmy's cousin."

"What about Jimmy's statement that he heard a door close?" Gabe asked.

"He did. Jimmy heard Levi Jackson hiding in the next office. And Levi Jackson said he heard voices when he was in the other office trying to destroy evidence of his embezzling. Those voices were Kristin's and the reverend's right before she killed him." I shook my head. "He didn't suspect what she'd do. I think the reverend simply wanted to make amends like he'd done with Mark."

"So, Levi hears the voices and someone leaving. Then Jimmy comes along and hears Levi slipping into the other office before he was caught shredding the incriminating books."

"Right." I sighed. "Plus, the warning she'd left on my car came after you'd arrested Levi. If she'd left well enough alone, she might have gotten away with it, but she had no way of knowing you'd arrested Levi before she left it. Making it impossible for Levi Jackson to have left the note. Once I realized Kristin had the medical training, I knew she'd put that knife out at the celebration to send a message to Frank that he was next."

"Well, it's a good thing you're quick on your feet." Gabe shook his head and patted my hand resting on the comforter. "Or I'd have another dead body on my hands."

Before I could comment, Frank Morelli entered the room with Officer Pete in tow. "Everything looks to be in order, sir." Officer Pete propped his hand on his utility belt, nodding toward Frank. "Do you want me to hold him?"

Gabe cut his eyes toward Frank and stared at the older man for a good half second before making his decision. "No, he's the victim here."

"I'm glad you understand that. A lot of coppers wouldn't." He lifted his chin and turned his attention to me. "And you, little lady, I owe you, my life. Kristin would've stuck me like a pig on a spit if it hadn't been for you and your quick thinking." His Italian accent hung heavy in his words.

"And my purse." I gave it a little shove, ashamed it could be used as a weapon.

"Well, I'm mighty grateful for that Kate Spade knockoff." Frank laughed.

"How do you know it's a knockoff?" I grumbled.

"The markings. It says Kate. No last name. My wife had a whole collection of various purses in her closet, God rest her soul. And I am an observant man." He made the sign of the cross as Catholics do when speaking of the dead, before he moved toward the end of the bed where his walker stood. "Now, if you don't mind, I'd like to finish my packing. I'm needed back in Atlanta." A sly smile spread across his lips. "A little family matter has just come up."

Gabe and I stood. Turning, I grabbed my purse. "Well, Mr. Morelli, it's been interesting meeting you."

He pushed his walker to where we stood and took my hand. "If you need anything, Amy Kate Anderson, you let me know. I don't forget about those I'm indebted to." Bending slightly at the waist, he lifted my hand and kissed it.

A flash of nervous energy skittered down my shoulders making the hair on the back of my neck stand to attention. I didn't like the implications. "You don't owe me a thing." With a forced smile, I said, "It was my pleasure to help."

Dropping my hand, he straightened meeting my gaze.

"It's true. Running into danger isn't anything new for her." Gabe shot me a lopsided grin. "She does it so often I'm thinking of marrying her just to keep tabs on her."

Frank emitted a deep and hearty laugh. "Then I'll expect an invitation when you do."

EPILOGUE

By the next Friday, Gabe and I were back into our routine. Hallelujah. I didn't care what any magazine article said. The man made me happy, and a routine meant dependability. Tonight, I'd ask him about being exclusive if it killed me.

He'd arrived at seven, our usual time, and placed the order for our usual pizza, pepperoni, and black olive.

After chatting about our day, I shared Flora's good news about her son and his wife expecting again. Which went a long way in explaining her bubbly attitude of late.

Now, Gabe sat at one end of the couch with Gizmo's head in his lap, scratching between his ears. The little scamp, so pleased with the attention, rolled over so Gabe could rub his tummy. We both laughed.

I'd picked out a movie on one of the streaming services that had been advertised all over the internet and looked perfect for tonight. We started the movie while waiting for the pizza. About forty-five minutes later, the doorbell rang. Gabe jumped up to answer it, disturbing the little sleeping terrier.

I paused the movie and stretched my legs out onto the couch, anticipating the waft of cheese and pepperoni that would fill the space. But instead of pizza, Gabe turned around holding a large cardboard box, the kind used to ship goods.

"What is that?" I asked.

"I have no idea, but it's addressed to you." Gabe's eyes filled with mischief. "Have you been on the super shopper site again? I know how you love that web page with its flash deals and unadvertised sales." Dimples framed his upturned lips.

"No, I haven't." Standing, I dashed over and grabbed the box out of his hands taking it to the kitchen table.

Gabe followed.

Pulling open the junk drawer, I found a pair of scissors and slit the tape. I opened the flaps and removed the shipping paper. "Oh, wow."

"What is it?" Gabe leaned closer to get a better look.

I snatched the item out and held it up so he could see it.

"It's a purse," he murmured, his tone flat and unimpressed.

"No, it's a Kate Spade with her whole name on it." I squealed. "Oh, my word. Do you have any idea how much this cost?"

"I'm guessing from your reaction, a lot." He moved the box toward him and closed the flaps.

"What are you doing?"

"I'm trying to figure out who sent it." He inspected the flaps, but the address was for the merchant who sold it, not the person who'd sent it. A sour look covered his face.

"You're scowling." I put my hand on my hip and held the new prize in my other hand. "Why?"

"I think I know who sent it."

"Really, who?" I pressed my lips together to keep from squealing again.

Gabe shook his head. "You mean you have no clue? The great Amy Kate, amateur detective extraordinaire, is stumped by something so simple?"

Annoyed, I set the purse on the table and pulled the box over to me. I opened the flaps and took out the rest of the packing material. There at the bottom of the box sat an envelope. "There's a note." I glanced up and met his gaze. "So, who do you think it's from?"

He chuckled. "No, this is too good. You go ahead and read the note." A smug gleam radiated from his eyes. Gabe was having way too much fun with this little mystery.

I reached in and grasped the envelope. Sliding my pointer finger under the flap, I pulled out the note.

Dear Amy Kate,

This is a little thank you for what you did for me.
Here's the real deal for the real deal.
Love, Frank M.

I plopped into the kitchen chair behind me. "I can't keep it." Tears threatened to form. I stroked the beautiful pale blue leather. "It'd be wrong to keep something from a known mobster, right?" My voice squeaked with all the longing in my heart rushing into my words.

Gabe sat in the chair next to me. "Amy Kate." The way he said my name, soft and tender, told me my answer. The purse would have to be returned.

I placed the bag in my lap and opened the clasp to look inside. So much room, so many zippers. And there to one side, a matching wallet. "Oh no." With a wail, I held up the wallet.

Gabe laughed. "Only you could make a gift into a crisis of conscience. That's why I love you so much. You *are* the real deal."

Tearing my eyes from the wallet, I met his gaze. "You love me?"

"Yes, I do." His smile spread across his lips causing his dimples to appear. Taking the wallet from me, he gathered my hands in his. "I know you hate the fact we're in a rut. But, Amy Kate, I love it. For the first time in my life since the Marines, I feel like everything is right in my life. You're right in my life."

"Oh, Gabe. I'm so glad you think so because I've been wanting to talk to you about being exclusive. But I wasn't sure how you would feel about it. I planned to speak to you at the wedding, but everything got turned upside down. Then I read that stupid article." My head hung for letting an article dictate my relationship. Deb, our waitress, was right. I'd found the genuine article, and I wasn't about to let him go.

Gabe lifted my chin with the crook of his finger. "You can always talk to me about anything. But especially about us. If I'm moving too fast, tell me. But I've known since the moment I pulled you from the garbage dumpster with that lettuce leaf in your hair, that you were the girl for me."

"Oh, Gabe." I slid my arms around his neck and planted a kiss on those strong red lips, wondering why it had taken me so long to realize how much I loved him too.

A buzz from the doorbell sounded through the apartment. When it buzzed a second time, Gabe broke the kiss and laid his forehead against mine. "The pizza is here."

"Pepperoni and black olive?" I asked, knowing the answer.

"Pepperoni and black olive." Gabe touched my cheek. "Just the way we like it."

The End

Bonita Y. McCoy is an award-winning author who hails from the Great State of Alabama where she lives on a five-acre farm with two dogs, two cows, four cats, and one husband who she's had since circa 1989.

She is a mother to three grown sons who have flown the coop and a beautiful daughter-in-law, who joined the family from Japan.

She loves God, and she loves to write. Her articles, devotions, and novels are an expression of both these passions.

On any given day, you can find her walking the dogs, reading her latest great find, or drinking coffee with her hubby on the front porch swing.

She is an active member of both American Christian Fiction Writers and Word Weavers International.

Drop her a line at www.bonitaymccoy@yahoo.com or sign up for her newsletter at www.bonitaymccoy.com.

Other Books by Bonita Y. McCoy
Amy Kate Mystery Series
Twisted Plots
Family Twist
Twisted Vows

Sawyer Sweet Romance Series
No Room in His Heart
Truth Be Told
Seeds of Love

Stand Alone:
Merry Christmas Mix-up

Only for the Summer

Contributed:
Coffee with God

Coffee and Cookies with God at Christmas
Chicken Soup for the Soul: Thanks Dad edition
Handy Tips for Homeschooling Parents: When You're Feeling Overwhelmed

www.amazon.com/author/bonitaymccoy

Sign up for Forget Me Not Romances newsletter and receive a special gift compiled from Forget Me Not Authors!

Join our FB pages to keep up on our most current news!

Forget Me Not Romances Readers and Authors
Take Me Away Books
Winged Publications
Soaring Beyond

www.ingramcontent.com/pod-product-compliance
Lightning Source LLC
Chambersburg PA
CBHW070502200726
48293CB00007B/2337